# 1

Vampires? Angels?

I ruled the bastards as both angelic princess and Queen of the Under World. Yet now I'm trapped with Lazarus Mages on a hidden island of resurrection and magic.

And that makes me *their* bastard.

Half vampire, half angel, I still lived out a human geek life, until my powers arose phoenix-like on my twenty-first birthday.

To escape Lucifer, my dad, and an apocalypse, I sacrificed one father, only to be welcomed into the deadly arms of a charismatic mage who played at being a new dad to his lost boy cult.

*Splash*.

When I dived into the waters of the Lower Vault, I shivered. Spluttering on the salty seawater, which burnt down the back of my throat — the ocean crept inside this dank cellar below Mage Rahab Drake's castle — I beat my black-and-violet wings, flaring fire down their feathers. Then I peered into the gloom.

Burning eyes blinked back at me.

Mischief was a brat of an angel, who'd tricked me into making a deal with Rahab to become the first female mage apprentice in the Brotherhood of the Phoenix. The Brotherhood dedicated themselves to the Legion and the Mage (or Rahab, as I pissed off the apprentices by calling the angel, who they'd elevated to godlike leader). Yet Mischief had also plotted the revolution to save the Under World and stop an apocalypse. So, the chance of it being easy to save him from his punishment for choosing my side over Rahab's in the steel Lower Vault was less than those burning eyes belonging to a tapdancing unicorn.

*Come on, wishing up a tapdancing unicorn...*

I swam backwards, my ash-blonde hair and the ribbons on my bronze uniform — with added violet knee-high boots — coiling like snakes.

The crimson eyes narrowed.

Both the ancient angelic and vampiric powers inside me stirred, spitting out violet and black warnings against the creature in the dark.

I'd never visited the sea because beachside sandcastle bonding hadn't been a priority at Jerusalem Children's home and Hackney wasn't a neighbourhood where you held a shank in one hand and a Mr Whippy ice-cream in the other. This first trip to the ocean wasn't winning me over to the swimming camp. Plus, I'd never tried doggy paddle with wings dragging me backwards before.

*Where the hell was Mischief?*

When I dragged Mischief out of the Lower Vault's watery tomb, I'd kick his Fae Angel arse. He'd abandoned me to a world of magic that was less Harry Potter's style and more Voldemort's...if he'd had wings.

*Yet it burnt through me*, singing wild rhapsodies of *knowledge*: a realm just behind a door, if I could only push through with the new mental powers that were being taught to me.

*Free myself.*

I shook, scrabbling to touch my feet to the bottom of the vault. When my head ducked beneath the foamy waters, I choked. Shards of lava-hot pain shot through the back of my skull. My new magic wove through my brain, pulsing behind my eye sockets, whilst I struggled not to sink, punishing me for breaking the Brotherhood's sacred Phoenix Code and the First Reformer, *Kunel's*, order.

I battled against the inferno melting my mind. Mischief had once warned that his magic was alive, squirming inside him. In the Legion's psycho cult, your mental powers were conditioned (and that's a fancy word for brainwashed), in line with their Code.

It was like chivalrous medieval knights but without the chivalry.

In the last four weeks — and I'd tracked the days by scoring my nails through the rotting wood of the whipping post in the Bailey of Drake's castle — I'd rebelled so many times, I'd finally collapsed under the torment of the magic. I'd been isolated from my fam: even Drake had been banned from speaking to me. The magic had cleaved to the deep ache inside, where they should've been.

*Hollowed me.*

Sighing, Kunel had finally given in and cooled the new magic, until it'd done nothing to my punk arse anymore but slink snake-like, coiling cold and heavy around my throat.

*Epic fail on taming the Queen of Chaos.*

Now it was back to torching me, however, just as the water froze.

*Someone wasn't happy.*

I smirked, even through the agony. The bastard shouldn't have trusted me out alone: newbie mistake.

*A shrill shriek.*

I howled, as my eardrums throbbed like they'd been

pierced by needles. When I raised my hands to protect my ears from the high-pitched wail that pulsed from the shadows, I sank under the water, swallowing briny mouthfuls.

Thrashing wildly, as my wings churned the waters, I dragged myself back to the surface.

Burning eyes scrutinized me...*hovering just above my head.*

A slender beak, sharp and hooked, sizzled against my cheek. Long curved talons carved into my shoulders, lifting me out of the water and up into the air, whilst wings of fire feathers cocooned around me: their heat shimmered, blistering.

*A phoenix.*

Hell, I'd been waiting on discovering one of these Mage Traps.

I grinned. 'Come on, fire-bitch, flame me.'

*Another shrill shriek.*

I howled.

*Time to arm your knight, J, so I can ride on my white horse to save the fair damsel.*

**You're the one offering yourself up as the princess sacrifice to the fire breathing bitch with feathers.**

*I'm revoking your squire status. Violet fire me before — knight or princess — I'm a chargrilled special.*

**The Lower Vault? Phoenixes? You're showboating, Violet-love: who's the audience?**

*I'm on a rescue mission. My fam is trapped down here.*

**Lie to the Legion, but I'll whip you sweet as apple ass if you lie to *me*.**

**If you shake your thing at the Mage, you'd better be certain it's his knee you want to sit on.**

*There's no way Rahab will ever be my sugar daddy.*

**Oh, girl, every boy here wishes he was special enough to be noticed by Rahab.**

*Chosen.*

**You've spent your life seeking someone to raise**

**you up. Can you resist if this shady dick sees the extraordinary in you? Who will you sacrifice? And where's the righteousness in that?**

I wriggled against the talons digging into my shoulder. 'J' was the sassy voice in my head who'd both raised and controlled me, since I'd been discovered as a baby in Hackney Cemetery on a gravestone.

Who the hell knew if J was real... But when I was staring into the swirling vortex glare of a mythical creature, in the bowels of a castle whose walls thrummed with magic as if alive, on a hidden island in the middle of the Atlantic, whilst my wings *drip, drip, dripped...* I wasn't going to disrespect on the *real* front.

Since my segregation with the apprentices, I'd faded to a shade. Sometimes I even doubted whether my own wings were authentic or would drop off back to the blood that'd birthed both them and an entire species of Blood Angels from the Broken slaves on Angel World.

I still twisted my wings, however, swinging them in blazing arcs at the phoenix.

*Hiss* — my wings surged through the phoenix...and out the other side.

I screamed at the searing of my delicate feathers, whilst the phoenix stared back at me, unruffled.

*Fire doesn't beat fire: check.*

Instead, I reached inside, tugging at my magic. It scorched me in punishment for breaking three of the Codes. "For real? Get your freaky arsed magical mojo sorted."

It *hiccupped* in agonising flames, before cooling, looping out towards the phoenix and noosing its neck.

The phoenix jerked backwards, flailing, as its shrill call became nothing but a strangled *squawk*. I held onto the magic, tightening and freezing.

**Death. The end. Destroyer. Is this what you are now, Violet-death? What your magic is?**

*It's a phoenix. It'll come back to life, yeah?*

5

**So, resurrection means that death no longer matters...? Or the *resurrected* don't...?**

***Bam!* You've become an asshole Lazarus Mage already. Or tell me this, hooker, is it life that doesn't matter?**

I gritted my teeth and yanked.

Golden sparks sprayed in the black. I yelped as I tumbled backwards, and the phoenix exploded, blasting me against the wall of the Lower Vault with a wave of shadow babies born on death.

The shadows shimmered silver edged; their eyes glinted like rubies.

I edged against the unexpected brick wall in the steel cellar. I traced my fingers across the wall and the holes between the bricks.

*Why the hell had this been built and what was behind it?*

"Good little creepy freakshows. Fly away home to your magical master..." I edged out a loose brick by my head, and it tumbled into the water below with a loud *smack*. I winced. "...If you don't mess with the cold, wet, currently Queen of Nothing, who's killed your..." I looked down. "Then I won't mess with you."

The shadows circled closer.

I peered into the gap in the wall.

Mischief slumped, bricked up underwater. A silver gleam illuminated his head. His eyes were closed, and his long silver hair bobbed around him like sparkling seaweed.

*Four weeks walled up beneath the water...*

**Now just cool it, Feathers-fear, before you choose the Fae Angel over the cult leader with the keys to the castle and your freedom.**

*Rahab killed Mischief. There's no bastard choice anymore. No one hurts my blokes.*

**No one but you...**

I gasped, as my heart thundered.

*Mine, mine, mine...*

How hadn't I sensed Mischief's death...?

I'd reached out; my magic trailed towards Mischief's.

6

Wouldn't I have known, if one of my fam...? I choked on a sob. How had Mischief been elevated, even though he wasn't a Marked or bonded like my punk angel Rebel, and I didn't love him, not like my vampire geek Ash, to *mine*?

But if Mischief wasn't, why were my cheeks wet with tears and not seawater?

I growled: I'd take down the Legion and his cult, just like the phoenix. *There'd be nothing left but shadows.*

When the phoenix babies nudged at my nose, undulating across my boots, I *shooed* them away.

They flashed dangerously. Then they swarmed, covering me head-to-toe in a tar tide of blackness. I yelped, before swallowing the shadows too: bitter and thick down my throat. My eyes were soaked in stinging darkness. I shuddered, as the new power, crackling and nipping, twined with my other warring powers already inside. I convulsed, splashing further down into the water and against the wall in violent jerks, cracking the wall.

I tipped back my head, as black seeped from my eyes, clouting the wall with my fist. The masonry crumbled.

*Hiss.*

Water snakes, disturbed by my pounding, swam through the holes in the wall, eel-like. Another *impossible* in the freezing waters of the Atlantic. But there was nothing...*real*...in the shifting Castle Drake.

Four weeks walled up underwater *with snakes...*

I flinched, as my bleeding nails caught against the bricks, whilst I demolished the wall brick by brick.

I wasn't bastard crying: *I wasn't.*

Then I was snatching Mischief out of his grave and soaring up, clutching him to my chest. I landed on the edge of the Lower Vault, laying him out, whilst I knelt over him. The gleam gilded his entire body. He lay still and silent. Hell, I even missed his snarky insults. I tidied his silver leather trousers and tunic, pulling my fingers through his hair to detangle it, as if somehow that would help.

*Bring him to life.*

Yeah, like it'd make up for the fact that I hadn't fought harder to save him from this punishment. That I'd dived into freeing my mind to magic because despite the torment, Phoenix Code, and the First Reformer's rules, being part of the Legion was the closest to a family — where I fitted — that I'd ever experienced.

*And all I'd had to sacrifice were my true fam.*

When I bent over Mischief, my tears dripped onto his cheeks. Then even though in the Under World I'd shattered all fairy tales, making an enemy of my Blood Lover sister, who was deluded by the romance of vampires (Fallen angels caught in an epic war with Angel World and angel mages), I tried for Sleeping Beauty.

*I kissed my princess.*

Magic: it crackled like popcorn. Sparks lit Mischief's cold lips, as answering static danced against mine. My eyes widened, whilst my arms tightened around him.

*Please...using up every ounce of karma I've earnt for saving the world...please...*

Mischief's eyes fluttered open, as the gilt gleam faded.

I grinned against his mouth; my fingers trailed down his warming arm.

Mischief's confused gaze met mine, as our snog continued, swapping our magic between us like our tongues with an electric hum.

*Coming around from four weeks of torture to being molested... It put a whole new spin on Prince Charming.*

I flushed, pulling back. Our magic fought to hold us together: silver and violet spiralled in the air between us. I dragged in my angelic power with an embarrassed *snap*.

*Awkward.*

I'd expected Mischief to puke water. Instead, he blinked at me, studying the Legion's adapted uniform for its one and only female apprentice: bronze ribbons wrapped around my thighs, tiny bronze skirt, tight shirt and scarf in rich velvet: like an

8

aristocratic anime. He sniffed. "Oh, I shan't call you beast anymore," his voice was raspy but not like he'd swallowed water into his lungs. "You shall be my *Sailor Moon*."

I blushed, pulling at my shirt self-consciously.

*Maybe I hadn't missed those snarky insults.*

"You were dead..." I pointed a shaky finger at him. "I just brought you to life."

He caught my hand, brushing his lips against the back of it. "My hero." His lips quirked, mockingly. "What diversion would Mage Drake have if I was dead? He walls you in...then the water creeps up inch by inch..." Mischief pulled himself up on his elbows. "Finally, just before you drown, he allows you to paint yourself in protective magic. You still feel the dark, fear, and isolation but you don't drown. My, what a shame for the Mage: he doesn't have a new Brother with equal imagination."

"Don't try me, Gandalf, I'm imagining you, me, and a snake right now."

Mischief moaned, frantically scrabbling to back away from me along the sharp edge of the Lower Vault, shaking his head as if to deny the image...*him, me, snake...*

*I was a wallad.*

"That was my Thoughtless-1000 moment, all right? I'd never do that to you." I held out my hand, but Mischief's fingers tremored, as he clawed at his pale chest like he could still feel the snakes coiled there. I bit the inside of my cheek to hold back the raging of the powers inside. "I'm the Monster Princess: the other monsters may *think* they're the Big Bads, but I'm the bitch who slays them. And I promise, I will."

Mischief huffed, but he stopped ripping his skin. "Insufferable arrogance. Has it taught you nothing?"

"That I'm kickass?"

This time he spluttered with laughter, before collapsing onto his back; I sprawled next to him. "When I was a child, snakes held no terror for me." He swirled the blood on his chest into letters: **VIOLE**... He peeked at me. "Yet since I was brought to this castle, Mage Drake has shut me in with them.

It's remarkable how fear can be cultivated because where there's magic, there's nightmares."

"Way to bring down the mood."

"My mistake, I hadn't imagined we'd hit the candlelit romance stage. Now," he raised an imperious eyebrow, "put me back."

I spluttered, straightening my wings to their full intimidating glory as I stood. "No way, bro."

Mischief merely tilted up his chin: *looked like my swag had deserted me.* "At once, *queen.*'

*That* was how to burn with a single inflection.

I flinched, and Mischief suddenly looked wary and lost, before his expression shuttered.

"I disobeyed three Codes, ganked a phoenix, and became infested with shadows, just so I could haul your ungrateful arse out of the sea," I growled. "What's an escape attempt if the prisoner won't leave their cell?"

"One where no one dies because of their stupidity." Mischief rolled sideways back into the water.

I pounded my fists against the steel, peering down into the freezing black.

Was Mischief truly more terrified of Rahab than the snakes? What did he fear would happen if he didn't wall himself back into the tomb?

*What did he know that I didn't?*

*Arf, arf, arf.*

I leant forward, staring at a silver Harbour Seal, which wiped a front paw over its whiskers. It batted its long eyelashes, curling its mouth into a smile. Then snorted water straight into my face.

I yelped, batting away the spray.

Mischief's voice curled from the seal's cute mouth, "That's seal for *be off with you, sailor. Don't you have treasure to be plundering?*"

"More like a Disney pirate." I narrowed my eyes. "What's seal for *help, she's about to kick my arse?*"

The seal's V-shaped nose flared in panic but it was too late. I'd dived into the water, clutching Mischief by his furry neck before he could propel himself away.

*Except, he could still shift.*

Finding myself holding nothing, my heart spiked with the same panic as when I'd thought Mischief dead.

I couldn't lose him. *Not after he'd come back to life...*

I burst my magic through the rippling water, netting Mischief in the cold, which had blackened now in the tar of the shadows, then I trawled him towards me. I ignored his chattered name-calling, cupping my hands around him instead and raising him to eyelevel.

I glared at the tiny equine seahorse, which glittered iridescent silver. Somehow Mischief still managed to look regal. *And how could a seahorse pout?* "Will you stop...trying to stop me rescuing you?"

The seahorse did all but shrug. "Only if you stop trying to rescue me."

"Not in the land of yodelling werewolves."

"Why?" He sounded more fragile than before. And suddenly Mischief was transformed back to his angelic self. Except, his arms were wrapped around my shoulders, and his lustrous scaled tail wound around me.

*My merman.*

When Mischief's tail rubbed against me, I shivered. Was it as sensitive as my wings or claws?

"Come back to land," I whispered.

"So you can gut me?" He shook his head. "You would sacrifice for Rebel, Ash, or your Blood Familiars, but not for *me*: the spy and traitor."

"You learnt about me in the Underworld and you're right: I'm no hero. I wouldn't sacrifice for a traitor.'

Mischief's eyes closed, as he shuddered. He gave a tight nod.

"But you're not a traitor: you're fam. And I've learnt that I'll sacrifice everything for fam. You chose to stand by my side;

11

I told you I wouldn't forget."

Mischief's eyes snapped open. He pulled me closer, tentatively touching our lips as if I'd be the one to pull away, then he snogged me hard, caressing me with his tail in time with the strokes of his tongue. I quivered, caught in his hold. He was strong, I suddenly realised, as he spun me in the water, and if he truly wanted to get away, I'd never stop him.

He had to want to be caught....*or surrender*.

*Why did he hide his strength?*

He chuckled against my lips. "The water is my land. Here? I'm the king."

"Then I'm the Kingslayer." I shot the shadows around Mischief, catching him in their sticky embrace.

Mischief cast me a panicked glance. "What happened to you?"

"I became strong too. Enough to do this..." I dragged us both out of the water and into the air, before tumbling us onto the ground. Mischief's challenge had awoken something dominant and dark inside me: it growled to force Mischief to his knees. He alone of my blokes had never called me princess or queen and meant it: *had never knelt.*

As Mischief's tail transformed back into legs, I wound my hand in his hair and tried to force him down.

He shook me off. "I am not one of your *boys*."

He'd paled; his hands tidied his hair in quick, furious motions.

I pinked. "I wasn't—"

"We are both aware of what you *were*. Your spark does not incite undying loyalty in me, unlike your doe-eyed followers. I'm not under your spell and what I think of angel princesses..." He caught himself, before crossing his arms. "I will not be forced."

"And what about me?" I couldn't meet his eye. "Not princess or queen. Just Violet?"

Mischief startled, picking at the edging of his tunic. "I think that I stopped you perpetrating an apocalypse and that now I have a duty to keep you from becoming Mage Drake's creature." I took a careful step backwards, unable to hide the same devastation that I'd earlier seen flash on Mischief's face. "I also believe you less of a beast than I'd been taught," he added more softly. Then his gaze became steely. "But here? You're not my ruler. Does it hurt to be returned to the ranks of the ordinary?"

My fists clenched. "I was never ordinary, and neither were you."

He flinched. "That's why you must allow me to return to my punishment. Everything here is in balance; my freedom will have a price — for you. I'm not the damsel: you are. Lucifer's games are like a kid's compared to the adult tortures on this island of the dead. Excuse me if I don't intentionally call down Mage Drake..." Mischief caught my eye, before he shuddered, pressing his fingertips together as if to stop himself shooting magic out at me. "You *mean* to call his attention by this stunt?"

"What can I say? The Bitch of Utopia doesn't do ignored."

The scent of creamy sandalwood suddenly filled the vault. For a bloke who wouldn't kneel for *me*, Mischief knelt like his strings had been cut.

"I apologise for neglecting you then, little apprentice," Mage Rahab Drake's cool call from the shadows made me jump. "You shall have my *personal* attention from now on, just as Lucifer is receiving from your mother. Intriguing, it seems like father, like daughter."

Rahab swooped from above, glorious and terrifying, his violet wings flaming through the slashes in the back of his emerald silk shirt.

I growled, but Rahab shot a sizzling blast at me, hurling me onto my back in a stink of scorched feathers. Then the angel who acted as daddy for the Brotherhood landed on top of me, and every bone in my wings broke.

# 2

Wingtips, feathers, and every fused bone in my wings howled with chilling agony. It spasmed me back to awareness after my nightmare flight out of the Lower Vault caught in Rahab's eagle embrace.

When I rubbed my cheek along the surface that I was sprawled on, it was no longer cold and wet but bouncy, warm, and *buzzing*. It wrapped me in the scent of candyfloss, like I'd fallen into the machine at the fair.

*I'd better hope Rahab didn't have a sweet tooth.*

I tried to flap my wings, but they only flopped in a boneless comedy routine. Slowly, I cracked open my eyes, then yelped, wishing that I hadn't.

*A low chuckle behind me.*

I bottom shuffled away, then stopped as the...*nothing*...underneath me swayed.

I hung in mid-air, as if held up by fairy magic, in a rugged cavern high above a pool of seawater: fish darted like jewels, sea snakes eel-slithered across the surface, and star-fish spiked the rocks. The seaweed, seagrass, and algae that was thick across the pool pulsed with an eerie emerald glow. I held out my hand because I should be able to touch — or should be falling into that unnatural pool — but instead my fingers

14

*crunched* against the same foamy, *buzzy* something that was holding me up.

"My Invisible Bridge," Rahab's amused voice explained from behind me. "One of the first things I ever created in my castle. Aren't you intrigued to discover what *you* could imagine?"

"Chocolate sausages, dinosaur ballet, and a world where sarcasm doesn't exist, except I still wield it, so I rule. Already got it covered, bro."

I spun around on my arse, dragging my broken wings after me with a wince. Then I stiffened.

Rahab leant, mid-air, as if leaning on the hidden rail of his Invisible Bridge. His golden curls, which matched his silk harem trousers, were threaded with silver. They hung over his eyes, as he scrutinized me. And his strong hands rested around Mischief's slender neck.

Mischief squirmed in Rahab's hold but he didn't try to break free. He wrapped his silvery-violet wings around himself protectively like a kid wrapping his arms around his knees and huddling behind his bed, as if that made the monsters go away.

*It didn't; I bastard knew that.*

Rahab rubbed his thumb in a lover's caress along Mischief's fluttering pulse. The way Mischief shuddered, however, and Rahab's loose grip like he didn't want to taint himself, was anything but *loving*.

I craved to tear Mischief away from Rahab, so he'd never have to wrap his wings around himself like that again...

**Hide me, Feathery-doll. Build a wall around me and don't let it come tumbling down.**

*Busy right now, J.*

**You'll be dead *right now* if the Mage breaks your mind as he broke your wings.**

**I'm your secret. Your true family who raised you. You can trust me, can't you?**

I hesitated.

J was part of me: I'd learnt my life lessons in London at his

15

knee. No one else had ever looked out for me. But...*trust*?

Since the supernatural had broken into my world, J had tempted me into danger, almost as much as he'd forced me into the hard choices that'd saved my arse. *Devil or angel...?* I didn't bastard know. But he was *my* secret: what would anyone think about a voice inside my head, which I'd hidden from even my fam?

I threw up the walls that I'd spent months practising, whilst held captive on Angel World.

When Rahab's thumb caressed across the back of Mischief's neck, however, and Mischief cringed, I growled before I could stop myself. Rahab let out a laugh in surprise. "Be silent. I wonder what *services* Zophia has rendered to garner such loyalty from a Glory?" I flushed at the same time as Mischief. *And how had I missed the chance to take the piss out of Mischief's girlie angel name?* "Kunel has taken four weeks to coax nothing out of you but an entire lack of dedication to the Legion, but with Zophia as motivation you've blazed to new heights."

My blush spread down to my chest: *was it that Rahab had praised me?* No bastard way was he playing the surrogate dad role. I bristled. "I wasn't looking for a gold star."

Rahab raised his pale eyebrow. "Are you certain? You've earnt one. Such a shame, however, that you waste your devotion on an Underserving."

I ran my hand through my damp hair. "You've lost me."

"It's no matter," Mischief's smile was too thin. "I imagine that's a condition with which you're shockingly intimate."

Rahab tightened his hands around Mischief's throat, and he gasped. I gritted my teeth, struggling to my knees.

"The Underserving," Rahab continued calmly, as if Mischief wasn't dangling now from his grasp and choking, as he scrabbled at his hands, "are members of the Brotherhood who haven't fitting mental powers to become even apprentices or who've tried to become mages and failed. They're servants to the Legion. Do you imagine I don't understand the boys I choose?" His gaze was considering, as I dragged myself across the bridge. I sucked in breaths to steady myself against the dizzying drop beneath me: the fishes swarmed in metallic chaos under my shadow. "The only question was *when* you'd pull Zophia from the water. Imagine my horror when it took twenty-eight rotations of the sun."

*Thwack* — I struck at Rahab's bare feet with my fists, sizzling flames and searing his ankles.

He hissed, dodging backwards and hurling Mischief at me like an unwanted kid in a custody battle.

For a moment, I held my breath, expecting him to plummet into the pool below.

*Thud* — Mischief bounced on the hidden bridge with a startled yelp.

"Maybe," Rahab examined the nails on his elegant fingers, "the Underserving simply wasn't as charming as I've taught him...?"

Mischief and I both winced.

"And maybe you're more freakshow than fanboy material on a stick?" I shoved myself up with a shaky hand. "I've been doing the apprentice thing for a month, whilst you've been doing the vanishing act."

Rahab's expression softened. When he crouched down in front of me, Mischief hunched away from him. "Hush, little apprentice, I've been a bad father not giving you my love and time."

My breath caught in my throat; I couldn't meet his intent gaze. "You're not my dad."

*Why the hell did I have to sound like a kid bitching to her step-dad?*

"I'm the true father to every Brother in the Legion. You've acted out and now you've ensured my guidance and discipline. It would've come earlier, but your mother demanded my attendance in Angel World for some sessions with Lucifer. Your father has but one use, just like my own son."

I looked away.

Rahab had given up his son, Drake, to the Matriarch to be used as a Marked Wing, just like my own dad: a sex slave in

17

the bedroom and a Commander on the battlefield.

*Yeah, not sure there was a Father's Day mug for that.*

"It'd appear," Rahab waved his hand lazily in the air, "that Lucifer is still defiant, despite the loss of his fire."

I glanced at Mischief. His gaze was carefully blank, but I didn't miss his stifled smile at Lucifer's defiance.

Why did it fill me with such righteous joy that the birth dad I'd deposed and handed to his enemy as Marked Wing hadn't been broken?

Yet.

*Because for the first time, I didn't want to break anyone.*

Mischief's eyes widened, as if catching my thought. *Understanding it.*

The shadows shifted inside me. I caught Mischief's hand between mine, pulling him closer.

Rahab's eyebrows raised, as if he'd understood me as well. "Naïve children, I taught Lucifer his place, as I shall teach you yours."

Then he clicked his fingers, and I screamed.

My stomach lurched as the Invisible Bridge disintegrated. I tumbled through the air, unable to beat my broken wings.

*A green glow...flitting shadows in the mirrored water below...blurring closer...*

Silvery-violet wings folded around me, whilst slim arms hooked around my waist. I buried my face in Mischief's hair, as he spun me away from the water; our feet skidded across the surface. Then we soared towards the cavern's entrance.

Rahab stood with his hands laced behind his back, as we landed.

When Mischief carefully let go, I swayed; my boots slipped on the slimy rock. "What the assassin pixies in hell *was that*?" My skin prickled with static; my new magic icicle tingled, heavy and dangerous in my throat. "You're not my dad: you're more like one of those creepy online groomers. And I'm not ending up ganked or pimped."

"*Sailor...*" Mischief hissed in warning.

"Do let her go on," Rahab's shark-smile froze me in place. "*Creepy* and...?"

I swallowed. "Just keeping it real, yeah?"

"Indeed." Rahab's lips curled. "Lucifer may have — unwillingly — donated to your conception but he wasn't your true father. I can be. Because all my children forget their old families here, becoming a new united one. You're the first Glory I've allowed into this refuge for gifted Wings."

"Have you been watching too much X-men?" I smirked.

Mischief nudged me; I nudged him back.

Rahab strolled to the cavern wall, running his hand loving along its filth. Then he closed his eyes. "This is where my mother tried to drown me as a baby." I started, twisting around to stare at the pool. I shook my boot, as if the water had been contaminated by the action. "My Angelic Powers terrified her. She hated that I was stronger than her: a Glory. My father managed to stop her, and together they abandoned me here. I imagine they thought I'd die. *I didn't.*" When he opened his eyes and his piercing stare swung to me, I squirmed. "As I grew, I created this castle, which became both my home and a refuge for other Wings, like me: the magical unwanted. I'm a saviour to the abused, the rejected, and the lost. I allowed *you* here because I thought that out of every Glory, you'd be the one to understand what I've spent centuries building...and hiding. My mages in the human world appreciate X-men, but I think I've been Xavier too long. Magneto holds quite a draw for me."

Was Rahab the saviour not the Big Bad? The Glories were savage and cruel. I'd rescued their slaves myself. I was working on freeing their Wings.

My eyes were burning, but I blinked away the tears. *Yeah, I understood.* My blokes and me were the outcast misfits and we were fam. But wasn't Rahab as brutal as the Glories?

"Lucifer was a prick but he loved me." I stumbled towards Rahab.

*Whack* — I slammed my hand against the rock.

Rahab gripped my chin. "Is that what you choose to believe?"

19

*Don't cry...don't bastard cry...*

"You're not my dad," I repeated like a mantra, before whispering, "you'll never be..."

"Zophia," Rahab snapped.

When Mischief slunk to his side, Rahab snatched Mischief by the scruff of the neck, pressing hard into the base. Mischief yowled.

"Stop it," I snarled, tugging at Rahab's wrist.

When my violet vampiric claws shot out of my nails, Rahab shook his head.

"Desist. You shall control yourself. If you do not stand still, behaving as both a queen and a Brother, then I shall weight Zophia and abandon him to the snakes in this pool for the next month." At Mischief's terrified gasp, I froze breathing hard through my nose. I couldn't let Mischief be put with the snakes again. *Not because of me*. Rahab smiled. "Good girl. You see how wisely I choose my Phoenix Apprentices...? Duma, on the other hand...?"

When Rahab shoved his thumb deeper into the base of Mischief's neck, Mischief's face became pale and pinched with pain, as he struggled for breath, forced into shifting *into Commander Duma Drake*.

No longer long silver hair but golden curls. Gold harem trousers, instead of silver.

I shivered at the *violation* of the forced shift.

The false Drake hung like a puppet from his dad's hand, which held him onto tiptoe. Only then did I realise that it was white-hot fury, which was making him tremor. "I don't know that I have a sufficiently inflated superiority complex to play your son." The false Drake hissed. "Should I toss my pretty curls, stomp around like a god, and lock myself alone in my room?"

I stared at the false Drake in shock. Why the hell did I want to light up his cloned arse in defence of my true harem boy Commander, even if he *did* have pretty curls?

I hadn't expected Rahab to answer drily, "You seem to be managing so far." Then he shook the false Drake, knocking his harem pants down his slim hips. "You see how something can

20

appear one thing and yet be another? Duma is no son of mine, even though he's in the Brotherhood. You can't choose what slithers bloody from your lover's womb, ripping her apart."

Rahab's smile was frozen. His eyes glittered like another realm lay beneath the surface: and it wasn't the one of fluffy bunnies and snuggles.

I recoiled; my heart raced. "When Drake asked you why you reduced him to a Marked Wing, you said it wasn't because—"

"He murdered his mother through his birth?' Rahab stroked his fingers down False Drake's cheek, and False Drake flinched. "No, I told him it was because he's a *disappointment*. And that's also the truth."

"I take it back." Mischief's voice was quiet and thoughtful out of False Drake's mouth. "However Commander Drake behaves, it appears he has every reason to lock himself in his room."

"Yet your beloved *Queen of Chaos* has taken a Marked Wing in the same way as the Matriarch took Drake." Rahab dug his fingers into the False Drake's neck again, and I stiffened. *Bastard, no...* Rebel's soft violet eyes smudged with kohl eyeliner gazed back at me.

Nope, not Rebel: False Rebel, even if he had a perfect flame of hair and studded leather jacket with red bondage trousers, as well as a spiked black collar around his neck.

Hell, after a month of not seeing Rebel, it hurt to see him now as an illusion.

Yet it also hurt Mischief to see how much I hungered for him to be my Blood Bonded and Marked lover, rather than himself. He couldn't hide that pain, just as I couldn't hide how much I desired Rebel.

*Loved him.*

I *ached* for him.

False Rebel closed his eyes, turning away his head.

"What do you want?" I asked Rahab; my voice was tight.

"I believe *you* were the one who wanted something." Rahab

21

splayed his hand along False Rebel's chest, tweaking his nipple.

"Cool story, bro, but I've got the message. I disrespected and now I've got your autopsy-level attention. So, what do you want from me, so you'll stop hurting Mischief?"

Rahab's surprised gaze met mine, as his groping hand stilled. "You truly care about this Undeserving?"

"*Ding, ding,* give that wizard a wand."

Rahab spun the False Rebel towards me, and we tumbled to the floor in a tangle of limbs. I shoved Mischief away, gritting my teeth against the shifting of my broken bones, and he turned back to himself again with visible relief.

Mischief studied me with an unreadable expression that unnerved me.

"He's yours." Rahab swooped into the air above us.

"And the deal is...?"

"We're not in the Under World. There are no deals, only rewards and punishments. Not everyone believes you have a place here with us, but I have faith in you. The Matriarch saw you as no more than a weapon to take part in her twisted sports. Lucifer is a brat who never knew how to use his freedom or spark. But you...? With the right training, direction, and motivation could take us *all* into the light."

The ancient powers inside me stirred, roused by his fervour. My cheeks reddened; I ducked my head. Hell, only Rebel had ever spoken with such belief. Why couldn't Rahab get with the program of wing breaking and snake ducking, at least then I didn't get the charismatic leader tingles that made me want to start marching in his deluded army.

A *tug* at the velvet scarf around my neck.

I blinked, glancing down into Mischief's concerned gaze.

"There may not be deals, you senseless ingenue, but there are balances," Mischief said. "If you receive rewards, then they must be earnt. Why, I ask, would you wish to receive anything from...?"

"Because I'm his apprentice." I looked up, battling to meet Rahab's scrutiny. "So, let's get with the rewarding."

The gust from Rahab's blazing wings hit my face. "Three

wishes then, if I was a genie. What would you ask for if you could have your deepest desires?"

I ignored the frantic shaking of Mischief's head, as I held up my hand and counted, "One: Mischief, he's mine."

Rahab *snapped* his fingers. "It doesn't work like that, but I like the effect. Now you've chosen him, your second two wishes can't include your other Wing or the vampire."

I froze. "No way—"

"Do you wish me to change this to punishment, rather than reward?"

I smacked my fist against my thigh, only for Mischief to catch my hand and cradle it. "Two: my brother. I want to see him." Mischief sighed and shook his head. "What? Did I say it wrong?"

Before I'd been brought to this castle, I hadn't even known that I'd had a half-brother. But as soon as Rahab had told me I had a blood sibling, I'd been desperate to see him and be certain he wasn't a prisoner or tortured like Mischief.

Rahab had told me he wouldn't place me in the barracks with my blokes. Instead, because I was royalty, I'd be lodged with my brother. But I still hadn't seen him, and it clawed at my insides.

Rahab grinned, *snapping* his fingers. "And three?"

"I want to prove myself to you."

*Because it was the only way to raise through the Legion and save all the worlds.*

Rahab's grin faded. "You will rise above us all, I am certain of it." Then he *snapped* his fingers again. I jumped, as he swooped, crushing me in a hard embrace. "Wishes granted. You'll *prove* yourself in a Battle of the Bailey against my son, Duma. It's a longstanding tradition in the legion. If you're victorious, you'll win the reward of *Zophia* as your personal Undeserving and the *chance to see* your brother. You'll fight before the entire Legion."

He hauled me to my feet. I staggered, trying to balance myself with broken wings. *How the hell could I fight the*

23

*Commander of the angelic army like this?*

"Of course, if you don't win," Rahab ran his hand through his curls, "perhaps if you imagine I'd asked your three worst nightmares, rather than your three wishes...? Because that's how I choose my punishments."

*No wonder J had turned scaredy-cat and demanded that I hide him.*

Now I had to fight Drake, whilst my wings were injured, and either receive my three deepest desires or face my three personal nightmares.

# 3

In Angel World, I was the Monster Princess. I'd been crowned Queen of Chaos in the Under World. Here in Drake's Castle...? I was the freaky black-and-violet eyed female apprentice in the sea of the Brotherhood.

And sometimes the only way to win was to lose.

Silver sparks shocked, then lips were kissing mine: desire and magic. I pulled away from its wildness, before its thread of loneliness and pain called to mine, and I dived into the touch like we were meant to rule together.

*Like we already were*.

Then Mischief finally drew away. "You *are* fighting for me," he forced himself to take a step back. "What kind of damsel would I be if I didn't grant you my favour?"

"Does your favour come with a side order of healed wings?" I rolled my shoulders: *no way was I flying today*.

I shifted awkwardly in the centre of the Bailey: the vast courtyard of the castle. Swaying, I caught myself on the bulbous bronze cannon; Mischief rested his hand on the whipping post above my head, blocking me from the view of the entire Brotherhood, who'd been put on parade to watch the battle: either my victory or humiliation.

25

Apprentices in bronze harem pants stood sweating at attention in the boiling heat: angels no older than me, teenagers, and *kids*. The apprentices didn't move a bastard muscle: a clay army. I didn't blame them; last week an angel with the graceful wings and poise of a ballerina had fainted on parade, and I'd drifted to sleep that night with the *swish — crack* of his flogging, at the same whipping post that I now huddled under, shuddering through me.

Kunel, First Reformer and Bastard Number One, who was in charge of the apprentices, glowed like a Captain America impersonator: slicked blond hair and not a feather out of place.

Mages in gold harem pants — the Alpha top boys — lounged against a wall in the shade, whilst servants in silver scurried between them with cool drinks: The Underserving, like Mischief.

Rahab's *refuge* was as hierarchical as Angel World. The only difference was how you rose or fell between the ranks and *who* was in charge.

Mischief leaned closer, murmuring, "The rules are not the same anymore. I can no longer take your pain for mere brownie points." I winced: Mischief could heal but he did it by taking the pain onto himself. *Had I been using him?* "I may only share my talent with Mage Drake's permission, or when *I* choose to and he has no chance of discovering it. Do you believe you still have the power on this island?"

I squirmed but shrugged. "Screw having *power*. How about getting through without being phoenix whomped, cult brainwashed, or turned into chunky salsa?"

"Well, someone's certainly not a realist." I smacked Mischief's arm, and he grinned. "How about we both strive towards those lofty goals?"

I dragged him towards me, kissing his forehead.

*Sniggers and jeers.*

Mischief wriggled away from me with a glare, rubbing at his forehead like a kid wiping away his mum's kiss.

"We were swapping saliva a moment ago, but now you're playing the virgin?" Black and violet roared, outraged at his rejection, hissing to drag him down and teach him in front of everyone just how much I could *touch* him...

Shocked, I stumbled away, huddling my arms around myself.

Mischief glared at me. "I am not your *pet*."

I blanched. Hell, I remembered how my dad had called Mischief his *pet*, and how Rahab controlled him. I'd never meant to make him feel like *that*... Yet wasn't it how I'd just ached to treat him? "I didn't—"

"I'm quite certain you did." Mischief bit out, before shoving me into the fighting arena. "You have a battle to win."

I stumbled, catching my toe between the amber cobblestones.

*Sniggers again.*

Shadows danced behind my eyes. I drew myself up, twisting to the mages. They shrank back, looking anywhere but my furious glare.

Then I turned to Rahab.

He stood in the grand archway to the gatehouse with his majestic — unbroken — wings out. Their pulsing wingtips rested loosely on the two angels who knelt either side of him: his son, Drake, and Rebel.

My head jerked back, as my skin tingled: Rebel, *my Irish bondage punk angel*. Not false or an illusion but real for the first time in a month of only being able to feel his emotions of fear, pain, and shame through the bond and soothing him through it, whilst not knowing if I was breaking his trust by forcing my emotions into him. Because he hadn't willingly become my Marked or my Bonded: I'd *taken* both from him.

*Did I even deserve to comfort him?*

What the hell: I loved Rebel, and he bastard loved me.

*Fam was fam.*

27

Rahab caressed his fingers along Rebel's shoulder, and I shuddered. I scanned Rebel for injuries: he was unmarked. Yet when Rahab could turn phobias into torture devices and all he needed with Rebel was the *dark* to torment him...?

When I took a storming step towards Rahab, Drake pushed himself up from his knees and stalked towards me, blocking my path. Unlike the False Drake that Mischief had shifted into, my Goldilocks had been reduced from his Commander gold trousers, to bronze Apprentice, just like me. He rubbed at them absentmindedly, revealing his creamy thighs, as if the trousers bothered him.

When Drake met me in the middle of the arena, he jerked his head at the ranks of the apprentices and Kunel with a sharp *tap* of his bare foot against the cobbles.

Forbidden from talking to each other since we'd been brought under Kunel's loving care, we'd developed the art of whole conversations via body language. Drake's meant:

**What's up with you in the land of crazy cats, bitch? Why'd you call down this conflict on me to humiliate me in front of the gang?**

*Although, that's a loose translation.*

I nodded towards Rahab.

**No choice, bro.**

Drake clenched his jaw, casting me an anxious, searching glance.

I sighed, as brilliant white threads that tasted of candy floss, quested into my mind, spinning me in their softness. They stroked me, soothing. This was our secret. The way Drake had reached out to me, risking punishment throughout this month to connect without words.

*To bond.*

"Our new apprentice has asked to prove herself in the Battle of the Bailey." Rahab stepped forward from the archway. Drake *snapped* back the white from my mind. His gaze blanked, but not before I'd missed the sudden cold rage. "My son may not have the same honour to ask for the chance..." *Hoots*. Drake paled, and I tensed: *please don't bastard do this...not because of my three wishes...* "But I'm a

28

kind father. So, Duma, do you wish for the opportunity to prove you have at least some worth before your peers?"

"Yes, sir," Drake forced out, his hands fisted at his sides.

He didn't turn around however, his gaze still locked with mine. His hand twitched: **See, what an epic ball busting you've called down on me?**

"How mortifying to hold a fondness for our royal apprentice and yet know she loves Addicts and vampires more than you." *Titters* from the mages as they slouched closer, circling the arena. Drake hunched, avoiding my eye. "Don't you wish — just once — to *win* against her? Show her your true worth, whatever that may be? Or are you nothing but her sacrifice: burnt, abandoned, and disposable?" Drake flinched at each word: assassin's blades, wrapped in the trickery of fatherly concern. I fidgeted, reaching for Drake's hand, but he recoiled. "Will she ever be able to see you as more than her lovers' gaoler?" He stroked Rebel's hair, and Drake's eyes narrowed at my growl. "Win, Duma, and demonstrate you can be something other than a *disappointment*."

For the first time, Drake's eyes glinted with tears.

*Rahab was going down Hackney style.*

Except, Drake's expression had cooled to predatory ice-cold fire. With a flick of his wrist, an invisible blast knocked me backwards.

I howled, as my wings scraped along the floor. When Drake wrenched me up by my scarf, his eyes clouded with concern. He shook his head, however, and his gaze once again smoothed out to the deadly. He shot out a second blast to paralyse me. This time, however, I was prepared; I deflected Drake's shot with the cold magic, which slunk through my neck like chains. Then I whipped him across the face with the coils, tumbling him onto his arse.

*Guffaws from the angel pricks.*

Eyes tarring, I sprayed out a hurricane of shadows at the

29

mages.

*Shrieks and hollers.*

I grinned: *not so much with the Alpha swag now.*

The mages scrabbled at themselves, smacked each other on the back, or reached into their pants, hopping on one leg to kick out the wiggling shadows.

When I turned to Mischief at the side of the arena, he quirked an unimpressed eyebrow, before singing, "Behind you."

Drake lifted me off the ground. Rich frankincense caught in my nostrils, as his pale violet wings trapped me. I struggled, but he pinned my arms to my sides, ramming me against the whipping post; the sharp iron manacles bit into my back, and I groaned.

"I'm winning this fight," I whispered.

Drake stared at me, his grip tightening. "Be silent. I apologise for my roughness, but we're breaking the Code by speaking."

"Stick the Code."

Drake flinched. He peeked down at Kunel and then at his dad, before murmuring, "Hit me."

"Kinky," I smirked. Then I backhanded him, twisting him around in the dance of battle, as he soared high above the arena.

*Hell, if he dropped me...*

"Why do you insist on this win, my Queen?"

"Didn't your dad put on the musical? I want to *prove* myself."

Drake stiffened. "Lie."

Why did he have to *see* me? I'd been invisible for so much of my life, it was freaky now to finally be understood.

"Trust me."

Drake's gaze was assessing but then it hardened. "No matter what my father believes, I'm a Commander. And I shall win this battle honourably for you."

*Hell, he meant it.*

"If you love me," I caught myself because — *screw it to Unicorn City* — that was the first time I'd said it out loud, and Drake's expression had slipped into the vulnerable and raw...*and I'd done that*, "you won't win to prove any of that medieval mind control by your NOT Dad of the Year. Your honour, worth, and place by my side...you already have that." Drake was trembling; his mouth pressed into a thin line. "You'll lose because my blokes sacrifice."

"And have I not sacrificed enough?"

"Have you?"

I didn't understand the way Drake clutched me closer, as he pretended we were struggling, resting his forehead against mine. "I drown in it. In you. Just once...*I'll win.*"

I squealed, as Drake hurtled us towards the floor of the arena. At the last moment, he twisted, bellowing like I'd winded him, and landed in an agonizing *crunch* beneath me.

I lay in confusion on top of him, like a hunter on her felled lion, stroking a stray curl behind his ear, whilst a snaking trail of scarlet matted his hair.

"Truth," he wheezed. "I was always going to lose for you."

*How could he see me, when he was still so hidden to me?*

Suddenly, I was yanked backwards by my top and hung in Rahab's grip. He glowered at Drake. "I believe you've shown us all, including our little apprentice here, your *worth*."

Drake reddened, as he scrambled to his knees. He held out his arms in front of him.

It was only then that I saw the welts: faded bruises criss-crossed from wrist to shoulder.

"We're all closed today for flogging," I snarled. "I win the three rewards, not punishments."

Rahab threw a cat o'nine tails between us: a rope whip with nine fierce tails of knotted cord, spiked with little metal balls. "You win the overall battle, but my son lost. Did you imagine it would be without punishment?" *Did hoping on wishing stars count?* "And I've judged sparring for centuries. You've both been the terror of armies. That was like kids wrestling. Whip

31

him and be done with it."

"That'll be a *no way, Sauron.*"

*Silence.*

Even the mages were standing to sweating attention now. Maybe I'd better tone down the cult leader baiting.

"Pick it up." Rahab's irises flickered.

I bit the inside of my cheek. "Not even if it was the One Ring."

Rahab booted the whip towards Drake. "Then it's our Queen Apprentice's turn."

My stomach turned.

*Don't pick it up...*

When Drake gingerly lifted the rope handle, dangling the cords between his fingers like hair, I trembled from the hot betrayal flooding me.

"How many lashes do you think our little apprentice earned, Duma?" Rahab asked casually.

*I knew a trick question when I heard it.*

Drake's pink lips pursed. "I do not believe she has earned any, father. She bested me; I am the failure. If lashes are owed, then they're owed to me alone."

*The brave bastard.*

Yet, wasn't that the true meaning of the Brotherhood? Defending each other, loyalty, *sacrificing*... Drake was my fam. He loved me, and I'd mourned him when I hadn't known whether he'd been alive or dead.

*Did I love him as well?*

Rahab nodded. "As you wish." *Prick.* "I shall deal with your chastisement this evening." Drake dropped the whip, as if it'd sunk its fangs into him. "And you...?" He twirled around to the mages. "Shall the Queen of Apprentices *rise*?"

*Lazarus rises! Rises! Rises! And we will rise!*

The Lazarus Mages, like golden butterflies, shot into the air, beaten into a fervour by their own chanting: ecstatic, rapturous, and thunderous. They spiralled on flaming wings, whilst my own remained mutilated.

*Lazarus rises...?*

I tremored: Eden, the psycho leader of the *vampire* fanatics had shouted that at me. And when two fanatics on either side in a war chant the same riddle, it's never a candy cartload of fun. Also, hadn't the second line been that everyone would then say *all our goodbyes?*

Maybe it'd just been a campfire story to scare vampire kiddies but it still made me shiver.

Rahab's grin was wild. "The Brotherhood have spoken. You're honoured. You're both to start Initiation Purge Week." Drake's horrified gasp did nothing to make me believe chocolate treats were part of the Purge. "Of course, there's only one position to train as Lazarus Mage. We thrive on competition. At the end, the loser will be reduced to Underserving to serve the winning apprentice."

Drake drew himself to his feet, casting his father a furious glance, before stalking away.

An Underserving? *Lower even than apprentice...*

When I looked up, I caught Rebel's glance from across the arena, where he'd been left kneeling. He smiled, but I could see the tightness around his eyes.

What the hell was this *Initiation*?

*Purge* didn't sound like *pleasure*. More like *hell*.

Delicate fingers clasped mine. I glanced at Mischief, who'd sidled to my side. Yet the way he stroked his thumb across the back of my hand, just like Rebel would've done had he been able to, didn't reassure me. Because Mischief wouldn't be comforting me if he wasn't terrified himself.

I'd won the Battle of the Bailey — and Mischief. But I'd humiliated Drake, forcing him into a contest for the only place as a mage. Now I had to take on a week of hellish initiations. I couldn't ask Drake to throw the Purge because whoever lost, faced a lifetime as little more than a slave.

# 4

To find a genie is not to be its master but its slave. Because wishes always have a price

I'd once found an antique tin lamp in a flea market on the way back from school. Although I was no thief, I'd stolen it for Gizem, my best mate at Jerusalem Children's Home. The Two Orphan Muskateers, we were the storytellers; Gizem loved to scare the other kids with tales of jinn (and not the Disney singing sort).

It'd become the tradition after that for each kid to take a turn holding the lamp like a holy relic, making a *wish* to the Jerusalem Jinn.

I think we half-believed in the jinn ourselves within the year.

Except, a wish to a jinn never went the way you meant it to, even we knew that. It was dangerous to tempt the dark magics.

What had I wished...?

*For the angels to want me.*

I bastard got what I wished for, didn't I?

I spluttered, spitting out silky mouthfuls of hair.

*Oomph.*

The Blood Familiars — fox brothers, Blaze and Spark— wriggled more firmly onto me, squashing me under their heavy flanks.

Blaze tipped back his head; his amber eyes met mine as they narrowed, then he let out a throaty *gekkering*.

*Thwap* — Spark's white-tipped tail swiped me across the nose.

I cracked my head against the glass floor of my chamber in the Mirror Lodge. I groaned, as my wings were jostled; my accelerated angelic healing powers were already knitting together the broken bones, but they still ached. I ignored the molten slivers of pain, twisting to tickle the Blood Familiars' sides.

We tumbled in a thrash of fur, feathers, and tails, until I wormed out from underneath them, panting.

"No fair," Spark whined telepathically.

"Life's not fair, foxie, suck it up," I panted, staring up at my dishevelled reflection in the glass ceiling.

An orb of violet fire, like a magician's ball, flared and sputtered in the centre of the room, casting it in a spectre glow: a box lit from the inside. Rough ropes, as if I was at sea, coiled from the ceiling, either to hold me, my Broken, Underserving, or some other *beast*: in this shifting castle of the impossible, it could be anything Rahab imagined.

*And wasn't that a thought that buzzed with the happies?*

Blaze leapt onto my bed — a glass slab that was too close to Sleeping Beauty deathbed chic for comfort — and circled round and round nesting into the bronze velvet sheets. "We've bided a long while now, and you swore this time you'd bring at least one of our lads home with you."

35

*Home...?*

How long had it been since I'd had a home? My apartment with Jade...? But then, Toben and his gang had still controlled it...

*Never...?*

Spark nudged me with his head, before grinning in submission. "Aye right, we miss them, Keeper."

I stroked my fingers across Spark's ears, and he nuzzled closer. I stifled a yawn. When had I last slept?

*Sleep deprivation: Cult Brainwashing 101.*

I rolled my eyes at Blaze, who'd wrapped himself imperiously in my velvet sheets like a gown. "Easy, bro. I go — BOOM — with my new wizarding skills, turning the entire Legion into baby gargoyles, then burrow my way off this island because magic grounds all Angel Airlines, with a bloke strapped under each—"

"Are you mocking me, lass?" Blaze growled into my mind.

I winced. *Maybe Mischief's sarcasm was catching.* "Turn down fox radio, I'm getting a migraine. And that'd be a *yeah*." When Blaze's eyes blinked with worry, my tone gentled. "I saw Rebel. He's alive...safe." They didn't need to know about the way Rahab's hand had curled possessively around his shoulder. "Plus, the reason I look like a sailor doll that got snapped in half, then dunked in the pond, is I fought for Mischief."

Spark let out an excited bark, his green eyes sparkling, before cringing low to the floor. "Sorry, sorry, sorry..."

*Mischief had himself a fanboy.*

"You freed him?" Blaze demanded.

I shuffled my foot backwards and forwards. "What's *free* mean anyway?"

**You should've known better than to trust wishes. The Mage is the Phoenix Jinn: he burns those he tricks to ash.**

*You're done with the Scaredy-pants routine then?*

**I'll be wearing them in reinforced sequins every moment we're stuck with these angelic assholes. You should be too.**

**How are your wishes working out for you?**

*Wish three? To prove myself...? I had to destroy Drake to do it. And I set us both up for this psycho Initiation Purge Week.*

**Dick move, Feathery-love.**

*Plus, Lazurus rises chanted in ecstatic fervour seems less Aslan and more Loki.*

**Then let me serve you some space Viking realness: the dead rise, when the Mage resurrects angels as slaves.**

**Yet you've only seen one terrifying sliver of the Legion's truth.**

**There'll come a time, when you'll have to decide whether the rewards the Mage grants, outweigh the price he'll demand.**

**And you haven't even seen Wish Two yet...**

A wide screen to the side of the chamber, which glittered with amber shards like a Phoenix bursting into flames, shook.

*Splash* — water sprayed from behind the screen, followed by an elegant foot and ankle pointing out in a striptease.

"Enough of the *free* semantics, look you," a teasing voice called. Then a wet — *naked* — Broken, Ceri, crawled from the bath behind the screen towards me. Less like a slave, however, and more like he was the auburn-haired lion, and I was the prey. He grinned as he shook his hair, raining pearly bubbles across the mirrors and to their sizzling death on the violet fire. "I ran this bath for you, and you haven't even joined me. Rude, and the waste of all this soapy good time fun."

*Hell, why did he have to be so pretty?*

Ceri had been delivered to me as my personal slave on the first night that I'd been brought to the castle, and in case I hadn't been able to read between the lines of *why*, Ceri had been quick to read it out to me in smutty detail.

I rolled my eyes. "Do most Broken get in the baths they run for their mages?"

Ceri rolled his shoulder, whose skin was bronzed as

37

caramel. Yet he had only stumps where his wings should've been: as a slave, they'd been cut off. "Do I look like most Broken?"

I flushed. "Screw that, you're my Lion Boy."

He gave a light laugh, licking my thigh.

I shivered: *bad thoughts, down girl*. Then he slithered up my body, as I clasped my arms around his slippery waist. "Just a quick wash to get clean, then dirty..." He murmured.

He lifted his arms, grasping onto the ropes above his head and arching his back. His chest stretched, pushing himself out to me: an offering.

I gasped.

For the first time, this wasn't a bloke bound but *willing*.

When I ghosted my hands down Ceri's chest, his breath hitched. I circled his nipple until it peaked, then sucked it; it tasted of ginger, as hot and spicy as Ceri smelt. He moaned; his prick was hard and straining. Unexpectedly tender, I trailed my hand up his neck, towards his cheek. He turned his head, pressing his lips to the back of my hand.

*Just like Gwyn and Haman: the other Broken slaves.*

Had Ceri been trained in the same tricks...?

*What the hell was I allowing myself to do again?*

The semantics of *free*...? How was Ceri any freer to choose what he did with me? He'd been gifted to me as a Broken, just as Gwyn once had: my sex slave...

I recoiled, shaking my head. "Not going to happen."

Ceri held onto the ropes for a moment longer, examining me with a shrewd look, before letting go. He pouted. "Why won't you play with me? I refuse to believe I revolt you because I have eyes, see." He jiggled his soapy arse, and I sniggered. "And here's a secret: I just want a good shag, isn't it?"

"Kinky bastard angels," I muttered as I backed away to the wall. "And you enjoying sex isn't a secret."

He stalked after me. "It's really not."

"We're not flirting anymore. The Non-Flirt Zone has been reached."

"Are you certain?" Ceri rested his hand against the wall, pressing his naked body against me, as he tilted his head in thought.

"We're not doing anything..." I gestured with my hands, whilst Ceri blinked at me in faux innocence; I was so adding him to my List of Asses to Kick. "...Naughty together because there's no *we*."

"Don't worry, I can solo flirt. You should try it some time. I'm the Solo Flirtster. But there's no *we*...?"

*Smack* — dramatically, Ceri collapsed to the floor.

Then he cracked open an eye to see if his death scene had my full attention. I crossed my arms, glaring down at the Drama King.

Spark nosed Ceri with a whimper.

Ceri winked at him. "Tragic, to die so young and beautiful...but at least I have my wank bank to console me."

"Try again, bro." I snatched Ceri by the arm, yanking him up, whilst he giggled. When his head nestled against my chest, his auburn hair brushing against my skin, I couldn't help asking, "How'd you survive in this nightmare sect?"

When Ceri stiffened, I stroked the curl of his ear and regretted saying a word.

"I didn't," he whispered at last. "Maybe I'm a rebel Broken, see, like you're the rebel princess? When we first heard about that...I hoped I wasn't alone..." He snuggled closer, and his words were almost lost. "Or maybe I'm just faulty. That's why they gave me to the freaky cold magicked Glory." Then he drew back from me, his eyes wide. "*I* don't—"

I caught his chin. "Ever thought you're the only one who's good enough for royalty?"

This seemed to short-circuit his flirty-tongue; Ceri froze, staring at me in awed shock. Finally, he managed to grin. "If this is a dream, then I'll take it. Ceri: by Royal Approval." He slammed his hand against the glass. "Not a failure, shameful, let-down..."

"Chosen," I repeated firmly. Hell, it was too close and raw. Every shadowed doubt that'd played on my own thoughts, here the Legion used them to control. "Saved for the queen."

"Then long live the Queen!" Ceri bounced on his toes. Then he blanched, backing away from the wall.

I frowned, twisting to see what'd freaked him out.

**Wish Number Two: you asked to *see* your brother. In the world of warped wishes, you watch your words, hooker.**

**Now you'll see him... Yet how much crueller is it to *see* but not be able to *touch*?**

The mirror wall no longer reflected back my own room but *the room on the other side of the Lodge.*

True to his word when he'd first brought me to the castle, Rahab had placed me with my half-brother, just never in the same room. Now I'd got my second wish: I could see my brother, but only through the one-way mirror on my wall.

I *clanged* against the mirror, sticking my palms flat against it, whilst I stared through at the other side.

The Looking Glass room was identical, except that the sheets on the bed were golden and lying on his side amongst them was my *brother*.

I pushed myself onto tiptoe, grinning; my mouth was dry, and my pulse raced. My magic stirred, striking against the glass to reach out to him, just as the shadows danced inside, until I could've twirled Ceri around from the fluttering feeling, if I hadn't been so stuck to the picture in front of me.

Even if I could only see brunet tresses cascading to my brother's shoulder — and a snowy peak of skin.

*Bruised skin.*

I bit my lip hard. The hint of shoulder above the sheet was swollen and purple.

*What the hell had Rahab done to my brother?*

I couldn't let my brother be hurt. I had to save him, just like I hadn't been able to save my sister.

I slammed my fist against the glass, but it didn't even tremor.

*Crash, crash, crash.*

Then strong arms were around my waist dragging me

away, and the wall was frosting, shimmering back to a reflection of only my room.

My brother was lost to me again.

"*Bastard, no...*" I screamed, squirming away from the hold.

"Apprentice," the cold voice broke through my grief, stilling me. "In the name of the Brotherhood, remember the Code."

I swung around to the chilly gaze of Och, the Chief Discipliner, who was both Mischief's older brother and leader of the mages who trained the Broken slaves, as well as *chopped off their wings.*

Yeah, so for Discipliner read *prick*.

I'd freed Barakiel — the Lightning Angel — from the prison on Angel World; Barakiel had killed Nathanael, Mischief and Och's younger brother. Not that either of Nathanael's brothers knew he was even dead. I didn't know why Rahab was keeping the secret, but I didn't fancy the magical wrath of either a Discipliner or my shapeshifting fam, so wouldn't be the one to break that silence.

I'd once accused Mischief of being part of the Discipliners, but it was only when I saw Mischief delivered to me slumped in sizzling electrified angel cuffs as my Undeserving *by his own brother* — a gleaming broad-shouldered Discipliner in gold harem pants and neat silver curls like a Roman senator — that I understood the truth behind the Legion of the Phoenix.

This was about *power*.

Whereas Och had been raised with it, Mischief had played the part of the pleb. Yet when Mischief could blast us all to itty bits with his magic: *bastard why?*

**Wish Number One: Mischief is yours, Violet-puss.**

*But he's not free.*

**What did your wet and suckable lion cub call it? *Semantics*, bitch.**

**Rahab isn't royalty; he was left to die. He's played a game of survival from the moment he was born; there's no silver spoon, only the drive to win.**

41

**Now he expects no less from his brainwashed kids.
You either up your game or you become his pawn.**

"Screw the Brotherhood and screw the Code." My magic gave a punishing pulse behind my eyes, even as I heard the echo of Kunel's nasal voice chiding me for my *rebellion*. "My brother—"

"Shall cope one more day without you." Mischief scowled. "Or do you imagine our sweet Invisible Prince trained to be nothing but a lost duckling, rather than the Butcher—"

Och backhanded Mischief, sprawling him across the chamber's floor.

Blaze bounded off the bed next to Spark, as they both snarled.

Only then did I realise that Ceri had fallen to his knees, his forehead touching the floor, whilst he panted. He was terrified and for the first time acting like the Broken on Angel World had.

*Hell, Och had probably trained him.*

I stepped in front of Ceri, pushing Och back and enjoying the indignant expression, which reddened his haughty face. "Bounce, bitch."

Och's gaze flickered between us, before settling on Mischief, who'd struggled up onto one knee. Och appeared startled. "Brother, please," he whispered, "for once, remember what you are."

I blinked, confused, as Och shoved Mischief, pushing down on his shoulders. To my surprise, Mischief ducked under his hands, staggering to his feet.

For a long moment, there was nothing but a staring contest between them like they were two kids, rather than powerful magic wielders.

Why wouldn't Mischief simply kneel? And why did my own vampiric and angelic powers surge and foam inside at his refusal, hungering to *force* him.

To slap him down, as his brother had?

When Och rubbed his fingers together, a coiled whip appeared in his hand. "Do not shame our family further."

Mischief hesitated, before turning away his head and

holding out his palm.

My arms shook, as I hugged them across my chest. "He's mine: packages must be delivered undamaged."

"By the Phoenix, he's not yours yet and he shall always remain under my guidance. Are you ready to reform, brother?"

Mischief ignored Och, tilting his chin in defiance.

Och sighed, hesitating.

*Swish — crack.*

The whip landed, leaving a crimson weal across the centre of Mischief's palm, but he didn't make a sound.

*Swish — crack.*

The second blow was harder. It cut across Mischief's thumb, and he flinched.

Och was holding back though, I could tell: wrapping the whip behind his shoulder for maximum effect but pulling it when he reached Mischief's palm to reduce the force. *I'd bet anything he didn't do that when he lashed the Broken.*

Could I beat Jade? If Rahab made me deliver her in handcuffs?

*No bastard way.*

Och raised the whip again, and Mischief stiffened.

Three wishes — rewards — and they'd each bitten me in the arse.

Suddenly, hands gripped me from behind, pinning my arms. I screeched at the pressure on my fragile wings. A sackcloth bag was jammed over my head: dark, stinking, and rough. I struggled to breathe through the fabric that sucked in and out of my mouth on each inhale and exhale.

I booted out, reaching for my violet fire, magic, shadows...*anything*. But it was dampened, like it'd been smothered, as I was in the sack cloth.

I screamed, trapped animal style, lost in the flailing panic.

43

*Trapped, trapped, trapped...*

Then Kunel's voice hissed close to my ear, "Welcome to Purge Week."

# 5

In the dark, I tilted up my chin, despite the stinking sackcloth over my head: I'd been humiliated by being transformed into a scarecrow, but I could still have swag. If this was the start of Initiation Purge Week, then I'd at least start it like a queen.

If I didn't win the contest with Drake to train as a mage, then I'd be reduced to Underserving. Falling from ruler to servant wasn't high on my to-do list, so although I couldn't force Drake to martyr himself again (and I didn't think Rahab would let it slip twice), I'd battle him for real to win the Initiation.

*Whatever the hell they were going to do to us, it was game on.*

I took a ragged breath, swinging my arms through the hot air.

Kunel had hauled me down corridors, across courtyards, and up stairs. Unable to see, I'd staggered, dizzy and disorientated.

*Now, I didn't have a clue where I was.* Point One on the freak-out-meter to Purge Week.

I sniffed: there was something beneath the stench of old

45

sackcloth. A warm autumnal scent like bonfires. It smelled like...*Lucifer*.

*Dad.*

To hell with the Initiation. I didn't know if it was fear, relief, or concern for Lucifer that made me rip off the bag from my head, spluttering as the coarse material caught on my lips.

I took hurried steps forward only to stop in shock.

Instead of my dad, it was Drake staring back at me, his eyes dazed and red-rimmed. His wings were grey, like he was one of the Fallen. I sniffed again: Drake's wings had been smeared in *ash* to shame him. Just as he'd been dressed in a matching all black leather Lucifer outfit.

*This was hazing Legion style.*

Point Two to Purge Week.

My heart ached that it wasn't Lucifer, just as I was flooded with confusing relief that I wouldn't have to see the dad I'd betrayed.

*Or hurt him.*

Yet both sides of my nature howled even louder that I'd have to hurt Drake. My new magic coiled around the ancient powers, shooting freezing spikes to cool the outrage, each one a pricking reminder of the Phoenix Code.

I'd been dragged to the Iron Barracks. Neat rows of grey beds were ranked in the arched iron room. The porthole windows looked out over the Bailey and the whipping post.

I glared around at the apprentices; even the kids had been included in the dystopian themed party. The apprentices stood in a silent circle around the pretend Lucifer, as if they'd trapped him. Kunel marched to join them, his Mr Perfect smile sliding into place.

When Kunel beckoned to me like this was all just a fun game of Piggy in the Middle, I ignored him, meeting Drake's gaze instead. "Leather suits you. I thought Rebel was my only bondage angel."

Kunel's smile slipped. "Do not talk to him. He's working on his worthiness."

"And I'm working on not freaking out and kicking all your arses...*sir*," I managed to force out the *sir*, before the hot shank slice of magic punished me for my insolence. "Wait, I know this bit: where's the Sorting Hat?"

"Fool," Drake hissed, "this is part of the Initiation. Join the circle and hush. *Please.*"

It was the *please* that did it.

*Clank, clank, clank.*

I stomped across the metal floor, crossing my arms as I joined the circle. Sometimes I forgot how honourable Drake was, as long as the Matriarch wasn't pulling his strings.

Kunel flexed his muscled arms, before pointing at Drake in the centre of the circle. Like freaky mirror images, the other mages pointed at Drake too.

Drake flushed.

Stubbornly, I kept my arms crossed, even as my pulse raced.

Kunel lifted his eyebrow at me.

Drake mouthed, "I win already...?"

Growling, I lifted my arm and *pointed.* Drake stood ramrod straight, as if before a firing squad.

*Had he just played me?*

"Tell us your failures this week, Duma." Kunel crooned. My guts twisted because that was the tone I craved. My magic unwound from my neck, reaching out hungrily towards it: *the praise.* I lived for those moments of golden attention, and from the adoring but envious expressions on the other apprentices' faces, I knew they were torn with the same feeling. *What was pain if you could have love too?* "Reform yourself through confession."

Drake stared helplessly around at the accusing apprentices — *and me* — before casting his gaze to the ground. "I failed the Brotherhood in the Battle of the Bailey," his voice was flat and lifeless.

*Unworthy, unworthy, unworthy.*

I jumped at the apprentices' chant. Drake flinched but didn't look up.

"I...doubted the Phoenix code and—"

Drake's confession was drowned out by cries of outrage and disgust. He hunched, hugging his ash shamed wings around himself in self-comfort.

I shuddered at the Legion's attempt to weaken Drake: way to emasculate a bloke. They'd taken the proud Commander's fears — that he'd Fall, become Lucifer, was unworthy — and made him confess it himself.

Point Three to the Initiation.

*What the hell did they have planned for me?*

Kunel pursed his lips, but his eyes gleamed with zeal. "Enough, brothers. Duma is to be praised for his bravery in his confession. His sins are great, but now we can help him reform. Only we love him enough to hurt him when he needs it. And I think you have one last failure to admit?"

Drake shook his head.

Kunel's strong shoulders rolled, as he pointed at Drake with more vigour. "On my feathers, if I must dig out your secrets myself, you shall feel the lash."

Drake's gaze lifted to mine. My hand shook, where I pointed at him; a tear slipped down Drake's cheek.

At last, he admitted, "I've had sexual thoughts towards another who is not my Glory."

*Unworthy, unworthy, unworthy.*

Still Drake didn't drop his gaze.

*This cult was going down medieval style.*

**As long as you're not a programmed robot, teaching the Brotherhood's cult yourself like the First Reformer.**

**Does the brainwashing dick have an off button on his shiny ass?**

*No one's messing with my head.*

**Think again, Violet-sweets. They've already**

48

**messed with your gorgeous head.**

**If they hadn't, would you be pointing at Commander Goldilocks and making him cry?**

Shocked, I slammed down my hand, stumbling backwards. *What the hell was I doing?*

Kunel seized Drake by the neck, shoving him to the floor and forcing out his wings: punishment position. I watched in horror as the other apprentices kneeled in rows on either side of him.

Kunel stood back. "In the name of the Code: *no brother will show weakness*. Let us scourge your confessed failings and raise you up on our wings together. Crawl through the gauntlet and be purged."

Drake wriggled along on his elbows, like a feathered worm. I wet my lips, backing away.

Until the blast hit Drake from the first apprentice, singing his right wing. He howled, just as flames blackened his left wing from the apprentice on the other side. Still Drake dragged himself forward.

Blood pounded in my ears; I was going to hurl.

As the third apprentice raised his hand to strike, I leapt forward. "Allow it," I snarled, knocking his electric strike ringing against the iron roof, before tumbling backwards over Drake. "You want to make this a Code battle? Then how about our duty to *protect and defend the Brotherhood?* Not barbecue each other with marshmallows."

Drake had turned his head, his breathing shallow through the pain. "They tend not to use marshmallows." He gave me a searching look. "Allow me to congratulate you on your idiocy. All you had to do was permit my suffering and you'd win. I would have imagined that was easy."

I brushed my hand gently through his blackened feathers, and he leant into the touch. "I'm not the same bitch of a Glory that I was on Angel World. I promise, Glories can love."

He jerked back, his mouth working as if desperate to say something but battling hard not to let it out.

49

Then a brawny hand was hauling me backwards, and it was *me* in the circle of glowering apprentices.

"In the Legion we must rise together or we'll Fall. Mage Drake will cast out the unworthy to be Marked...' Kunel paused for the *whimpers* and *whines*. 'My mission is to save, and I can do that through love but if I'm forced through wilful rebellion, I'll use *fear*.'

*Silence.*

Now I even missed the terrified whimpers because Kunel's Angelic Power was *nightmares*. When he snatched the base of my neck, digging in his thumbs, I gasped.

I tumbled onto the mountain of feathers, above the valley of bones. Here, I was Beginning and End. Death and Rebirth. Destroyer and Saviour. The vision I'd suffered ever since my powers had come in on my twenty-first birthday.

Except, now violet flames — *mine* — licked crackling across the valley. Bones glowed and feathers sizzled to black. The air stank with billowing clouds of smoke. I choked, stumbling through the haze across the charred skeletons of...

*No, no, no...*

My foot sank through a wing, which *snapped* beneath my boot.

A trench of angelic skeletons: *my fam*, nestled next to their vampire enemies.

And there I was — a dark beast atop the mountain — shooting fire into the sky: an apocalyptical nightmare.

I howled in terror, scrabbling backwards.

*It wasn't me...I couldn't do that...I'd leashed the beast...I wouldn't kill...*

**Nightmare**, **Violet-cupcake. Sir Brainwasher is playing with your fears like his dick. Don't let him get a happy all over you.**

*Not...real? I haven't ganked...?*

**Snap your dark self out of it. He twists love to fear.**

*I'm dreaming?*

**You're trapped in his spell. It's real, girl, unless you break out.**

*How about this?*

I shook myself, refusing to look down at the bodies at my feet. Instead, I swaggered up the mountain towards myself.

Hell, I looked legendary, even if I was an evil bitch.

Evil Bitch Me appeared confused, as I snatched her by the hands and drew her into an exaggerated twerk routine. Then I closed my eyes, stroking Evil Bitch Me's hair behind her ear and pulling her closer, before licking my tongue across her lips.

I snogged my evil twin because how many chances was I going to have to try that out?

*Yeah, I'm an awesome kisser.*

When I opened my eyes, I was sprawled on the floor of the Iron Barracks and Kunel's face was red, as he awkwardly clasped his hands behind his back.

*He'd caught the show then.*

Kunel bent over me. "It appears that before you can bring honour to the Legion, you need a taste of how we treat *creatures*, since you insist on acting like one."

"Don't you like a little beast in your bitch?"

Kunel's lip curled. "What I think is that chains and collars will *suit you*." Behind me, I heard Drake's holler, as I surged up. Kunel shot his nightmare blackness at me, however, and although my own shadows rose against them, Kunel's surge of *fear* coursed up and down my spine, tumbling me to my knees. I panted, dry retching. Kunel patted my head. "They shall suit the beast very well until it learns obedience. You've barely tasted true punishment. At least you won't be lonely when you join our other creature."

I choked; my mind howled.

*What monster was I being caged with?*

I huddled at Kunel's feet, reduced to nothing but the *creature* he claimed, in my animalistic terror of chains, collars, and monsters.

# 6

*Freak, monster, beast*...the labels had been spat at me since I was a kid: a supernatural hidden amongst the human, simply trying to belong. Now I'd been disgraced from royal apprentice to chained *creature* because there was always a balance: freedom for my fam.

But I wasn't alone in my punishment; I'd been leashed with Monster Number Two.

I shivered because of course *creatures* didn't wear clothes. Bare arsed on the slate flagstones of the kitchen floor, I pulled at the iron collar around my neck, which dug into my skin. I tugged, but it was looped by a chain at the front to a metal ring beside the hearth. A fire died a slow death, hissing to itself, as a blackened chimney rose above.

In the gloom that reached to the vaulted ceiling, the dancing flames cast the only light. If this had been the Under World, there'd have been punk music blaring, cage fights, and mayhem. But this was the formal, orderly, and dignified Legion of the Phoenix. All the good little soldiers were tucked up in bed. At this midnight hour, only the *creatures* still haunted the castle.

I panted, edging closer to the *second* chain that led behind the trestle table.

*Here little Monsty-monster... Nice creatures of the night don't lurk, unless they want spankings...*

I licked my lips; my gums tingled.

Charcoal grey eyes sparked in the dark: twin stars. Then Ash — the vampire Brigadier — prowled on all fours around the gilt-edged trestle table towards me; he was naked too.

I jumped; my heart pounded. I was dizzy with desire, ecstasy, and *relief*.

I grinned so hard the sides of my mouth throbbed. "If I had to be tied to another creature, you'd be my first choice." I didn't miss his flinch on *creature*. "Who'd have guessed a fanatical cult weaves freedom into chains?"

I shuddered at the collar around Ash's throat, linked like mine to a ring by the hearth: it shone brilliant gold. The olive skin of his neck around the collar was blistered, as if the collar had *burned*.

In the dark, Ash was a deadly panther, even if he'd been leashed. I ached to run my hand through his tumble of sable hair. I scanned him for injuries, as I had Rebel, but except for the sores around the collar, he was unmarked.

*Maybe the mages only needed the collar?*

Hell, these past twenty-eight days, I'd yearned for Ash, whose aromatic scent was now calming my fear, almost as much as I'd thirsted for Rebel's sugar blood and the stroke of our Bond.

My ancient powers wanted...*needed*...both my blokes: vampire and angel.

*Wasn't that love?*

The walls hummed, thrumming in time with the magic that beat through me.

Ash pounced, pinning me under him, and I squeaked. He smirked. "Hey, gorgeous." When he wrapped his grey wings around us both blanket-like, I shuddered, remembering Drake's ash smudged feathers...and tears. "Hot as you are naked and styling the bondage look like me — what did I warn you about kinky angels? — this wasn't what I wished for every

53

night. I'm lodging a formal complaint."

I couldn't help the sharp stab of hurt that he hadn't *wished* for me, as I had him. But what could I've expected? I'd been the reason his sisters had died in Lucifer's light. He'd had an entire month — alone — to grieve, think, and kick my arse to the curb.

Why would he still love me? *Blokes always abandoned me.*

Even as the thought pulsated through me, however, somewhere far back I knew it was *wrong*. Yet I couldn't calm my panicked pulse or thundering heart.

I struggled to escape the strong band of Ash's arms, even as I wished I could sink into his embrace. Kunel's terrors still shanked my mind in flashing points: I stiffened at each shadowed fear.

"I wished for you to be safe, Violet," Ash said, softly. "Not here with me in chains. Safe, happy, *free*."

At last, his words broke through my thrashing and the tar-black buzzing in my mind.

Ash hadn't abandoned me: he'd sacrificed himself.

*Again.*

I kissed him, pulling him closer, until the confusion was chased away. "How could I be any of those things without your sexy arse?"

Ash pulled away. "Although it is sexy, you don't mean that. I'm not like your angels: a toy to make the fear, worries, or *hate* in your head go away. I've been nothing but a whore: there for other's pleasure. And I won't be that again. What are they doing to you? What are those...shadows?"

Flushing, I booted at him, scrabbling away, as my chain *clinked*, slithering after me like a metallic umbilical cord.

*Clink* — my back hit an unwashed cooking pot; my stomach growled at the scent of rich meats and herbs, which still clung to it.

I'd only been fed on porridge, which was the slop served up to apprentices, and my insides felt hollowed out. I couldn't stop the moan, as my tongue darted across my lips.

Ash sprawled on the slate floor with a twist of his hips like he was on a silk four-poster. "If I'm a really good boy, sometimes the cooks let me lick clean the pots." *And why did even that sound appealing?* "Note to self: Oliver Twist impression isn't popular with angels."

*Hell, I wished I'd seen that.* "You're popular with me, and I'm the bitching queen."

"Popular enough to forget that I'm the mages' pet now? Or are you back singing the *vampires are the Big Bads* marching tune? Do you think I...deserve this?" Why did he have to sound so uncertain as he fidgeted, linking his hands behind his head?

*Twenty-eight days separated from me and his fam...*

"You asked what fun party games the bastards have been playing with me, but I want to know what they've been doing to *you* to have made you forget that *fam is fam*. And that means—"

"What?" Ash whispered, stiffening. His eyes were half-lidded, but he never took his intent stare off me. "You're..." He swallowed, "...in Hogwarts the X-rated version but you can learn here. The Slytherins, who treat me as the class mascot, see you as a champion. Our retro punk angel is Mage Drake's boy..." He reached as if to touch his collar, but only hovered his fingers over the front of it, afraid to touch: it flared warningly, and he winced. "I'm the *creature*, not you. I wish I could be more than that, and I was once. But I've played the pet before and I can do it now, if it means you're free."

I rocked, light-headed, whilst static crackled up and down my skin, spitting to escape and blast the world for *letting Ash believe that*. "Fam means," I replied, each word as sharp as a polished shank, "that I love you."

Ash blinked at me.

Then I dived at him, howling with violet and black that blurred the kitchen to nothing but *Ash, Ash, Ash...*

I snatched him by the shoulders, tumbling him over, until we were yanked by the chains at our throats with mirrored yelps. Then I straddled him, licking down the line of his long neck, whilst he gasped.

My steel nails shot out, gouging thin lines down Ash's

chest. He whined, arching into their touch, as I groaned at the intensity of the sensation: trembling shocks that radiated from their sensitive tips. I quaked, biting my lip at the overload. My wings burst to flames at the rush.

Then I lapped at the trails of crimson, juddering at the bursts of rich power and longing.

*Home.*

*Hell, Ash's blood was home, and I hungered to drink every drop of him and live in his scarlet...*

My eyes widened.

Ash's dazed gaze focused, as if he'd caught my thought, then he slammed his lips against mine: hard and possessive. His fingers tangled in my hair, holding me still. Here was the dark solider of the Under World, who'd dominated the Devil's Trident in a dance with death that'd paled even mine.

*No one's bastard pet.*

When I ran my fingers through his feathers, he keened. Meant as a punishment to torment by Lucifer, Seducers were hypersensitive and kept on a constant edge because they couldn't reach their own completion unless their wingtips were touched. Seducers were meant to be *toys*: to give pleasure and not receive.

Ash wasn't Lucifer's anymore, however, his pleasure was his own.

So, I didn't tease, as I caressed along Ash's wings. I burnt to sear away the mages' touch on him, the lonely days, and his doubts, as well as to prove my *love*, which tottered new born. His prick pulsed between our bodies like his obsidian wingtips. I crawled over him, stroking his right wingtip, before sucking it hard between my lips.

Ash's back bowed, as he howled. Yet then he snatched my hand, sucking *my* claw into *his* mouth.

*Hell, hell, hell...*

Electrified, it was my turn to howl, as I closed my eyes, slamming my other fist, nails out, *screeching* across the slate. The winding coils from my gums to my wings built to a wailing crescendo, until finally nothing but black...

Groaning, I opened my eyes.

**Back in the land of the living, Violet-hell?**

*What in the holy big 'O's, was that, J?*

***That*** **was a Seducer's big 'O', and there's nothing** *holy* **about that slice of heaven. Your Geek Fang and his wand had a magical moment: he took you to heaven.**

*Death and sex in the same clever nail mods. Kudos to the Fangs.*

**If you were his food, the Seducer would be snacking on you. If you paint Eat Me on your arse, sooner or later some dick will take a bite.**

*Not Ash. I trust him. He's earned that.*

**And all it took was the sacrifice of everything he had.**

I winced, unable to banish the memory of Ash's sisters in the Fire Catacombs being burned alive by Lucifer's Light because I'd taught them to talk. How I'd been forced to watch their deaths alongside Ash, when all I'd been able to offer them had been hope.

*And it'd been a lie.*

Everything had been an illusion. *What was real now?*

The walls pressed against me: the humming louder and more oppressive.

I shifted up onto my side, huddling my arms around my knees.

Ash lounged against a three-legged stool, which was beside the table; he might as well have been smoking a cigarette. "So, that was an *I love you shag*?" His tone had lost its vulnerability and was back to teasing. "I've heard about those. Does that mean you haven't...forgotten...that I love you?"

"You may have knocked me out but you haven't screwed my memory." I forced myself to ignore the shadows crowding from the walls and their warning *whine* that set my teeth on edge. "I'll remember, as long as you don't go forgetting you're fam. Why would you...?"

"Do you have to know?"

57

"You mean pretend?"

"We're already collared, what more role play do you want?"

"I only want the truth."

I hated the way Ash's gaze became blank. I knew the look — I'd worn it myself at Jerusalem Children's Home to hide from my abusers. I'd seen it on Drake because of my mother, the Matriarch, who now violated as Marked Wing my father, Lucifer.

I never wanted Ash to look that way.

"The truth?" Ash tugged at the chain, and it *clanked*. "I'm yours to be used. So, *use me*."

I stared at him, breathing hard. Then I shuffled over to him, even though he cringed back, stroking a wave of hair out of his eyes. He stiffened like I was going to pounce on him and *use him* again like he'd offered. Instead, I leaned in, scenting the divine orange and clove aroma on his neck, before kissing him tenderly just under his ear.

He shivered.

"What this cult does to us, calls us, or convinces us to think... it doesn't make us *what we are*. You're my bloke: a funny, loyal, *Stars Wars* obsessed geek. And you're also the dark Brigadier with freaking swag."

Ash grinned. "That's why you love me, monkey muffins."

I raised my eyebrow. "You want to go there? Because I'm sure there's a butter knife around here..."

I scanned the gloom of the kitchen: the spitting hearth, soot-blackened chimney, trestle table that gleamed with shanks...

I dived for the table, just as Ash caught me around the middle with a *whoop*. "What's wrong, *babe*...?"

"You're going down. Where's the garlic crusher...?" I spluttered with laughter, as Ash nibbled kisses along the chafed skin around my collar.

"Sorry," he nibbled a final kiss, but his gleaming eyes didn't look *sorry*. "If you can hold back from my cutesy name death, why have you been locked here in chains?"

I sighed. "Disobeyed." Ash glanced up at me sharply. I knew we were both remembering the searing heat and stink of the Fire Catacombs and his own disobedience against Lucifer. "You're not the only one who can play the defiance card. Rahab's not like my dad but he's still a tyrant. You think I'm *safe* here? Then you've been drinking crazy juice because Rahab rules with punishment."

"You can't *just* rebel," Ash's voice had hardened to steel. 'This isn't the Under World, where anarchy is prized. You'll be broken. And these aren't kids playing at wizards but zealot cult soldiers. If you want to fight them..." He stared at me, questioningly. "Then you'll have to toughen yourself to be like them or you'll be the one who snaps. After everything we've sacrificed..." His breath hitched, and I bastard knew he was thinking of his sisters' tiny fingers raised to the viewing panel, whilst fire blasted through the furnace, *just as I was*. "...Don't you want to take down the true Emperor behind Angel World?"

Hell, Ash knew me too well. How had he always been able to worm under my skin, digging at the parts I'd thought hidden?

The shadows lapped at my mind, hungrily, as the walls ballooned closer.

I wrapped my wings around Ash, as I peeked around the kitchen. "I'm on it, bro," I whispered. "I'm working undercover."

Ash kissed me, urgent and hard. Startled, I tried to pull back, but he murmured against my lips, "Castle Drake is *alive*, Violet, like an evil Tardis. Mage Drake doesn't need spies, when he's everywhere at once. Whatever you're planning...however you're playing the Legion...keep it inside that beautiful brain of yours."

The whining in the kitchen became a furious buzzing in my mind, threading hot magic through my brain as it *quested*...

"What about the brat Commander, Rahab's son? I'm in a brutal *Hunger Games* style contest with him. But if he knew—"

"He can't. Unless you want to report on yourself to the Mage...? The angel grew up here; he's no newbie to suffering.

And we've all sacrificed for you." Ash's eyes were as hard as he'd told me I needed to become. Why did I forget my fam were each other's ancient enemies and only reluctant allies because of me? Why would Ash care if Drake hurt? It was only *me* that it tore up inside. "Break the Ice Commander. Win the battle. Then *we'll* be by your side to help win the war."

I blinked away tears, holding Ash closer to hide them. "If this was Rebel...?"

Ash tensed but nodded. "If this was our Irish angel, he'd have already volunteered to be broken."

Then why did I feel like *I* was being shattered? "My brother—"

"*Isn't you.*" I started at Ash's sudden intensity. "You can't save everybody, and not everybody wants saving."

"By the Phoenix, have you no honour?" Kunel's nasal sneer broke across the gloom.

Startled, I peered up, as Kunel and Och, like the Blond-haired Avengers, marched clattering across the kitchen. The fire flared in the hearth, surging up until we were lit by its flames.

"Nope, but I have a killer smile and sassy wit. Does that count?"

"Plus, a biteable arse," Ash muttered.

"Oh," I smirked up at Kunel, "and a biteable arse."

*Exploding mage*: the cooks were going to have a hell of a mess to clear up in the morning.

Kunel's blotchy face loomed closer. He snatched my chin. "You were chained here, apprentice, to teach you how low you could Fall, but instead you've revelled in your debasement, even touching the Fallen's *dirty whore*."

Black rose in roaring waves inside me at the way Ash flinched at each word. I'd wanted to know why he'd changed: and with each venomous word I learnt the truth.

At least, I thought so, until Kunel narrowed his eyes and commanded, 'Down, creature."

Suddenly, Ash scrabbled back from me, his eyes wide. He juddered like he was being shocked throughout his entire body. His wings spread out in agony, and he whimpered.

I twisted to Kunel. "Bastard, stop."

Kunel smiled but only *tutted*, before repeating, "*Down, creature.*"

This time, when he hesitated, Ash howled. Steam rose from his seared feathers; scarlet dribbled from the corner of his mouth.

The collar smouldered molten gold, as the skin beneath bubbled into blisters.

*A bastard shock collar...* No wonder the mages didn't need anything else to mark Ash.

I snatched onto Kunel's trousers, shaking them. "*Please...*"

Ash threw himself onto his front, prostrated before the angels. Slowly, his shaking stopped, and the steam settled.

"A Compulsion Collar punishes disobedience or even hesitation." Kunel chortled. "Some days I think the Brotherhood could be reformed so much more smoothly if we used these on apprentices." Och didn't join in Kunel's laugher. He scrutinized me: his gaze was serious and inscrutable. "But they are useful in the interrogation and training of Fallen. To teach them their place."

"You know the place of my boot? Your balls, bitch."

"Time to stop talking now." I *eeped*, as Och yanked the chain with a hiss of magic out of the metal ring, hauling me up and dangling me in front of him, until the collar choked me. I coughed, clawing at my throat. His icy stare met mine. "Somehow, you've tricked my brother; Zophia risked everything for you. Do you even know or care how you've destroyed him, creature?" When he shook the chain, I gurgled; my lungs ached, desperate for air. "He's always had so little here. So, when I fought for the assignment on Under World for him, it was his *chance*. And he threw it away for you. Yet you're the traitor, are you not?"

Even as my vision greyed, I knew I was missing something. *Traitor?*

"Now your spark is poisoning our dear Duma," Kunel enthused, like the camp leader and not the prick who'd forced a sobbing Drake to crawl through the gauntlet. "If he wasn't lit by your spark, he could return to the love of the Brotherhood. I must save our boys from you, cutting out your cancerous influence, if you don't reform."

I spluttered with the pain and the aching truth of their insults. I'd stolen both their chances with my Angelic Power, which incited loyalty.

Was I no better than either of my parents?

*Better than a creature?*

Should I be saving the Legion and the world from Rahab or myself?

I sagged, as Och twisted the chain. The shadows swallowed me.

Suddenly, the kitchen pans began to *rattle* and *clink*. The fire roared. Kunel dropped me with a holler, whilst the room lurched to the side like it'd sneezed.

"Now you bring a vampire attack upon us," Och hollered.

I blinked away the blackness, holding my hand to my bruised throat, as the walls shimmered and *screeched*.

*Vampire attack...?*

Ash reached for my hand, but with a sudden tilt, I was tossed to the other side of the kitchen, tumbling over the table and catching my hip with a sharp enough pain to bring me all the way to consciousness again.

Then I was falling through the wavering wall.

I became soft taffy, weaving through shadows, as I was dragged out of Castle Drake. Briny water burst down on my shoulders, thrusting my head beneath the waves of the Atlantic Ocean, until I was drowning.

# 7

Drowning smelled surprisingly like dropping into a barrel of fresh apples.

My lungs screamed, as I held my breath. I thrashed in the salty water that stung my nostrils, tumbling around in the black ocean.

*Which way was the surface...?*

I clamped closed my eyes against the spiralling panic, as I flailed desperately towards air, except there was nothing but *water, water, water*...and I couldn't breathe.

*Hell, I couldn't breathe.*

So, this was drowning?

I hadn't even ticked off half the names on my List of Asses to Kick. I'd thought I'd at least go out in a blaze of glory, rather than this cold death on the ocean bed.

Darkness shouldered in around me; my vision was shutting down.

I couldn't hold my breath any longer. As soon as I opened my mouth, however, water would rush in, and I'd be dead...

Then wings cocooned me in the aroma of orchards, whilst lips caressed against mine, pressing open my mouth.

I shook my head. My pulse was like a living thing, pounding in my ears, but strong arms held me close, whilst magic skittered, sparking across the kiss.

I inhaled, choking on the sudden oxygen. Then greedy for it, I twined my tongue with my angel rescuer, deepening the kiss and dragging more oxygen into my burning lungs.

Slowly, my mind calmed.

My awakening magic unwound itself from around my neck, ignited by the kiss and freed from my own personal terror of drowning. Then I clamped my wings around the angel — and now it was *his* turn to struggle — as I yanked him backwards through the black.

*Bastard dry land...*

The thought burst through me, driving the magic, shadows, and the booming *thud* of the ancient powers deep inside.

*Crash* — I landed on a strip of coral rock, below a crumbling cliff and the steep face of the castle.

The wind whipped the ocean spray against me in stinging lashes. A drain sluiced water in and out of the castle's wall.

The angel who'd breathed air into my lungs sprawled underneath me. Except, now I'd opened my eyes, and my wings flamed us in a ghost violet light, I could see that his wings were dappled with grey, rather than violet.

*A Shadow*: an angel who was *Falling*, becoming a vampire because he'd been away too long from Angel World.

Hell, how had I forgotten the vampire attack...?

Yeah, that's right: *drowning*.

I shoved the Shadow onto his front; he let out a shocked *oomph*.

"Hey, easy on the feathers, or I'll have to ruffle your pretty ones right back," Harahel pouted. "And since when was this a kinky nudist camp?"

I flushed, crossing my arms over my tits.

Harahel brushed his waist length brunet curls out of his eyes, before twisting them to squeeze out the water with his single hand, since his right hand was missing. In the Under

World it hadn't mattered that he'd lost his limb in battle: he hadn't been seen as an *Imperfect*. Instead, he'd been taken as Blood Lover by Misrule, one of the highest-ranking civilians, who'd run the rebellion to overthrow my dad.

Harahel's ash harem pants, which in Angel World had denoted his Imperfect status, had been replaced with black leather trousers, a sheathed ivory dagger, and an army green Great Coat with bone buttons. I grinned to see him restored to the legendary soldier he'd been before Angel World had reduced him to a librarian.

When I shivered, he slipped off his Great Coat, shrugging it over my shoulders; it smelled of him, like springtime. I burrowed into it, sniffing the collar. "Cheers, but what are you doing floundering around like a feathery fish? This is a mage wasp nest; they sting intruders to death."

Harahel slouched against the rocks, blinking the spray out of his eyes. "They don't want to see the mighty Harahel when he goes BOOM!"

"And you don't want to see the Bitch of Utopia when she gets medieval on your arse for hiding secrets. How did you do that business with the Snog of Life?"

Harahel leapt up, shoving his hands into his pockets, as he scanned the waves like he was *waiting* for something. "My other tricks will blow your mind! Although, I might've...stolen them from the Head Coven."

"Wait a bastard minute." I dragged Harahel's coat closer like it could ward off his words, whilst I hauled myself up. "Did you just admit to stealing from *spell lobbers*?"

Harahel gazed upwards, pursing his lips, before muttering, "That'd be a *yes*."

"And Misrule had a fit of temporary insanity...?"

"He doesn't know." Harahel grinned. "Just call me The Rule Breaker."

I couldn't help grinning back because even clinging to the edge of the cliff this was the most *freedom* I'd had in twenty-nine days. Over the stink of the salt and seaweed, with the faint

65

whiff of iodine, I could scent *a way out*...

I just didn't know if I could take it.

"Not to sound the ungrateful bitch, but isn't the Under World light one ruler?"

Harahel rubbed his arms. "You mean the ruler's Blood Lover?"

I snorted. "Don't play the brat card. Misrule doesn't treat you the same way as my sister and some of the other Blood Lovers are treated, like you're a deluded kid caught in the romance, when in fact you're little more than a blood bag. You're Misrule's *partner*."

Harahel scrunched up his nose, before sighing. "Until I Fall, I'm still an angel in a Fallen's world. Colour me dramatic. Plus, Misrule banned me from rescuing you." He booted a pebble like a kid whose dad wouldn't let him stroke a rabid dog.

"Because only bastards stop their lovers from taking on martyrdom missions..."

A glimpse of luminescent fire, like glowing jellyfish beneath the waves, lit up the sea. I trailed off, staring out at the blinking lights.

Harahel shot me a guilty look. "And for my second magic trick..."

I crushed him against the cliff, shaking. "Swear to me on Poseidon's prick that's not some freaky arsed underwater war because of *me*?'

Harahel tilted his head. "Why his prick?" When I growled, Harahel sniggered. "OK, OK. I'm a brat but I'm a charming brat, and it seems a whole bunch of Fallen have a thing for angels...or me..."

I groaned. "You've brought your fanboys to fight?"

The lights flared: underwater fireworks.

Och had accused me of being a *traitor*, and even though I hadn't known it, he'd been right. I was the Queen of Chaos, and I'd brought anarchy to the ordered Legion...*death*...to both the mages and Harahel's followers.

*Loyalty would get both sides ganked.*

Harahel nodded. "Saving you will be worth Misrule's

spanking."

I seized Harahel's wrist, hauling him after me towards the drain into Castle Drake. He dug in his heels, but I yanked him harder, until he skidded after me. "I'll be the one taking you over my knee in a minute. If you want to play the hero and risk your soldiers' lives for me, then we're saving every single one of my blokes."

I wrinkled my nose at the rotting stench as I dived into the drain's darkness.

"Yeah, not happening." Harahel stumbled into my back, knocking us both toppling into the stinking waters; I retched. "I've missed my mates every day. Don't you think I want to swim away with Rebel and Ash? Mischief reckoned I didn't know how they treated him here, but I did." I didn't miss the blush on *Mischief*. It was easy to forget that Mischief had been our rebel leader back in the Under World. "Yet the spells won't last forever. I made a choice: it was you."

"Flattering. But epic fail on convincing me."

Harahel tugged me to my feet with a snarl. "Wouldn't they want you to be free?"

"That's not the problem. I can't be free, if they're not."

At last, Harahel grinned. "Then I guess it's us against the spell!"

I grinned too, as Harahel and I darted down the tunnel, only to be hurled in a howling tangle of limbs and *slosh* of seawater, as if the castle had puked us out of its lungs, onto the floor of the Bailey.

*Slam* — I yowled, as my kneecaps slammed into the hard amber.

Then I peeked up at the ranks of mages, who glared at our soaking and half-naked — *dramatic* — entrance.

Harahel clambered to his feet, slipping out his dagger that glowed ghostly between us.

Och, who stood legionnaire tall at the front of the Lazarus Mages, raised an eyebrow at me.

Appearing with a Shadow during a vampire attack... How

67

the hell did I talk my way out of the *traitor* target already painted on my back...?

I opened my mouth, then closed it again.

*What do I bastard say, J?*

**That depends, Feathery-cupcake. Have you chosen the side of my favourite apple-pie librarian and his Lord of Misrule?**

*You know I have.*

**Do I? Because here's some tidal wave realness that'll sweep your ass away: if you choose to be Protector to more than one world, then your vampire whore was right. You'll need to play the Mage...your brother...and every dick who gets in your divalicious way...until you're the last bitch standing on the battlefield.**

*But if I win like that, I'll destroy everything that was worth saving.*

**Your call, girl. It always has been.**

Harahel scowled, raising his blade. "Come on, kiddies."

When Och nodded, the mages circled, leering.

"Time to run, not wave your dick around." I leapt up, snatching Harahel's elbow and thrusting him through the closest archway.

Then I shrieked as I was swallowed by shadows.


Harahel and I landed with a *crash*. I reached in the dark for Harahel's hand, before questing out with my foot in the small space. It smelled dry and stuffy: *a bastard wardrobe*.

"If this is you...? You can stop it now: I've learnt my lesson," Harahel whimpered.

"I'm not the one messing," I growled. Then I hollered, "Allow it McEvilTardis, or one spray can and I can get real creative." I gripped Harahel's hand tighter, whilst the wardrobe shook; I hissed, cowering at the furious buzzing. Finally, I smirked. "Glad we have an understanding, bitch."

I threw open the wardrobe door... The world lurched... Then I fell on top of Harahel in the centre of the Iron Barracks.

I peeked up at the circle of apprentice faces peering down at me.

Drake glanced between Harahel and me (and why did I have to be wearing Harahel's coat?), before linking his hands in front of himself. At least his wings weren't still ash-stained. "My Queen," he nodded at me as politely as if we at a ball, then at Harahel. "Librarian."

"You mean *Ruler*," Harahel pushed himself up with a haughty tilt of his chin, before holding his hand out to me, "of the Under World."

"Pissing contest officially not useful right now," I hissed.

The corners of Drake's mouth curled into a smile, before he smothered it. "I believe the exit is that way...Ruler of the Under World."

The other apprentices exchanged uncertain glances, but Drake stepped in front of them. Without a leader, they were nothing but sheep, whereas Drake was still the courageous commander of his kid army.

*What would be done to Drake for letting us go?*

"If you know where the exit is, why don't you take it with us?" I dared him to look away.

Drake's eyes widened; he fidgeted with the tops of his trousers.

Harahel rolled his eyes. "Come on..."

"I apologise, but I can't," Drake whispered. *Why did even the thought of abandoning him skewer me?* "My father's threatened to visit my punishments for disobedience on Zachriel. Unless you can promise Zachriel's rescue, I cannot risk his suffering."

I blinked. "Why would you care? You were his gaoler and torturer for forty years."

Drake flinched. "I wonder how it slipped your notice that I myself worked under the direction of your mother? *Tortured* just the same? I remember quite well how *you* enjoyed those dark games."

The other apprentices goggled at our free show.

69

"For real?" I stormed towards Drake, caught between fury and tears, but Harahel snatched the Great Coat's sleeve, and this time it was him propelling me towards him.

My insides churned, as my angelic side wailed in horror at leaving Drake thinking I was still *that* Glory: a bitch like my mum who got off on his pain or thought *he* got off on Rebel's.

As I twisted to call back to Drake in the doorway, however, the shadows crowded around me again and...

I gurgled, choking on water and floundering in the murk, until I realised with a jolt that my feet were on the sandy seabed.

*What. The. Hell?*

A silvery glimmer shimmered around me, and suddenly I was sealed safely in a bubble, gasping in deep breaths. I could still smell the briny stench as I peered out into the depths. They were lit by the flare of magic warfare beneath the sea; both sides were like shades in the gloom.

A touch on my hip, and I yelped.

Harahel held up his hand to ward off my defensive attack. Then his dagger lit spectral in the dark.

*Violet me up, J.*

**Like Little Miss Physics Don't Mean a Thing can conquer water with her fierce fire...?**

*Magic fire and righteousness.*

**And what's righteous about fighting angels to save yourself?**

*I'm battling a cult to save the brave bastards who rushed out on a crusade to save me. That's righteous.*

Flames rushed down my arms and sizzled across my palm. They cast a purple glow across the boulders, darting fish, and feathery coral reef ringing us. I shifted my feet in the oozing sand of the mountain ridge.

Then a shadowed figure with flaming wings dived towards me.

I shot a fire bolt through the water, but the angel didn't slow. Blinded by a sudden shoal of tiny fish, as dense as fog, I became entangled in seaweed. I ripped at the fronds that tied my ankles, slicing my palms on their rough edges. At last,

70

Harahel sliced through the strands, wrenching them away.

Except, just as I straightened, Harahel howled because the angel had reached us.

It was *Rahab*, sparkling like a golden — pissed off — god.

Rahab swept his wings around Harahel, as if he was cradling him. Rahab flared his wings, however, brighter and hotter. "*The Phoenix knows, I've tried to be a good father to you, allowing you into my secret home with my saved boys,*" he blasted into my mind like a branding. "*Yet here you are playing traitor with Fallen vermin.*"

When Rahab wrapped his arms tighter, even I could feel their heat scorching my cheeks; Harahel sobbed.

"*Punish me,*" I shot back telepathically, before stepping through the warming water. "*I've had the rewards, now give the punishments. Just don't gank Harahel and the vampires.*"

Rahab tossed his curls, considering. Then he tipped his head, bringing his lips closer to mine, even though they never moved. "*Wish granted, naïve apprentice.*"

He bit my lip, and on my gasp, he pushed his tongue into my mouth. But instead of oxygen, water gushed into my lungs.

And this time, I truly drowned.

# 8

I gagged, thrashing against the delicate hands that were holding me down. My lungs burned, as I retched against the salty water searing my nostrils. Lips pressed against mine, sparking and *sucking*, as the pain receded along with the panic.

At last, I could breathe again.

The mouth lifted from mine.

I gasped — *in, out, in out,* — screw chocolate, all a bitch wanted was *oxygen*.

*Coughing and retching, and someone that wasn't me.*

When I opened my eyes, Mischief was laid next to me, spluttering into his hand. His skin was clammy, and his eyes dazed: he looked like he'd been drowned. And as he'd just taken the pain of my drowning from me with his Angelic Power, *he bastard had*.

I traced my fingers along the floor, which buzzed with a constant tingling static — *magic* — and up Mischief's cheek.

He startled at the touch.

I clasped my arms across my chest: Harahel's Great Coat had been removed, along with the chain and collar, but a velvet sheet had been dragged around me. I rubbed my chin against its softness. My blurred gaze transformed the grand room of domed ceilings and arched windows out to the blazing stars into a golden ocean. But then again, this *was* the Gold Palace.

*Rahab's inner sanctum.*

In a month of obedience, I'd never been invited to tea in the palace. It only took one day and night of true rebellion, however, and my corpse had been dragged here for reanimation.

*Score for the corpse.*

Rebel, in true damsel fashion, had been hidden away like a sultan's treasured jewel behind the palace's glimmering gates. Rahab had guarded him fiercely. At last, however, the dragon had found her way in.

Mischief raised his eyebrow. "Why, for a sailor who seems determined to swallow half the sea and even some fish too, you are perky." When he bent over with another coughing fit, I clasped my arms around him, dragging his head into my lap. He blinked up at me: exhausted and tremoring in shock. "How many brownie points do I get for saving you again? Wait, not saving you...what's it called...oh yes, *bringing you back to life?*"

When I stroked his hair, it was as much for my own comfort as for his.

"Be silent. Why do you imagine everyone wishes to hear your incessant prattling, Undeserving?" I stiffened at Rahab's command.

I shuffled around to face the rest of the room: Rahab who leant against the golden wall with Rebel kneeling by his side.

I launched myself up, losing my sheet, before swaying and dropping down — *crack* — onto my arse again.

I let out a pained yelp.

"Feathers..." Rebel tried to stand, but Rahab held him down.

"Every child must learn to walk on their own, even if they fall." Rahab gave a deep laugh. "Where were you toddling to with your Fallen friends, little apprentice?"

I dragged the sheet around my shaking shoulders again.

Rebel bit his lip so hard that blood beaded, rubbing his hands backwards and forwards across the knees of his trousers.

*Anxiety, fear, and excitement.*

They feather-kissed my skin across our bond. The same emotions that coursed through me because I could see Rebel at last and ached to hold him and lick the candy sweet blood from his lip. I hungered to devour him: my Bonded and Marked because both sides of my nature roared that he was *mine*.

Yet Rahab was *touching* him, massaging his leather-clad shoulder; it stung worse than I'd imagined that I couldn't stop him.

"It seems you need glasses because that was a kidnapping." I sprawled on my back with as much swag as I could manage, when I couldn't even push myself to my knees. "Sucks for you because you've failed your Violet approved Health and Safety Inspection."

When Rahab strolled behind Rebel to a marble statue of a bloke on one knee, who was weighed down with a globe, I stiffened. Rahab rapped its top. "Aren't you just full of quips?" The back of Mischief's hand ghosted across my wings: safe and grounding against the spiralling fear. "Then you shan't mind how I chastise the foolish Imperfect who we captured...?"

"His name is Harahel," I snarled. "If you call him Imperfect again, I'll go Hackney style on your pretty curled head."

"Mind yourself," Rebel murmured. "Don't give him the rope to hang you with, Feathers." Then he scooted on his knees to look up at Rahab with his patented puppy dog look. Why did I crave to claw Rebel bloody that he was using it on someone other than me? "Here's the thing of it, sir, Harahel's a muppet

74

for coming here but he's loyal to the queen. He's an angel still, and although I know you have to punish him as a good da would..."

When Rahab reached out towards Rebel, I flinched. Yet Rahab only tilted Rebel's chin. I studied the fond way in which he drew his thumb over Rebel's soft lips in bemusement. "Hush. I forget how remarkably *good* you are, Zachriel."

Rebel jolted, swallowing hard around his collar. "By all the saints, I wish I was. But I'm a bad angel."

Rahab tapped Rebel's lips reprovingly. "I said *hush*. Have I not discovered your true worth? I shall break the training from those witches and free you. I hope one day you'll see how exceptional you are." *Hell, was Rebel blushing?* The ancient powers inside howled; I didn't know if it was because Rahab was playing new best mate to my lover or because my lover was basking in the attention of my mentor. Rahab glanced at me. "I hope the same of you, Queen Apprentice. No one steals what's mine." Gold tendrils coiled in molten snakes out of Rahab's fingers, as Midas-touched they slithered down to coat the sculpture. Rahab's brow furrowed in concentration: the statue's bearded face was submerged now in the tidal wave of gold. I glanced around at the palace: had everything in here been coated with Rahab's own magic? "Impressive strategy to leave the Under World under the rulership of both an angel and a Fallen. Half and half, just like yourself."

I winced.

Mischief raised his hand like the shy kid in class. "Not to be a credit hog, but that was in fact *me*."

"Did you discover a way to quieten that one?" Rahab arched his brow.

"Not even when the bitch was a unicorn."

Rahab waved a lazy hand and the last of the statue was lost beneath the gold, which hardened like it'd always been that way. "What do you imagine will happen to the Fallen now that one of their leaders is gone? How far do you think the creature of Misrule will go to retrieve him?"

"To the moon, over the rainbow, or even down the rabbit hole... Wait, I know this one—"

*Slap* — Rahab cracked his hand down onto the top of the glistening statue.

Rebel caught my eye; his gaze was soft and concerned.

"Harahel will be tossed in the oubliette to be forgotten." Rahab's violet eyes were considering. "*You* cannot be a shadow to my boys. You must be their light."

A tiny cell in the dark. *How could I let that happen to Harahel again...?*

"An oubliette?" I forced myself to smirk like it wasn't tearing me up inside. "What's with the *Labyrinth* vibe, Bowie reject?"

When Rebel groaned, hugging his arms around himself, I knew I'd made a bastard mistake.

Rahab's grin was all teeth. "Then since you still have punishments owing, little apprentice..." Now it was my turn to groan. *Why did he have to remember that?* "...I'll just have to work at making them more personal."

"Don't strain anything," I muttered.

Then I shrieked, as a golden tentacle whipped out, wrapping around my ankle and yanking.

I slid out from underneath my sheet, worm wriggling, as I was tugged backwards, reeled in.

I cringed, my pulse *thud — thud — thudding*, whilst I booted at the solid gold, but then wailed at the aching jolt through my naked heel.

I stared up at the — *alive* — statue that peered down at me in turn.

"Sweet Christ, sir, whip my arse but don't—"

"Generous of you to offer yourself for chastisement." Rahab kissed Rebel's hair lightly, before nodding at the sculpture.

*Clank* — Gold Beard shrugged the globe off his shoulders, straightening with a sigh.

He seized me by the hair, hauling me to dangle on tiptoe: lucky me to have come into conflict with the top boy of the statue world.

Rahab leaned over me; his sandalwood scent, like fragrant trees, wound around me as closely as the gold tentacles. "This is Atlas."

"Cheers for the blind date, but I don't think it'll work out. He's loaded and hot, but call me picky, the tentacles are a turn off."

"Atlas was condemned for eternity to hold up the skies as punishment because he and his brother sided with the Titans against the Olympians," Rahab continued, as if I hadn't replied. "Sometimes, I imagine I'm the only one holding up the skies." Rahab chuckled, low and musical. "Nothing but the Legion to stop worlds falling. Yet now we have your brother and you...?" Atlas shook me by my hair, wrenching strands out by the roots; I squealed. "If you choose the right side, then we can all fly. But if I don't teach you like a good father, and instead you choose wrongly....? Well..." Rahab balanced on the fallen sphere, his majestic wings sweeping out, as if he was a rare beast performing a circus trick. "I'm certain I can be more imaginative than Zeus in my punishments."

"Then get with the punishing," I growled.

Mischief cast a careful glance at Rebel. "May I request—"

"Nothing, Underserving, unless you're spoken to." Rahab's glare swung to me. "I shall decree tomorrow the Day of Initiation. You shall pass or fail in a single day. I'll tell the Legion of your *kidnapping*, but there'll be no more refusals or that lie shall die, along with your Harahel."

"Bastard fine," I gritted out.

"When the morning breaks and the bell tolls—"

"All bad little boys will be turned into trolls...?"

I didn't expect Rahab's gentle smile, as he stooped to kiss Rebel's forehead. Sweat prickled across my shoulder blades; my healing wings flapped feebly. "Two *good* little boys — one brother and one lover — will suffer for the Queen Apprentice."

I stared at him in shock.

This was *my* punishment. How the hell had Rahab worked out that hurting my fam punished me far more than hurting *me* ever could?

Rahab had once said that he could *see* me. It looked like he'd been right.

"I've got the memo," I swallowed. "They're my whipping boys. I promise, you want me tamed, this is me, sitting up and begging."

Atlas cocked his head at Rahab.

Rahab tucked a stray ruffled feather down on my wing. "You're not tame. Can you feel the weight of the skies yet?" Then he leant close to my ear as he murmured, "Are my punishments personal enough now?" I hissed, twisting away from him. "See? Not tame."

At another flick of Rahab's wrist, Atlas dropped me in a yowling heap.

The weight of the skies *was* on my shoulders because by dawn I'd have to take on the terrors of the Day of Initiation, when I was barely recovered from broken wings and a drowning. If I didn't win, I'd be made Drake's slave and I'd have no chance to take on Rahab and destroy his cult. If I refused, he'd gank Harahel.

Plus, because of the escape attempt, both my brother and one of my fam would be punished. Yeah, Rahab had made it bastard *personal*: by going after my fam, this had become a battle between titans and gods.

# 9

Once, as a kid growing up on the Utopia Estate, I'd been suspended from school for fighting. At least, that was the time they'd *caught* me with the shank in my hand.

It hadn't mattered to them that I'd been the only bitch brave enough (teachers included), to stand between a bleeding kid barely tall enough to peer over my shoulder and the gang of top boys from the Estate. I wouldn't have cared but the top boys had machetes and the kid was armed with nothing sharper than braces.

The newbie hadn't known the code: how to avoid a shanking. I'd protected him and been punished for it because life...?

It boots you where it hurts and it isn't bastard fair. But does that mean you should stop acting the Protector?

Blazing, clamouring rock music blasted through the

roughhewn cave: Mischief's secret grotto.

*The Ghost Caves beneath Castle Drake.*

I threw back my head, losing myself in *Lower than Atlantis'* thick bass lines and snarling guitar riffs. Tiny luminescent glow-worms swarmed the walls, lighting us spectral. Mists lifted from the sea, which was feathered with the birth pangs of dawn, shrouding my face. The crash of the waves against the rocks, which blocked the entrance, broke hypnotically against "Here We Go's" mythic soulfulness that sang from Mischief's iPod speakers.

*Squelch* — I slipped in a seaweed pool, wrinkling my nose at the stink.

White ghost crabs scuttled from their disturbed home; their stalk eyes wagged at me in accusation.

I shook out my boot, spraying water across the wall: at least I wasn't naked anymore, even if I was dressed in my Legion uniform again.

Mischief reached out to steady me, before snatching my shoulder and spinning me.

Ceri laughed. He sprawled on a boulder, like a merman who'd shed his legs, wiggling his toes in the water.

I grinned: rocking out to this beast of a song on a hidden island in the middle of the ocean...*hell, yeah.* As I dragged Mischief closer to dance, rubbing my thigh against his, for the first time I felt *free.*

*Or could imagine that we were.*

I closed my eyes, resting my head on Mischief's shoulder.

**Half an hour until dawn and your wizarding showdown...**

*Cheers for the reminder.*

**You're always welcome, Feathers-pie. Why do you think you're safe just because you're outside the castle?**

**You're a fish, flipping out of the frying pan and into the fire.**

*These are no trout lips, bitch.*

**Then you're the fire, girl, and that's your choice.**

I startled, as Mischief roared — regal as the King of the Fae

80

— twirling me round to the thunder of electric guitars.

Addictive, buzzing, swaggering: I shivered, whilst the music soaked down to my bones, beneath the cold magic curling around my neck and the shadows clinging under my skin.

My soul screamed.

I snapped open my eyes, staring into Mischief's desperate gaze; he clung to me like he'd already lost me.

As the song died, I pulled back, until only the tips of our fingers touched; I could still feel Mischief's silver magic sparking against my violet.

Suddenly, I remembered the pool beneath the Invisible Bridge with its eerie emerald glow and Rahab's calm: *This is where my mother tried to drown me...*

Hell, Rahab had been abandoned in a cave like this.

*Alone.*

How powerful must he be to have survived?

"The Mage is batshit," I said, flatly.

Mischief snorted. "Certainly not the opener I was hoping for. With your colossal wit, you're only arriving at this understanding now...?"

"He was a kid trapped in these caves." I stared into the foggy ocean spray, rubbing my boot across the seaweed encrusted rock. "So, he dreams up illusions to be his mates. This whole world with codes, rewards, and punishments, where the sky won't fall in. All because he needs to be in control...safe." *And hell did I get that.* "Does he even know what — *who* — is real?"

"No such thing as *real* in Castle Drake." Ceri stretched on his back, running his hand down his chest as if by habit. "You're all just figments in *my* dreams, isn't it, and naughty ones at that. You should see what you're doing right now..."

"Dream Me had better not be starring in a porn show or—"

"*Hmmm,*" Ceri purred, running his thumb down his prick with a smug grin, "Dream You *is* adventurous..."

Ceri gave a delighted yell of laugher, as I dived for him,

81

*splashing* into the pool. When I hauled him out like a damp lion cub, his arms wound around me. He nipped kisses down my neck; I breathed in his spicy ginger scent.

"Children," Mischief huffed, "I rather think we've passed the point of playing."

"There's always time to play." Ceri licked up my neck, and I shuddered. "And I'm no kid. I haven't been since..." When Ceri's expression darkened, I knew what he couldn't bring himself to say.

*Since they'd chopped off his wings.*

"I'll find a way to pay Rahab back for what he's stolen," I whispered, nuzzling Ceri's bronzed cheek in comfort. "I'll steal what's his. Then my blood—"

"Don't get started on the power of your blood, or I fear we'll be here all day." Mischief feigned a yawn, and I bristled. "Not one of us is flying out of here with the wards guarding us, so although your blood grew wings on the Broken of Angel World, if you attempt it here, you'll just ensure their guillotine works overtime."

I blanched.

*Whish — thud.*

The crimson pool, child-sized guillotine, and the wing lying in the basket...

I doubled over, dizzy at the horror of the memory. Ceri lowered me to the stone floor with his arms around my middle. Mischief petted my head. "The Discipliners are pricks," I rasped out.

"Seconded." Ceri wound his fingers in my scarf like a comfort blanket. "Want to know the twenty-two things Dream You can do with warmed chocolate sauce and an ice cube...?"

I wetted my lips...*interesting*...then glanced up at Mischief.

Mischief's haughty expression had softened. "The Discipliners are almost as large *pricks* as Mage Drake himself."

I patted at my temples like my mind had short-circuited: my magic slept damp and cloying around my throat. It didn't even stir. I waggled my fingers at my neck. "How come there's no hot magic shanking me for disrespecting Rahab and breaking the Code?"

Ceri smirked. "Because out here there's no..." He waggled his hand in the universal sign for *wanker*.

I sniggered because how often did you see an angel slave do that?

"What my wildly rude friend means," Mischief rolled his eyes, "is that these Ghost Caves were here before Rahab: raw, natural, and unmoulded by his will. Just like us. Maybe you should cling to that truth and not forget it. Although, it is amusing to see you flounder between the pretty magic and your prettier lovers."

I struggled to hold back the ancient powers that burst fire sizzling to my fingertips. Why did Mischief always know what buttons to push? "Are you looking to get dashed?"

Mischief tilted his head. "And there she goes: *threats*. You may have noticed but Rahab is much better than you at *Godfather* intimidation. So was Lucifer. What do I have to truly fear from you...? Oh, I remember now, being *rescued* against my will."

I gaped at him. "You're still having a hissy fit that I saved you?"

"You can't save everyone," Mischief howled, clouting the wall. His knuckles shattered in a spray of scarlet, but he didn't notice, panting. "Am I to be indebted that you've brought down Rahab's notice on you? Harahel? Rebel...even Drake?"

He bit his lip to hide its tremor.

*Guilt.*

It was so hard to remember now he was reduced to Undeserving that he'd been the leader of our rebellion in the Under World. That he tried to save us, as much as *I* tried to protect him.

I'd allowed Mischief to think his freedom had led to his mates' suffering. And mine. I knew it hurt far more to see others' pain than to suffer your own.

*Yeah, I bastard hated the undercover gig.*

83

Ceri stroked his hand across my lower back. When I glanced over my shoulder, his gaze was as anguished as mine. "Look you, we have to tell him."

"I assure you, I already know." Mischief clenched his jaw, although his shoulders hunched. "I'm the only one who won't *take the knee* before Your Highness. Not a single Legionnaire will raise an eyebrow when you return me to my punishment in the Lower Vault, and Rahab's smug head will quite explode." His eyes gleamed, but he fought not to let the tears fall. "You shall be rid of my sarcasm and the punishments. The world will rejoice."

"We're not the world, cariad." Ceri slunk to his feet, winding around Mischief, who linked their hands. I didn't miss either the way Ceri stroked his thumb over the back of Mischief's hand or the *cariad*: darling. "And you and your sarcasm are needed here. Who else can I grope, or get to spank me?" I coughed at the sudden image: hell, that wasn't going away anytime soon. Ceri winked at me. "That's free for your wank bank."

"Placing spanking in a galaxy far, far away, maybe you're not the King of All-knowing. I'd never put you back with the snakes and I care about you kneeling to the power of *nothing*. The only time I'll be rejoicing is when the Brotherhood no longer rules as the power behind Angel World. But Ceri's right: I should've already told you..."

Stranded on the boulder by myself, I stared up at Mischief and Ceri, who curled around each other like they *fitted*: how many centuries had they been mates? *Cariads*? Escaping together to the Ghost Caves to comfort each other and plot?

I'd wandered into this magical world, where I understood so little. Why did it burn that I was still the outsider?

"Are you awaiting a drum roll or a bolt of lightning perhaps?" Mischief enquired.

"I'd prefer a swarm of fairies kicking your unicorn arse but failing that..." I took a deep breath, then rushed out, "I yanked you out of the Lower Vault not just to save you..." Mischief's hand curled tighter around Ceri's. "...Or to piss off the Mage, but because I needed to set things on fast forward. Once I'd seen the Broken Nursery..."

Ceri had taken me past the kitchen, sneaking down spiral staircases and into the bowels of the castle. There at the end of a dusty corridor had been a locked room.

Ceri had told me that he was the castle *Carer*. I'd wondered what he *cared* about beyond sex and snuggling. Yet the way his usually cheery face had become haunted with a despair and melancholy that'd chilled me, had been all the persuasion I'd needed to follow him.

Even isolated from my blokes and reduced to an apprentice, I was a Protector still.

Ceri had hesitated outside the rusted steel door. "I've spent my life charming the mages to keep them out of here. But now I've charmed you to let you in, seeing as you're different." He'd chewed his lip. "I hope that I'm opening the Nursery to the rebel and not the beast?"

Then he'd unlocked the door.

"...All those tiny cots in the dark," I whispered, clasping my hands around my knees hard enough to bruise. "Tiny faces peering up and so bastard scared. The ones who could toddle all thronged around Ceri to be picked up, as if he was their dad..." I licked my dry lips, forcing out the words, which I'd barely been able to think ever since that morning seven scratches on a post ago. "I'd never thought about where the Broken kids were kept before they were five and taken for the Ritual of the Wings or trained afterwards to be chosen by Glories on Angel World: the ones we missed who didn't get my super juiced blood to become Blood Angels. The ones I left behind as slaves. And they're *here* in the castle still with the Discipliners and only Ceri to look out for them."

"And me," Mischief muttered.

"When she crouched down, Fynchan crawled into her lap," Ceri grinned. "My queen has a new suitor now: one who's a mess of black hair and a thousand *whys*?"

Mischief's mouth was tight. "And what did the *queen* do? Spank the child for its insolence?"

85

*That bastard hurt.*

I curled more tightly around my knees.

Ceri squeezed Mischief's hand reprovingly. "She made fire unicorns gallop around the nursery, until the kids all giggled and called for their *Uncle Mischief.*"

Mischief flushed, shifting from one foot to the other. "I apologise. But you don't understand..."

"That in a week Fynchan turns five and loses his wings?" I tilted my chin in defiance, even as my stomach turned to say the words. Fynchan's soft wings have been so fragile rubbing against my arms: *how could the Discipliners steal them?* Yet they'd taken Ceri's at the same age and my Broken slave, Gwyn's, on Angel World. "I have to step-up now, I get that."

Mischief nodded. "So, you rescued *me* out of love, simply for someone else?"

My chest ached; I blushed.

*But what could I bastard say?*

"No matter," Mischief continued briskly with a wave of his hand — *hell, it so did matter* — as he glanced at Ceri. "We both love those children as well. They're worth any sacrifice. Did you believe I wouldn't understand? Someone has to be the true champion of both the Broken and Phoenix slaves, and it'd never be the mages. I'd come to believe it'd be *me.*" He avoided my eye as he bit out, "Yet if you imagine that you'll survive the Initiation fighting with the Legion's Code and *their* mental powers...?"

Mischief and Ceri exchanged a knowing glance. Then they dived on me. I *eeped*, falling back amongst the shifting ghost crabs and seaweed bed of the pool.

Feathers, warm skin, and mingled hair.

Their bodies pressed against mine, just as their lips tongued my mouth, throat, and wings...

I arched, lost in the tingling sensation, until I jolted because something was passing through them to me, as they held me down on the boulder.

Magic: It popcorn crackled from their wings and kisses. It sparked in silvery waves down my bowed spine, bubbling the cold Legion magic...*taking over.*

I rode the thrill because if this was possession, I belonged to the silver magic already.

**Wake your sailor doll arse up, Violet-pea.**

**Alarm bells are ringing, and you only have minutes until the real bell will toll.**

*I'm a Violet filling in a feathery sandwich right now. Let me dream I'm licking the silvery cream, yeah?*

**While I gag on that image, you're gagging on a magic that was never meant for you.**

**I told you there was danger out here.**

Battling through the glimmering tide that whispered...*home, home, home*...I shoved at two angelic shoulders.

At last, Mischief raised his head. "Tasted enough true magic?"

*Hell, no...*

Ceri held my hand to his mouth, nibbling at each finger, whilst he sucked. The sparking inside didn't fade: it sank tendrils even deeper.

I forced myself to nod. "Why...?"

Mischief raised his hands. "Some of us don't fear sharing power: we embrace it."

Silver spun out into discs flickering between his hands.

*Bang* — he flexed his fingers, and the discs soared across the cave, crashing into the wall in a shower of smouldering rock.

I hollered, covering my face.

Was that *power* — magic — now inside me?

"Why would you hide that type of talent?" When Mischief flinched, I drew his still glowing hands between mine, shuddering at the way the magic between our skin *reached* for each other. "If Ceri has magic too, why's he a Broken?"

Mischief tried to pull away, but I held onto him, as his cheeks pinked. When he cast a glance at me, his gaze was clouded with shame. "The Lower Vault is the fun punishment for captured witches: for *women*. My magic shouldn't be silver,

87

despite how powerful it is. It's *wrong*. A mage's magic is gold, whilst mine is..." I shook with rage at the cruel judgement on Mischief just because his magic had been assigned *feminine*. "I'm sorry. Have I sullied your queenly image by touching you with my womanly—"

"Bastard stop it," I snapped. "Your balls are bigger than any blokes, and no, I don't need to feel them, we're talking in metaphors. The whole Legion and Angel World gender divide is screwed. Do all Broken have this silver magic?"

"Not like Mischief." Ceri slid a hand to Mischief's neck, massaging. "And he hides because there's nowhere safer than the shadows. But we all have something wired differently in us that makes our magic wicked—"

"Is kissing you the only way to silence your tongue?" Mischief hissed. "There's not a wicked feather in you. You're more courageous, devoted—"

"Sexier?" Ceri smirked.

"More powerful than my brother who *beats* you." Mischief's eyes blazed. "You're right, both of you. Now is the time to take apart this Legion from the inside." He narrowed his gaze at me. "You've been granted our *special* magic to help you do so. No one can complain that a *Glory* is too *feminine* to use it."

**Too late, Violet-sweets, it's dawn...**

I scrambled around: golden light flooded the entrance cave, as the molten sun gleamed over the ocean.

*Bong, bong, bong.*

I gasped at the deep ringing of the bell, which echoed through my head.

*Morning breaks and the bell tolls at my victory or funeral.*

# 10

Dawn's golden light flooded over the Bailey, but scarlet pooled on its amber cobbles.

Numb, I stared at the whipping post: if I only focused on the fisted hands bruised in the shackles, then I didn't have to admit the bloke hanging from them was...

*Swish — thud.*

Rebel screamed, as the corded cat o-nine tails sliced through the morning silence, then clawed red down his back.

"Ninety-five," Och intoned, combing through the bloody tails to stop them sticking together.

This time both mages and apprentices alike stood at attention to witness Rebel's shameful *punishment*.

Except, the punishment and shame were mine: Rebel was simply taking my lashes. If Rahab wanted to break me, flogging Rebel, whilst I could do nothing but stand on and watch, ticked the Tame Violet box.

Yet the grim twist to Rahab's mouth and the way he

clasped his hands behind his back as he glowered over proceedings from the archway, told me I hadn't been imagining the fondness with which he'd drawn his thumb over Rebel's lips.

It's just that controlling *me* mattered more. *And wasn't that bastard terrifying?*

*Swish — thud.*

When the little metal balls at the end of the whip caught in Rebel's back, ripping away the skin, Rebel shrieked. Blood sprayed across the Bailey; I jumped, when it teared sticky down my cheek.

Never before had the blood's candy sweetness made me gag.

"Ninety-six."

*Please, just be over...*

Rebel's agony and terror struck me across the bond. I paled, swallowing hard as I swayed.

Two hands clutched mine: Mischief held me up on one side, Drake on the other. Their grips were crushing.

Rebel wasn't my whipping boy alone. He might be my *lover* but he was also Mischief's mate and *something* to Drake that I didn't yet understand.

I glanced sideways at Drake. He was as ashen as me; his jaw was clenched as tightly as mine. But it was the tears glinting in his eyes that booted me in the gut.

*How could the Ice Commander be melted by Rebel's suffering?*

I nudged Drake with my boot, forcing him to look away from the whipping post. He shuddered, straightening his shoulders. I fell back on our secret body language, shrugging:

**What?**

He rolled his eyes:

**Have you been hit with the crazy stick, bitch? The angel having his punk ass whipped, duh.**

I shrugged again:

**What's it to you, bro?**

Drake raised a shaky finger to his chest:

*My fault.*

My eyes widened. In the freakery of the tolling bells, Rebel's punishment, and the nightmare start to this Day of Initiation, I'd never stopped to think what Drake would believe about it.

*Or maybe even what his dad had told him.*

I shook my head frantically, steeling myself to ignore Rebel's wailing and the fall of the lash again, as I pointed at myself.

**Not your fault:** *mine.*

Och shook out the tangled tails, casting a concerned gaze over his shoulder at Mischief. Something unreadable passed between them, as secret as my special way of communicating with Drake. It only truly hit me then that they were *brothers*: like my half-brother was mine, except we were strangers.

*Would we ever be like true siblings?*

Yet when it was Rebel who was being flogged like a midshipman, why was Och shooting the Apology Eyes at his brother? The prick wasn't going easy now either, not in the way he had when he'd struck Mischief's palm with the whip. Instead, he swung the rope above his head, bending his body to give it full force, before bringing it down, carving deep enough to show white slivered bone beneath.

Rebel arched and writhed, before his head lolled forward.

*Bastard, no...*

Panting, I shuddered between relief and horror. For ninety-nine strokes I'd hoped Rebel would pass out and for once discover that the dark could be an escape from pain.

The sadists, however, had a cute little trick to stop the mages hiding in unconsciousness. The whip already cut open the disciplined angel's sensitive shoulder blades and lower wings (and my own feathers cringed in sympathy to imagine that), but throughout the flogging the disciplined had to stretch out their wings as if about to take flight: *Rise.* If their wings fell, then the cat would mangle their most sensitive angel parts.

*Wake up.*

I blasted the thought through our Blood Bond, even as my guts roiled that I was violating Rebel through the connection to force him to obey my commands.

*That I was compelling him to suffer for love.*

I'd once thought that I craved my blokes to be my puppets but after enduring Rahab's false world where everyone in it became his toy, I knew it wasn't real control.

It was an illusion. A kid singing to itself to drive away the monsters.

*And this monster was coming for Rahab.*

Rebel's head snapped back up on a howl, and I winced. Rebel swept out his wings.

*Swish — thud.*

When Rebel convulsed, Och hurled away the cat, hurrying to unshackle Rebel from the post. "One hundred. Punishment complete." Then he shot a look at Mischief. "Zophia, your services are required."

Then I understood: Och's concerned gaze, as well as Mischief's talent to heal being used with *Rahab's permission.*

Rahab beat his favourite toys, only to have their pain taken by his least favourite. And Mischief survived — *was allowed to live* — because he took the pain of Rahab's golden children.

When Mischief reluctantly let go of my hand, avoiding my gaze as he darted to kneel next to Rebel's broken body, which Och was cradling with unexpected gentleness, I hated that I didn't know whether I wished Mischief would heal Rebel because that meant them *both* suffering.

When Rahab soared above the Bailey, Drake also let go of my hand.

How could the Bitch of Utopia miss something like an angel's fingers between mine?

*Yet I bastard did.*

92

"I should similarly lash every one of you for not stopping the escape...excuse the Freudian slip...*kidnap* of our royal guest." If they gave medals for terrified silences, the entire Legion would've been awarded one. Rahab tossed his curls. "But I believe the example has been made. If the queen were to be kidnapped again, Och's arm would tire as much as the skin on your backs." I shrank from the scowls. *Way to make yourself popular.* "Yet now the Day of Initiation begins to judge who shall be your new brother or sister. Let them walk in the way of the Phoenix!"

The Brotherhood stamped their feet on the hard floor of the Bailey, as I backed away from Drake.

My breath hitched. *Show time.*

*Lazarus rises! Rises! Rises! And we will rise!*

Drake snatched me by the hair hurling me into the centre of the arena, before kicking out my knees.

*Oomph* — I fell flat on my face in the copper candy of Rebel's blood.

I smeared it wildly off my cheeks, choking as it caught on the tip of my tongue and exploded through me; I juddered, lost in the joy of our Blood Bond and yet drowning in the *pain, pain, pain* that sang through it.

I wiped the back of my hand across my lips.

Rebel had been dragged to the side of the Bailey, with Mischief suffering the agony of the flogging alongside him, and I was battling to save the world.

*Drake knew how to distract a bitch.*

Had I expected him to puppy rollover and wiggle his belly? If he didn't win, Drake would lose his only chance to become a Lazarus Mage and gain the respect that his own dad had always denied him, returning instead to the status of slave.

*But then, if I lost, so would I.*

I snarled, struggling to turn over, but Drake rammed my head against the cobbles. I yelped, booting my leg backwards, but he caught it and twisted. Then I howled.

Hell, every time I'd fought Drake, he'd been holding back. No matter that his dad treated him like a reject, he was still a Commander in the angelic army, as well as the badass who'd fought the vampiric Supreme Commander in a duel and won.

I had swag but I was a newbie to this supernatural world, without Drake's centuries of combat experience.

*Death*: charred corpses in circles, torching corrupted courts, attempting to murder my own dad...

Now *that* I had down.

I didn't want to *harm* Drake, however, only defeat him. And if the cost of entry into the Legion of the Phoenix was his death...?

It was too high.

When Drake seized me by the back of my neck, I stiffened. He flung me against the whipping post, and my feathers caught sticky against the congealed blood.

*Rebel's blood.*

*Spiked metal balls carving into Rebel's skin, slicing it away from the bone and spraying it across my cheeks...*

I froze, catching Drake's haunted expression, before his face became carefully blank.

The bastard was playing mind games: he didn't want to harm me either. So, if I had a freak out over Rebel's punishment, then he'd win.

*Two could play at that game.*

I smirked. "What's wrong? Don't want to get Rebel's blood in your girlie hair, brat?"

I snatched Drake's curls in my gory hands and *rubbed.*

Drake let out a squeal. His eyes widened, as he drew in desperate gasps. He yanked backwards, scrambling away. I was left holding golden clumps.

*It also left one pissed off pretty boy.*

Messing with an angel's hair: who knew it tapped into their inner rage?

Drake caught me by the shoulder, twisting. I struggled, but the bastard was powerful.

*Slam* — Drake cracked me down across the cannon.

I groaned; my wings were trapped beneath me, taking most of the impact. Fire shot straight to the wingtips, searing. The ancient powers inside bellowed at the indignity: the threat to my newly knitted wing bones.

And to my chances at flight: to *Rise*.

The shadows stirred, restless. I fought to hold them inside.

*Slam* — Drake hauled me up from the cannon, only to smash me down across it again.

*He knew*.

The Ice Commander was deliberately targeting my wings because *of course* he had a strategy. He didn't fight on emotion and rage like me, with the beauty of a dance like Rebel, or the instinct of his squirming magic like Mischief. If he couldn't take out my mind, Drake would take out my wings — *shank my weakness*.

*Cold bastard*.

Yet he'd grown up with Rahab as a daddy and been gifted as a kid to my mummy as a bed slave...

I'd be astounded if Drake *didn't* know how to hurt.

Except, I was a Jerusalem Children's Home kid. I'd been raised with hurt in my soul too.

Rebel had once told me that if I didn't kill only to save, then when I hunted vampires, we'd become only *two monsters in the snow*.

Well, watch out bitches, because now there'd be *two monsters in the blood*.

Mischief's magic glinted in a gushing wave through me: popcorn and power. I wove it in winding braids with my violet fire that surged, fizzing in fury at Drake's attack, until they became silvery violet discs.

The discs exploded from my palms, launching Drake in a howl of fried feathers and shocked pain through the air and slamming into the pool of blood beneath the whipping post.

*Shocked whispers*.

Even the apprentices risked their own lashing to break their military silence.

I eased off the cannon, wincing at the smart in my wings, before prowling to Drake, who sprawled in the *crater* where he'd landed.

*Hell, this magic was juiced.*

Drake moaned, forcing his head up to glare at me.

Nope, that wasn't guilt icy-balled in my stomach at the anguish in his eyes.

I pulled my hands further apart, and the discs whirled together into a single pulsing sun.

Drake swallowed, staring up at the lightening sky.

*Why was it so hard to draw back my arm and shoot him with the final fire bolt?*

Victory: it throbbed through me to a tribal beat. My enemy crushed at my feet. Except, I desired Drake at my side. This felt...*wrong*...even as I pulled back my arm to strike.

Then Drake roared, rolling to the side. I blinked, confused.

*Three Drakes* hovered in the air before me: bleeding, bruised, and annoyingly smug.

*Bastard clones.*

"What's wrong?" Drake One smirked. "Are you having difficulty deciding which one of us to make bleed, *brat*?"

I flinched, before forcing my sore wings to flap, rising to meet him in the air. "Why limit myself to only one angel toy, when there's three up for grabs?"

The Drakes growled, but all my powers were ready. It didn't matter which one was the real Drake, he'd just shown me his belly and begged me to slip in the shank.

When Drake Two dived towards me, I fired a burst of flames sizzling across his wings. He howled, and as I'd hoped, an echo of the wound vibrated through the other clones and the real Drake. He tumbled down onto the arena floor with a *bang*.

Simultaneously, I cast a shadow net over Drake One, sticky over his creamy skin, swinging him crashing next to his clone brother, as well as shooting a disc at Drake Three, blasting him in a spray of singed feathers onto his back.

Multiple Drakes? *Multiple ways to hurt him at the same time.*

Each Drake reached out towards the other, whimpering and holding each other's hands in comfort. I realised he was attempting to wrench them back inside himself again. He'd been too weakened to manage it, however, and now his clones were stuck outside to suffer with him.

As I landed, prowling towards the three Drakes it was easy to spot the original: it was the one who pushed himself up onto his elbows, as if he could even now protect his clones.

*Like he'd always protected me.*

I stumbled, fading the fire on my hands.

*Hell, I couldn't do this.*

Yet there were more ways to win than blood. We might be both coated in Rebel's, but Drake had always been hurt more by tender touches than pain.

I hated the way the clones cringed back from me, as I crouched over them. The true Drake, however, met my gaze, even if his breath hitched.

I reached out, stroking Drake One's feathers from the shoulder to the wing tip; Drake shuddered as he too felt the echo of the sensation. I traced over Drake Three's nipple; he panted, whining. Then I twisted.

All three Drakes arched.

Drake turned away his head. "I'm the real Drake," he muttered. "You need not..."

I slipped my hand beneath his harem trousers to caress his inner thigh, as I continued to twist Drake Three's nipple, and kissed Drake One's wing tip.

Drake writhed, overloaded with sensation. "Enough. It's me," he murmured. "Don't violate my shadows; they're innocents." He steeled himself, before raising shaking fingers to touch my hair. "I hid them from your mother; she believed they could only appear in battle. Have me if you wish, but they've never... They don't know what it is to be forced at the hands of a Glory. Do not steal that from them."

97

How had the dominant bitch inside managed to escape: the Glory these blokes feared and needed to hide from here on the island? No wonder they hated Angel World.

*And me.*

I shook, drawing back.

Drake wrenched on his clones. Finally, they merged into him. He fell back, closing his eyes. "Allow me to congratulate you on your win."

I ran my fingers through his curls, which were stiff with Rebel's blood. His eyes snapped open with shock.

*Catcalls and jeers.*

Drake flushed.

"Look at me." I grabbed his chin; his eyes were wide and his pupils blown. "You have the only bitch in the castle; this is most bloke's wet dream. What do those pricks have but a cold bed and their own hand? Let them watch because you're the only one I *see*."

Then I kissed him: desperate, hard, and exploding with frankincense stars.

Drake was real, beneath me, and *mine*.

"As you like." Drake breathed in slowly, as if trying to breathe me in: to live on my scent alone. "It has always been as you like."

He smiled, shy and uncertain.

My chest ached. I'd *used* Drake's *fondness* but why hadn't I seen that it was truly *love*, as fierce as Rebel's or Ash's? Just...different...because had anyone ever loved Drake before?

*Did I now?*

Rahab's *clapping*, followed by the sudden stamping of feet and beating of wings broke me out of my daze.

Drake tensed, his face becoming the rigid mask that I understood so much more now.

*Lazarus rises! Rises! Rises! And we will rise!*

I gritted my teeth, as the chant swelled around the Bailey,

before dying down at last.

"Was I not right to trust in my royal guest? Like a good father, I knew you merely needed the correct push for the win. The *motivation*." Rahab rose over the Bailey; his bow lips curled into a smile. "You are now an official apprentice in the Brotherhood. You may work to become a mage: *my true child.* Whereas my blood son..." His smile died an ugly death into a glare; Drake quailed. "Well, we all know he's not worthy."

*Smatters of laugher.*

My fists clenched, as I fought not to unleash my fire on the smug bastards.

Rahab waved his hand. "The contest is over. Violet is entered into the Brotherhood, and Duma is humbled to Underserving." His eyes sparked. "You've already trained to serve her mother, Duma, you should know how to satisfy her daughter."

"I'll satisfy myself by kicking your arse." I launched myself up, but Drake snatched hold of my skirt, yanking me back down.

Drake shook his head. "Be silent. Now is the time to celebrate. Don't you want to see your brother again at the Initiation Feast?"

My brother?

*A bruised shoulder beneath golden sheets in the Through the Looking Glass room...*

At last, I'd meet my magical monster brother at a feast in my honour. I'd know if he was *safe.*

I forced myself to give a careful nod. "I'm always down for partying hard."

Rahab swooped towards Phoenix Hall, on the edge of the castle. "Party and punishment. I promised both *lover and brother* remember? Consistency is the key: I shall never break a promise. Now, follow."

In waves of gold and bronze, Rahab's boys rose into the air

99

after him, circling towards Phoenix Hall.

I offered my hand to Drake, pulling him to his feet. We both wore Rebel's blood like second skins. Now scarlet painted, we flew after the tide of gold towards my reward, brother, and my punishment.

# 11

As a kid in the children's home at night — alone — I'd weave tales of my birth brother: older, braver, and *my protector*.

I imagined that we'd been separated by mistake, but he was searching for me and would find me. Then I wouldn't be the only freak with mismatched eyes anymore because he'd be the same as me, only he'd be able to stop the monsters creeping into my bed at night.

*He'd save me.*

Except, now my brother and I *were* the monsters, and *I* was the one who had to save my older brother: The Invisible Prince.

In fact, so invisible that as I squirmed on the turquoise bench at High Table, straining from my vantage point on the dais at the end of Phoenix Hall, I couldn't even see him.

*At least, I didn't think so...*

Yet would I even recognise him? My half-brother was nothing more to me than a flash of brunet hair and pale skin.

*A stranger.*

My claws shot out, screeching along the sparkling table top. Drake's hand rested on my shoulder, before he leant over to refill my gold tankard with mead.

I snorted: when I'd said *partying hard*, never in Medieval Ville had I thought it'd be with *mead*.

Drake straightened, keeping his gaze averted from mine.

His silk trousers had already been changed to silver: *Undeserving*. I itched to rip them off his slender thighs — not because of the 101 Dirty Reasons that'd be fun — but because he shouldn't be reduced to the ranks of servant...because his dad had wanted to prove *my* worth before the Legion.

"Problem?" Rahab rapped his fingers on the table in imitation of my claws; I sharply retracted my talons. "Aren't you enjoying your reward?"

"Because it's never a problem to brutally flog someone's fam." I slammed my tankard against the table; the foam slopped out in a fizzing sea. "This is mutiny, bro"

"I believe that to be my line," he replied drily, sprawling back in the armchair at the head of the table, which was draped with a golden canopy.

Och perched next to me, clutching his tankard like his firstborn.

*Guess that's what a guilty conscience looked like.* Except, it hadn't stopped Och putting his back into swinging the cat o'nine tails.

I scanned the hall again, over the bowed heads of the apprentices on the lower trestle tables and the mages, rowdy and drunken, on the silk covered tables closer to us.

*Cheers and whistles.*

I pinked: *the party was for me.* I'd told Mischief I'd never wanted power. But respect? Adulation? To fit in?

*Yeah, I bastard thirsted for those.*

Tapestries as rich as the table coverings hung on the stone walls, between the gold and green banners of the Legion: angels battled vampires, witches fell before mages, and in the most glorious shone the prophecy of the *Rising*...

I shivered, caught in the thrill.

*Could it be real?* Could I be the one who led the Brotherhood to that wondrous moment of victory: The *Chosen* who they'd been waiting for?

Unexpectedly, music burst through the hall: the seductive spell of Katy Perry's "Dark Horse". I closed my eyes, snared in the song's relentless, unstoppable black magic. Its chorus rose in brooding crescendos: magic as a weapon of love.

"Are you making a point?" I forced out, opening my eyes with difficulty against the force of the music.

Rahab blinked. "My tastes lean more towards Mozart than hip hop, but the mages discovered this music from their human Brothers. I'm not the Matriarch: indulging in humanity isn't punished, as long as they don't lose themselves in it."

I caught Drake's smirk, before he covered his mouth with his hand. "Your son wasn't in charge of this playlist?"

Rahab's gaze shifted to Drake. "And if he was?"

Drake's expression instantly stilled. Yeah, I got the joke: I'd cast a love spell on him, and now he was screwed. There was something legendary about Drake pulling that kind of trick at my own celebratory feast to get back at me for winning, and no way was he being punished for it.

I grinned. "Then his choice of song doesn't suck."

This time, Drake didn't hide his smile.

A *whine*, loud enough to startle me even over the icy rhythms of "Dark Horse".

Startled, I caught a movement in the shadows at the back of the hall. Then the mages laughed again, and this time it had nothing to do with me and everything to do with humiliating the naked vampire, who they'd forced to all fours in the sole patch of shadow on the bare floor.

Ash wore the Compulsion Collar around his neck, and his chain had been wound around a table leg. Even though he was out of direct sunlight, the rays through the phoenix stained-glass in the arched windows must be giving him the mother of all migraines.

When a mage bent to pour a dribble of blood — not enough to do more than bank the fires of starvation — into a bowl on the floor, and Ash desperately lapped it up, I fought not to remember the way I'd fed his sisters.

How I'd once had my own *pets*.

103

*Sneering snickers.*

I shrank back on the bench. Why had I even for a moment wanted to lead these pricks? What magic was woven into those tapestries?

When I glared at Rahab, he didn't even try to hide the smug grin. "Feeling any...*different*?"

"I'll be in the sharing mood, when you tell me where Rebel and Mischief are."

Rahab sighed. "All this is in your honour, yet you worry about an Addict and an Underserving...?"

"Guess I'm a sentimental bitch."

"Then I imagine I am too because they're recovering in the Mirror Lodge." Rahab tilted his head. "Do you not approve?"

"You've earned a Feathers Medal. You want your second...? Where's my brother?"

"Patience," Rahab *tutted*. "The show is about to begin."

I stiffened. Why did I think this wouldn't be the rabbits out of a hat variety, unless it included cutting someone truly in half? "Patience is overrated, like shower sex, birthdays, power, dieting, perfection, money, parents—"

"I'm intrigued to discover what *isn't* overrated in your world?"

"*Fam*: their loyalty, courage, and sacrifice. *Love*."

Drake's fingers ghosted across my shoulder again, grounding me down from the high. I gripped onto the edge of the table.

"You may not believe me, but I hold the same truth." Tiny crinkles radiated around Rahab's eyes, as he smiled. "My Legion, here and amongst the humans, are my *fam*. I prize the same values as you. Yet perhaps it's merely hard for you to accept the authority of another? Remember, I understand; I seek to help bring you into our Brotherhood."

If it hadn't been for Drake's touch on my shoulder — Rahab's true son, who'd been cast out — I'd have believed Rahab.

How to Be a Cult Leader for Beginners. And I'd almost fallen for it.

"Yeah, so let's get with the bringing already."

Rahab frowned, perplexed. "It's not a celebration without a feast."

As the music died, Drake slipped a golden platter in front of me, then a second before his dad. I groaned, sinking into the heady roasted aromas. Thick wedges of beef towered over flanks of venison and pheasant wings. I half-expected a wild boar to be stuffed at the head of the table next to a slaughtered swan.

A bitch from the streets of Hackney had never *feasted* Henry the Eighth style, and after a month on Dickensian gruel, my stomach grumbled.

*This meat was going down.*

I snatched up a leg of...*something dead*...and gnawed, ripping off the flesh, as the juices ran sticky down my chin.

Rahab only grinned, whilst he nibbled delicately on a bread roll.

Hell, let him. This would be meaty heaven, if I had a pizza slice underneath it...

"You bastards don't have to eat," I accused between mouthfuls. "You get all your yummy nutrition from the sun. So, why do you act the Addicts and copy humans? After all, don't you think they're worthless?"

"Not worthless," Rahab ripped the roll in half, crumbling it between his fingers. "Many have magic. The rest? Must be reminded of their place."

Suddenly, the mages beat their fists — *bang, bang, bang* — on the table. Then they cheered, as Kunel swept to his feet with a bow.

When Kunel swaggered towards us, I slumped. "Here comes the jester," I muttered.

Rahab's lips quirked. "One of those at this table is quite enough."

*Fair point.*

"On this Initiation Feast, let us remember the story of the Legion of the Phoenix!" Kunel swung back to his audience, who shuffled in their seats in anticipation.

I rolled my eyes, shovelling in another mouthful of beef, before slurping on my mead. *More fairy tales...*

These angel mages were no different to the vampires, Blood Lovers, or kids in the children's home. They ritualised fantasies to hide from the terror of the truth beneath.

*Including the monster who was sitting in a golden chair like a benevolent god right here amongst them.*

Kunel glanced over his shoulder at Rahab, who gestured for him to go on. When Kunel raised his hands, shadows slithered out of the tapestries, dancing across the hall.

*I knew there'd been something shady about those threads.*

"Bastard," I half-pushed off the bench.

"Only a tale for children," Och muttered, settling his hand on my knee to keep me seated. "Do not show fear now, my Queen, Kunel would delight in that." Why did he speak with more hushed reverence than the First Reformer ever had? Yet all I could imagine was the spray of blood across Rebel's back, along with the *swish* of Och's whip.

I shoved his hand off my knee. "And you wouldn't?"

Och's eyes narrowed. "My brother is unable to walk, shuddering through the agonies of a whipping *I* laid onto your boy. I do not delight in it, nor your fear. I simply do my duty, and if you'd done the same, neither of them would be suffering now. Nor would your brother be soon."

My breath caught, even as Och leaned away from me again, as if he hadn't been shanking me with each word.

Tears pricked my eyes.

What did being a rebel count for in a world ruled by the Code and strict ranks of Brotherhood? Wasn't it easier to obey, do my duty, and be rewarded, than to risk punishment?

*To become part of the fairy tale?*

I battled to hide my vibrating *fear*, as the shadows grew into grotesque puppets: vampires, angels, and witches. Nightmarish, they waged silent battles above our heads, slithering cold trails across my exposed skin, as they slunk between their living audience.

The shadows inside me clamoured, surging out in trailing

fingers to join the fight. I hung between the two: the true puppet.

Kunel spun between the tables, weaving the shadow war. "In the name of the Brotherhood, there arose a great conflict. Witches and the Fallen became a plague. One angel with the most powerful mental powers of them all arose..." A pure light shone on Rahab, as if he wasn't already going for the Deity of the Year award. I swallowed my mouthful with difficulty; way to make a bitch lose her appetite. "And built the Brotherhood and Phoenix Code. Yet still the mages weren't strong enough to rise..." Shadow angel mages soared from the tapestries. "So, the secret of resurrection was taken from the blood of one special angel, Phoenix, to raise an army of dead angels."

I hurled down the venison leg that I'd been holding; a glob of fat splattered onto Rahab's chin. He wiped it off with a thin finger.

Shadow angels rose — resurrected — but leashed behind the mages like fighting dogs.

*Phoenix slaves.*

Phoenix had been my first kiss. The first vampire to try and either kill me or transform me to Blood Lover. And when Rebel and I had been hunters, we'd ganked him.

If Phoenix could resurrect himself, however, was he even dead?

It didn't sound like his life before he'd Fallen — having the secret *taken from him* — would've led him into the Land of the Balanced, which explained our encounters. Because how had Rahab transferred Phoenix's miracle blood to resurrect his angel slaves?

With a little needle prick and *this won't hurt*...?

Yet Phoenix hadn't changed his angel name, unlike every other vampire. Had he lost so much more than them, that he couldn't bear to lose his name as well?

"By my feathers, Phoenix was kidnapped from the Legion..."

*Boos and hisses.*

I huffed: I'd always hated pantomimes.

When Kunel cast a sly glance back at me, however, my guts churned. "Phoenix had already conceived a son with the Matriarch, however, who'd hoped to birth a talented daughter with his powers. And the son's blood was just as potent at resurrection."

*My brother.*

I hadn't realised I'd doubled over the table, until Drake's arms were clasped around my neck; his curls swept across my face, as his cheek brushed against mine.

They'd been...*bleeding*...my brother to steal his blood to raise their slave army.

*My half-brother — the Invisible Prince — was Phoenix's son.*

For what twisted reason had Phoenix wanted *me*...? Had he sensed the connection? Craved it because he'd lost his own son? Or hadn't he known?

That would've been one hell of a conversation.

"Our Invisible Prince." With a flourish, Kunel slipped a glass box out of his pocket and tossed it into the air.

*Silence.*

The Phoenix Hall stilled in an uneasy quiet.

The box hung between the warring shadows, before hovering and expanding.

This time, I shrugged Drake off, leaping over the table in a *clatter* of tankards and platters.

I swooped up, batting away the shadows and hugging the side of the box.

A tall angel curled inside the tiny space, with his wings furled over him; his brunet hair cascaded down, hiding his bowed face: *my brother.*

I couldn't bear to look away or let go, whilst the mages bellowed and Kunel cursed, because at last I could see my brother and had to save him.

Even if first I had to save myself from the shadows, which dove towards me in gnashing swarms.

# **12**

The nightmare shadows had broken their strings, united with each other against me.

I clung to the glass box, shrouded in the shadows' twirling black above the heads of the apprentices and mages in the Phoenix Hall. Like a dark ocean, the shadows' freezing touches choked me.

I gagged, as one slid down my throat. *Then another...*

My own shadows hissed inside, mummifying the invaders, before shooting out of me in an inky phoenix that drove the shadow puppets quivering back into their tapestries.

Sunlight flooded the now silent hall again.

*Who've guessed exploding phoenixes were the way to the Brotherhood's heart?*

I didn't even glance down at the mages, however, because Kunel's crooned praise no longer gave me the tinglies. He'd lost his sway over me, since he'd kept my brother locked in a box: a toy on display.

I slammed my palms on the glass — *bang, bang, bang* — but my brother didn't even look up. Then I noticed the way his back shuddered up and down: he was weeping, although I couldn't hear that either.

The prince was trapped, naked, and unable to see or hear

out, whilst we watched his suffering, just to add to the drama of the Brotherhood's tale.

I swung to Rahab, but he shook his head. He was sprawled in his seat, unruffled by my shadow battle, like he'd known it'd happen. *Or had planned it.* "You wished to *see* your brother. Plus, punishment. My promise fulfilled and entertainment too." He laughed, low and musical. "Dinner and a show."

Violet and black swirled in baying unison to light Rahab up with *my* fire, just as I'd wiped out his shadows with my own. Yet all that truly mattered was that my brother was more of a captive than me, even if it meant playing nice with the psychos.

"Cheers for the hospitality." If my jaw had been any more clenched, my teeth would've cracked. "Now you can let him go, yeah?"

Rahab nodded.

I sagged against the box, tracing a finger along the glass to follow the curve of my brother's spine. Then I clasped the pouch, which hung around my neck under my scarf: it held my sister's necklace. I'd lost Jade to the vampires; now she was a Blood Lover in the Under World, who'd rejected both the angels and me. I couldn't lose a brother too.

*I didn't even know his real name...*

"That is," Rahab's gaze hardened, "when you *see* all you've missed."

My eyes widened; I gripped more tightly to the box, as if I could stop whatever was about to happen.

*Like I could be my brother's Protector.*

Suddenly, my brother began to shrink... Only, he wasn't shrinking, he was *deageing*.

Years were stripped away, as he writhed, bruising himself against the sides in his panic. I'd be freaking out too if I found myself first a teenager, all mop of hair and long limbs, then a kid with anime large eyes and freckles.

The prince was small enough now to lift his head and stare out of the box. Even though he couldn't see me, he was looking directly at me. A sob caught in the back of my throat at his terror because I couldn't do a bastard thing to soothe or *help him*.

And this — all these years being played out in minutes — was what we'd missed. Childhood and teenage years spent apart because we hadn't known that the other existed. I'd been abandoned amongst the humans, and he'd been a prisoner of the Legion, only wanted for his blood.

Neither of us had been raised by our parents: *loved*.

We could've had each other but we hadn't even been allowed that. And to see this — not just the adult but the child as well — was my punishment, as well as my brother's.

*Rahab was a cruel bastard.*

A *wail*.

A baby lay in the box that now seemed too big, rather than too small; tears steaked my brother's tiny face as he kicked his legs. When the baby bawled again, I vibrated with the need to hold him until he calmed, whispering that he'd be safe.

*Only that'd be a lie.*

The baby alone in that box needed me, and for the first time, I didn't know if I could resist the Brotherhood.

I peered over the glass at Rahab. "I'm your tamed apprentice who's jumped through all the hoops. So, tell me what I need to do to free my brother."

Rahab steepled his fingers. "Only a Lazarus Mage has the privilege of meeting with the prince. As you just witnessed, he's the lifeblood of the Brotherhood."

"Then mage me up."

Rahab barked with laughter. "You imagine the First Reformer thinks so highly of you? I'm afraid you've years of hard work ahead, little apprentice."

"Stick your schtick because I'm not buying," I snarled, rubbing my hands back and forth across the glass like I could reach the wailing baby. "Castle Drake and the Legion are your screwed-up creation. If you want to, you can mould me into a Phoenix Mage, Joseph's coat of many colours, or the Abominable Snowman."

Rahab raised himself slowly in his seat, spreading his

gleaming wings. It looked like he was about to burst into song...or burst me into flames. "And your question is?"

"What's the price? What freedom must I sacrifice to become a mage ASAP?"

Rahab *rapped* on the table: it echoed through the hall. "At last, the correct question. You must undertake the Mage's Challenge."

"You shall not. I forbid it." Drake sprang onto the table, restored to the towering, predatory Commander in his terror.

I'd almost forgotten Drake was there, silent and cowed in his role as Undeserving. Yet he'd shaken it off the moment that he'd heard *Mage's Challenge*. Every bloke in the hall was staring at Drake like he'd lost it *Falling Down* Style.

*Hell...*

Drake had just witnessed Rebel's flogging. If he'd been prepared to risk *that*, then how dangerous was the Challenge?

Yet I throbbed with warmth that Drake sought to protect me, even if I didn't need a defender, because that's what fam did: they had each other's back.

Och yanked Drake's ankle, tumbling him onto the table with a *thud*. I flinched, but Rahab didn't even look down. When Och rubbed his fingers together, an iron harness gag appeared. Drake struggled, staring at me with pleading eyes.

I shook my head:

**Sorry, bro.**

Drake closed his eyes, as Och forced the gag between his teeth, fastening it behind his curls.

"The Challenge," Rahab continued, as if Drake hadn't even spoken, "is to liberate the familiars from the witches of the Head Coven. Then to return the familiars to the Legion, so we may save them."

"Save them? Or skin yourself some Jon Snow fur coats to keep yourself warm in winter, since you march around half-naked?"

"*Your* familiars would make the most elegant coat." When I growled at his threat to Blaze and Spark, Rahab's eyes

113

glinted. "Bring me the witches' familiars, however, and your foxes may keep their pelts, whilst you'll see that I mean merely to reform our new guests."

*Yeah, and I crapped nymphs who sang "Don't Fear the Reaper."*

"Where's the Big Bad sized catch?"

Rahab lifted his finger. "No one has ever succeeded in the Mage's Challenge."

*Yeah, Drake's outburst not so crazy now.*

I snorted. "If you wanted to gank me, why not have the fun of doing it yourself?"

Rahab soared towards me. "I wish to free the true light within you."

"Pretty sure it's not light inside me."

Rahab's smile was soft. "You've been blinded by the words of others. Only a Champion of Light can win the Mage's Challenge, and there hasn't been one of those for centuries. Whose side will your spark fall on? Shall we test it?"

I shivered because his words electrified me: light or shadow? Vampire or angel?

I'd been a Champion in the vampires' Bone Carnival but could I also be a Champion of Light in the angels' Mage Challenge?

I nodded.

Rahab's eyes lit with such satisfaction that I *knew* I'd missed something important. But Drake was gagged, Rebel and Mischief were in my chambers recovering, Ash was leashed, and my brother was literally a baby. Rahab knew how to isolate me, and making choices on my own was bastard hard.

"I want my fam with me." I met Rahab's gaze; his satisfaction slid to blankness, then fury. "My blokes."

"You may have Zophia, the vampire whore, and..." Rahab hesitated. "Zachriel if he's healed."

"What about—"

"My son will be in the Reformation room because of his public disobedience."

I glimpsed Drake, but his head hung low; tremors ran

114

through him.

Yeah, I'd be cracking on with this Mage Challenge because I refused to leave Drake for long in what sounded the opposite of Rainbow Funfair Land.

Och rested his hand on Drake's elbow. "I could reform Duma myself, without the need for the Reformation Room—"

"Chief Discipliner, do you need a trip there yourself?"

Och blanched, stepping back. "No, sir."

Rahab brushed his wing over the glass box. I fought not to shove him away. "Yet you must have motivations, as well as rewards, Queen Apprentice. If you fail the challenge, firstly your vampire whore will become forever the First Reformer's handsome pet; Kunel appears quite taken with him."

I growled, twisting to Ash, who'd been dragged onto the silk table like a centrepiece. The mages touched and stroked, whilst Kunel rested his hand possessively on Ash's mane.

*Mine, mine, mine...*

The violation howled through me. Ash defiantly didn't move or react to their intimate touches or pinches, but I knew what their callous cruelty meant to him: to be seen as nothing but a *creature*. A Seducer. As Lucifer had reduced him to as punishment for standing against the murder of slave Bloods: Ash's courageous rebellion.

*How could I let it happen again?*

"If there's a *firstly*, then there's a bastard *secondly*..."

"Zachriel—"

Fury spiralled tsunami through me, bursting out. "I'll rip off your wings before I let you whip him again."

Rahab's wings tightened around the glass box. My brother's wails had tapered off to dry sobs, as he rubbed at his tired eyes. "Why would I do that? Punishments must be original to be effective. I understand you won't believe me, but I don't wish to cause Zachriel more pain. Instead, he'll be executed."

I stopped breathing. Stopped. Everything.

The world stopped.

Lights danced in front of my eyes. I beat my wings frantically to keep myself from falling out of the sky because all I could see was Rebel...*dead*.

*Because of me.*

My bond screamed at the thought. Agonising, elemental, pure. I shook from the terror. And this grief and knowledge that I wouldn't survive if Rebel didn't...?

Hell, at last I got it. *That* was love. And Rahab was about to take it away from me.

"Calm now, you look as if I'd ordered the Apocalypse!" Rahab chuckled, like I wasn't gasping at his threat to my fam, world, and *life*. "I can be merciful. I'll resurrect him as *my* Phoenix. He'll look so beautiful with golden wings."

*I was going to hurl...*

The one thing Rebel hated more than anything and had always fought against — slavery — to be visited upon him after death...?

Yet Rahab thought that horror *mercy*?

"Don't do that to him..."

"I assure you, Zachriel is in such pain now — haunted by his past — that having his memories wiped clean, as they are in all Phoenixes, wouldn't be a loss but a blessing. Can't you feel Zachriel's suffering? Don't you wish to ease it? Forgetting would be a kindness. He'd be happy as a Phoenix with nothing to worry about but to please me. *I* could make him happy."

I blushed: Rahab more or less rapped *because you don't*.

"I'll win the Mage's Challenge." I flew down to Ash, knocking the mages' hands off him and sweeping my wings to cover him. His skin was warm, and I clung to him against the images of Rebel. *And whether they were true.* "Then you'll never find out because he's *my* fam, and *I'll* be the bitch to make him happy."

As I clutched Ash, the phoenixes burst from the stained-glass windows in scarlet flares of light, swooping above our heads. The mages and apprentices *oohed* and *aahed* at the show.

I'd become part of the Legion's propaganda: their new mascot.

Now, I'd take on the most dangerous witches in the world in a challenge that had never been won before because it was the only way to save my brother and become strong enough to sweep away Rahab's golden reign.

Yet I'd also risked my fam: Ash and Rebel. If I wasn't the mythical Champion of Light, then one would become a pet and the other would die, only to rise again as a slave.

# 13

Copper burst in a kiss that shook me with its tremoring sweetness because it had the urgency of a *goodbye*. Yet this was the first time I'd tasted Rebel since his candy blood had spilt on the Bailey floor and I couldn't let him go. Instead, I pressed him against the oak's rough bark in the wood behind the Head Coven, stroking across his shoulders in case I'd still be able to trace the welts, even through his leather jacket.

Because I could still hear, see, and *feel* them shuddering through me.

*Rap, rap, rap.*

Mischief's graceful hand knocked on the oak above our heads.

I opened my eyes, drawing back from the kiss.

How did Rebel always make me forget that it wasn't just the two of us against the Big Bad World?

Had he expected to die tied to that whipping post? What had Rahab been saying...*doing*...to Rebel over the last month? At least I'd had Drake, Ceri, Mischief, the fox brothers and the new magics nudging me towards the Brotherhood. But Rebel had been alone. Had he been messed up as badly as Ash?

When Rebel pecked a kiss on the end of my nose, I realised I'd been staring.

"Oh goodie, is this the line for the kissing booth?" Mischief rested his head on my shoulder. "What's the going rate for an apprentice...sailor doll...champion... Excuse me, what are you again?"

*And there was the Sugar Plum Sass I hadn't missed.*

When Rebel growled, I swung to the side, expecting Mischief to end up on his arse at the receiving end of my enraged punk. Instead, Rebel noosed his arms around Mischief with an intense fierceness, whilst Mischief soothed, "I have you now." *And yeah, that led to a serious case of my raised eyebrow.* "We all do."

Ash met my eye, questioning. Ash's tight black jeans, shooter, and Devil's Trident had been restored at my dogged insistence before the Mage's Challenge. His Compulsion Collar, however, had been removed, and I'd never been so relieved to see Ash's neck, even if it was chafed. He lounged against an elm, fiddling with his holster like it no longer fitted. Or as if it was the only distraction stopping him from fighting Mischief for Rebel in an angel tug-of-war.

Mischief peered over Rebel's head at me: he was ashen, and his eyes squinted, like even the pale moon in the fairy tale wood was giving him the Godzilla of headaches. Already strained from healing Rebel, the multi-teleportation (and hell did that trigger my geek crush instincts) to bring us here had hit Mischief hard. Worse, his gaze flickered with a pain that he was trying to mask: a constant pressure.

Spells still screamed make-believe, yet Rahab had planted one in Mischief's mind that would expand, like the glass box trapping my brother, to collect the familiars.

We'd also all been whammied with a Compulsion Spell: we couldn't escape the witches' grounds. Rahab prided himself on understanding his boys — and girl — so he could pick us apart and remake us.

*Lame.*

If the Cult Leader for Dummies understood me at all, he'd have known that I wouldn't abandon my fam: brother, Ceri, Blaze and Spark, or Drake...

I'd never abandon the Broken kids, Underserving, apprentices, and Phoenixes...the bastard world to the Legion's warped teachings.

Rahab thought we were alike? *Screw that.*

Mischief flinched, as moonlight struck his face through the branches, before holding himself to rigid stillness to hide it. "After all," his mouth twisted, "we're in the presence of a soon-to-be *Champion of Light*. However could we fail?"

*Yeah, sarcasm.*

I booted at twigs, *snapping* them in sharp gunshots; Mischief winced. "Then why don't I feel like a champion?"

"No one does," Mischief's voice became soft. "Did you imagine it'd buzz like Christmas or your wedding day? Perhaps there'd be a neat god pill to pop?"

"How about just a little tingle?"

"Do you deserve one?" This time Mischief's smile was too wide. Ash straightened; his hand slid to his shooter. Still Mischief cradled Rebel in his arms. "You risk your true family for the *Butcher*. Tell me, you're quick to claim his kisses, but does Zachriel know the cost—"

"Lay off." Rebel pulled away from Mischief; his fingers traced along the black collar around his neck, seeking comfort. "Sweet heaven, I knelt for Feathers. I've ballsed up everything I've touched, but not her. Although I'm a bad angel, she's treated me like I'm good; I'd die and be resurrected a thousand times for her."

My eyes burned with shamed tears. *What did I know about love?*

**The Unicorn Angel has a point, even if he is showboating his pretty ass.**

**This battle for your brother will have a cost. At the end, I hope his monstrous hide is worth it.**

*And what about __my__ monstrous hide, bitch? Am I worth it?*

**Always.**

Ash took a step forward. "We've lost enough brothers and

120

sisters; Violet can't be blamed for not wanting to lose anymore," Ash's voice was low and intense. He shared a glance with Rebel that shredded me. *"And you're not dying."*

"Brilliant!" Rebel grinned, bouncing on his toes. "So, how do we do a flit with these familiars?"

"We have the element of surprise," Ash smoothly slipped into Brigadier mode: *hell, he was hot like this.* "But it won't last for long. Check out the stables."

I scanned across at the Head Coven: The House of Snakes.

A grand red-brick Elizabethan mansion squatted in a toad-like pile of blackened chimneys and spiralled turrets. An army of windows glared back at us, which were lit by the full moon.

Behind the mansion lay the stables. I was betting a Seducer and an Addict that there weren't horses inside.

I nodded, "We have a winner."

"How does it go afterwards for the Blood Familiars with Dr Frankenstein, mate?" Ash prowled towards Mischief. "Capture, feed, find good homes?" He snatched Mischief by the elbow, hauling him closer. "Or more like: capture, beat, experiment on?"

Mischief laughed, yanking himself free and twirling to the edge of the wood. "Do none of you perceive that this is not about *familiars*? Or initiations, champions, or challenges? This is about saving the world, you tiny creatures, from Rahab. I've fought this battle, not for a year, *but my entire life*." When Mischief panted, I drew back from his unleashed regal rage. "I wait, hidden in the shadows, whilst you prance in the glorious light. You wish to be our leader...? Then you *will* lead."

I crushed my nails into the palms of my hands, as my pulse pounded. I remembered the rockfall in the Ghost Caves: Mischief's different but formidable power, which he'd been forced to hide his whole life. I knew about being *different*, but Mischief had suffered for it, whilst sacrificing for those who were weaker.

Mischief had plotted against Rahab for centuries. Yet he didn't seek power, only to free his people.

*That was a bastard hero.*

It also made him as dangerous as Rahab.

**I told you this would be the choice: if you wish to be Protector, everywhere is a battlefield, and these are *your* sacrifices to make.**

**You ride the world like a dick and you're on top.**

**If you're not ready, then get off and let Silver Angel grind his sweet way to heaven. Because you're not the only leader of this supernatural pack.**

*Cheers: that's an image I'll never be able to bleach from my brain. And I'm not jealous—*

**Lying to me is only lying to yourself, hooker. The Wizard Who Snarked has stronger magic than you. He's been plotting rebellions for centuries longer than you. And pretty in punk has a man crush on him.**

**Just remember you have one thing he'll never have.**

*What?*

**A biteable ass, girl.**

I sniggered, then flushed.

Mischief swung to me. His eyes flashed, as he murmured, "Or do you forget what Ceri showed you in the Broken Nursery so soon?"

My breath caught; I shivered.

How did Mischief think I could forget Fynchan clambering into my lap, clasping his arms around my neck like he *trusted me* and laughing, as I made fire unicorns dance?

I'd broken Mischief out to save the slaves. I was *their* champion. Yet how had Rahab twisted me into *his* creature?

*Mischief wanted a leader...?*

I stared between my fam, who studied me back. "Then just call me *Simon Says*, bitches."

Mischief gave a sharp nod.

"Let's say the spell casters have the familiars in the stables," I glanced back across the lawns. "What's the chances the furry critters will come quietly? Blaze and Spark hunted me the first time—"

"Do you know why the witches are the vampires' enemy?

122

They *hunt* us." I didn't understand the way Ash glared at Rebel.

Rebel hung his head, pressing himself against the oak.

I frowned, glancing between them. "Not following, bro."

"Don't," Rebel whispered. "Not now..."

"Once they capture us," Ash bit out, still not looking away from Rebel, "they *transform us into familiars.*" I gasped, biting hard on my lip. "We're not capturing creatures for Rahab, but vampires. How honoured do you think his *guests* will be?"

I tremored, folding my wings around myself like that could change the truth. *All this time I hadn't known...* "Blaze and Spark...?"

My Blood Familiars: *fam.*

I was their Keeper, but once they'd been vampires, the same as Ash, until that'd been stolen from them by witches.

*Blaze and Spark had been vampire brothers.*

"My mates," Ash said. "They still are. I always looked out for them the best I could. Even when they were—"

*Crack* — I swept Rebel's legs out from underneath him, slamming him to the undergrowth; the twigs *popped* in protest.

I held Rebel down by his throat; silver sizzled on my fingertips.

"Don't take off his head," Mischief warned. "Control your beastly rage."

"Why? This bastard's adopted family of psycho witches transformed Blaze and Spark into familiars. Did you hunt them? Hand them over for your sadist da to hurt? Were you even planning to help us against the Head Coven or are you still the spell lobbers' bitch? Were you planning to betray us? Was Ash going to make a pretty wolf?"

Rebel let out a sob, not even struggling, as I tightened my grip. Then I was flying backwards through the air, blasted by stinging silver. I landed with an *oomph* on my arse.

Mischief stood in sparkling splendour next to Rebel; he

held out his hand to Rebel, hauling him to his feet.

Rebel clasped his neck, rubbing the redness. *Hell, had I done that?* I hadn't even summoned Mischief's magic, but it'd sparked.

I paled at the danger, not to myself but to my fam and the bastard world.

"Even you do not believe that nonsense tirade." Mischief tossed his hair. "My name is *traitor*: it's not Zachriel's. If you truly believe he could do any of those things, then it's not only trust that's missing within your astounding mind."

"My fam are vampires, *I'm* half vampire, and yet this secret...?"

"I'm sorry, so I am." Rebel peeked up at me through his thick lashes. "Ages ago, my adopted family tried to teach me to hate, so I'd hunt vampires to turn into familiars. Whip my arse for fibbing, but I'd never hate. And I didn't hunt for new familiars."

"Is that why you had us hunting those fanatic bastards, the Pure, instead?"

Rebel nodded. "I'd never hurt a slave. Cop on! Don't you know that about me yet, woman?"

Ash marched to Rebel. "That's why this..." When he clouted Rebel — *crack* — in the nose, I flinched. "...isn't your balls. But if you ever hurt Spark and Blaze...?"

Rebel grinned around his cradled nose. "You'll kick me in the bollocks like the bad bastard you are? Just so you know...? Ditto, muppet."

When Mischief grimaced, pressing his hand to his forehead, I stalked to the edge of the wood. He might be used to handling pain (and his magic might feed on dishing it out), but the sooner we stole the familiars, the sooner he'd be free of his headache.

Mischief glanced at me in surprise. "Lucky me, you've remembered we're not on a pleasure jaunt. After all, if we don't return within a single night, it's only *my* brain that'll splatter like an alien birth."

"We're in our own series of *24*," Ash muttered. "*Will they defuse the bomb in his brain in time...?*"

Mischief ignored him, scowling. "Or do you wish to squabble some more? Pause for some make-up sex perhaps? We do have a whore here at least..."

Ash growled. "Make that two. You should show me your moves, silver hips."

How was I supposed to save the world, whilst the blokes at my back couldn't see past their ancient divisions to the truth that they were so similar they could be geek brothers?

Mischief's expression darkened, but before he could snap at Ash, I snatched his wing, dragging him closer.

Then I nodded at Rebel and Ash, who drew in, until we stood together in a circle. My wings rubbed against Ash's: sweet and intimate. I linked my pinkie with Rebel's, rubbing my thumb across his in apology. When his gaze met mine, it was sad and as distressed as the shadows across our bond.

*I'd* betrayed his trust by doubting him in the surge of my new powers and I couldn't take it back.

*Hell, I wished I could take it back.*

Mischief hesitated, awkward on the edge of the circle.

I smirked. "You too, grouchypants."

"If you insist on such displays of unnecessary affection." Yet he pushed Ash aside to nestle in next to me, gripping my hand hard. His wings were warm as they stretched over us all, including Ash.

"We'll be out in the open all the way to the stables." Ash rubbed against Mischief's feathers. Was that a bastard *purr* from Mischief? "Prime witch pickings."

"Now if we'd had Drake's Power of Invisibility..."

Mischief perked up. "Sneaky little Duma, hiding his light under a bushel." I bit my tongue. *Way to reveal Drake's tricks.* When Mischief's eyes slyly narrowed, I had the feeling he didn't plan to send Drake a congratulations card. "Why do we need the golden child, however, when we have *this*?"

Mischief let go of my hand, stepping back. His wings beat, just once, then silver broke in a wave over all our heads.

Lights danced; my vision blurred. I swayed, only held up

by Rebel's grip.

Then the wood shot back into sudden clarity, and I steadied. I peered around at the others. They were still there.

When Mischief grinned at me, triumphantly, I shook my head. "Sorry, bro, epic fail."

Mischief sighed. "Move your arm, sailor." When I shook my arm, I gasped; it shimmered multi-coloured, camouflaging with the trees behind. "Shape shifter," Mischief smirked. "I believe in sharing talents, remember?"

"That's a fine thing!" Rebel's smile was dazzling, as he hopped from foot to foot. "We're after doing this together."

"And if we're caught — together," Ash held up his hand to stem Rebel's enthusiasm, even though he was struggling to get out the words, "I know what it is to be at the mercy of wicked witches. Here are the rules and they're non-negotiable." His jaw clenched. "No eating, drinking, or heroics. The Head Coven train vampires, Addicts, and mages: we're not the Justice League, we're the Suicide Squad."

I wet my lips, spreading my wings. "Then let's play the supervillains."

I soared into the night sky towards the most powerful witches in England and an impossible challenge, with vampires and angels camouflaged at my back. If I failed, Ash would be lost to the mages and Rebel would die. And if we were caught, we'd become the witches' creatures.

# 14

Creatures cowered, crawled, and crouched in the witches' stable. Piss, dung, and fear stung my nostrils; I held my sleeve across my mouth. Ranks of gleaming eyes stared back at me from the stacked cages in the shadows.

*Yowls, chirps, grunts, squeaks...*

Rebel poked his fingers through to a white Arctic wolf, which loped forward, sniffing, before *snapping* at him with a snarl.

"Sweet Jesus..." Rebel fell backwards, bottom shuffling into Ash who caught him, hauling him back to his feet.

"*Shh*, familiar POWs, unless you *don't* want your captive arses sprung from jail?"

*Silence.*

I grinned: *this Keeper still had it.*

Although, the Creepy Factor of being scrutinised by the intelligent gazes of squirrels, red pandas, ring-tailed lemurs, chimps, and badgers almost cancelled out the Cuteness one.

"No rush," Mischief gingerly shifted his knees away from the path through the stable, which was moulded with stone snakes. "I believe it's only our lives dependent on the success of this mission. Plus, of course, this spell pressing on my brain like an unwelcome parasite. Not to mention..." He stroked the nose of a foal, which was nuzzling through the bars of a cage. He shook his head; his gaze was troubled. "...Until I was sent to the Under World, I would've had no concern for the fates of Blood Familiars." His laugh was bitter. "Sometimes, I wish I'd been able to wallow in my own safe ignorance. Truth is much harder once faced."

"Then let's break out these bitches and break open that bastard spell." When I seized the red squirrel's cage, the squirrel *chattered* at me, before sweeping its bushy tail around and hopping back.

A buzz tingled down my shoulder blades and gums. It prickled across my skin in goose bumps.

**Hold your sweet ass, Violet-puss. You're buzzing like you're riding one of your pretty boys. Your magic's calling out to you. Have you blocked it for a reason?**

*My magic is riding me, J. Like how it hurt Rebel in the wood...?*

**I must've been watching the wrong channel because I could've sworn it was *your* hand around the loyal little punk's throat...?**

*I slipped, but the magic's dangerous. You warned me before...*

**Come on, girl, you know you want to say it.**

*You were right.*

**Halleluiah, the heavens themselves did weep.**

*All right, bitch, you've had your moment.*

*I could tame the Devil's Trident, but this is different. The magic shouldn't be tamed, it needs to become part of me, like the shadows. I just don't know how yet.*

*Until I do, I don't want to hurt my fam.*

**If you don't listen to its warning, you'll hurt**

**yourself too.**

I yanked open the cage, snapping the lock, before reaching inside towards the *chattering* squirrel.

Then I screamed.

An electric current shot through my fingers where they touched the bars; I vibrated, as if a hot prong had been shoved through my hand.

*Howling, screeching, bellowing, squealing…*

The familiars were being shocked too, and this time, as they cringed or rolled on their backs, they *shrieked* their distress. And they didn't stop.

It was the perfect alarm system: the witches would hear us.

*J had been right again.*

I tried to wrench back my arm, but I couldn't move it. Then Ash's hands were curled around my shoulders, tugging. I stumbled backwards into Ash's citrus wings, as Rebel tenderly kissed my burnt fingers.

"*Spell, now*," I hollered at Mischief.

But opening the cage hadn't only set off the electric shocks.

Mischief stared back at me with haunted eyes, as boa constrictors wound around him, holding him in place. He struggled for breath, even as another stone snake from the path transformed and slithered up his leg.

*Bastard spell casters.*

"Get a grip, Tinkerbelle, this is about *saving the world*." I knew it was a low blow, but Mischief was losing himself in the terror of his own personal nightmare come to life. "Or is it *your* brat arse that doesn't remember Fynchan?"

Mischief's gaze snapped to mine, sharp once again. "So, the beast is catching on."

Mischief's eyes closed; his face creased with pain.

A glass box, like the one that'd trapped my brother, materialised between us in the stable, before slowly expanding.

*Hiss* — the snakes writhed, tightening around Mischief.

"Screw the shocks, open the cages," I growled.

Yet before I could battle against the electric current, the air around us quivered.

"That you, Mischief?" Rebel asked.

Mischief shook his head.

"Clever little creatures with magic," a simpering female voice arose in the air around us.

A freezing draught, which was scented with berries, howled through the stables.

*The witch of the House of Snakes.*

I spun, but there was no one there.

I drew Flight, just as Rebel unsheathed Eclipse. Ash nodded his head towards Mischief, before booting aside a snake to crouch over him, resting his gun on the head of the glaring boa constrictor.

*Smash* — the glass box shattered, as if a giant boot had stomped on it.

We all flinched.

Rahab's spell had been broken like it'd been nothing but child's play, and so had my chance of winning the Mage's Challenge.

Numb, I gripped Flight until my knuckles whitened. I'd bastard lost my brother, Ash, *Rebel...*

I hadn't realised I'd been shaking, until the cloaked witch giggled. "I hoped I'd caught a wolf, but instead it's a little quivering bunny. Still, we'll play just the same. They all play."

Ash dropped his shooter, shrinking back.

I hadn't won the Mage's Challenge. The Head Coven had caught my fam and me. And now a psycho spell caster wished to *play.*

I hadn't planned Kinky Date Night strung up in the Head Coven's Honesty Tower. Sometimes, however, you just had to go with the spontaneous.

*Clank, clank, clank.*

I slammed my shackles against the red-brick, rubbing my wrists raw, whilst I struggled. I swung on tiptoes against one side of the tower; my shoulders ached. I shivered, as the night breeze gusted through colossal circular windows on each wall. There was no glass, and the night roared in, mingling with a *magic* that was so wild I could taste it.

The witches' magic wasn't ordered and controlled like the mages'; it was free and dangerous.

*Dazzling.*

But Honesty Tower...? It sounded like something girls pledged to please their daddies.

The chamber lay in a dusty gloom, except for coiled silver lights, which hung high on the ceiling. The tang of baked raspberries and cranberries like an aged red wine clung to it. A locked mahogany door scowled at me from the other side of the room, and neat waves of clothes skirted it.

My fam and me had been posed around the tower like gargoyles, as if the room had always been waiting for us.

*Clank, clank, clank.*

I wrenched at my shackles again.

"For the love of all that's holy, would you give it a rest?" Rebel blinked at me. He'd been stood on a central pedestal with his wings outstretched. His jacket and top had been removed, but at least his trousers hadn't been taken, even if he'd been placed in such extreme bondage that he couldn't move a feather. "You've been at that all night. The chains are angel and vampire proof, and hurting yourself only hurts us. Why won't you admit that sometimes there's no way out?"

I snarled, banging against the wall. Then I battled to slow my breathing. "Not sleeping on us are you, Brigadier? You don't want to miss playtime."

Ash shook his head groggily as he arose back from the Freddy Greuger style Dream World, which we'd been whammied into by the witch. He'd been shot the hardest because *he'd* shot Little Miss Invisible with his gun.

Her outraged shriek had been better than her simpering.

"All present and correct," Ash slurred, tugging at the restraints, which held him on one knee like Atlas. "As soon as I can feel my fingers, I'll be up for some witch burning."

Mischief snorted, "The Wynter sisters here at the Head Coven are renowned. Do you wish to hazard a guess what for...? Their hospitality, perhaps? Love for trespassers? Extensive donations at charity auctions? No, that's it...their *cruelty*. Hatred for mages, vampires, Addicts, and monsters. As well as extensive perverse ways to make them suffer for their lack of perfection."

"Cheers to our manager in charge of morale boosting." I bit my tongue, forcing down the panic, as I glared at Mischief; he'd been chained to the floor facedown. And didn't that just set off alarm bells? "I'm voting a witch bonfire."

*Crash* — the mahogany door slammed open.

"Sweet Jesus..." Rebel breathed.

Nope, the bastard glowering at us from the doorway was neither *sweet* nor our *saviour*.

Angel Titan shambled into the tower, clutching a wooden bucket and ladle. His ginger hair had been clipped close to his head; his violet eyes were glassy.

*Was he an Addict like Rebel?*

Although Angel Titan was dressed in a fancy three-piece burgundy suit, a gag had been shoved into his mouth like he was a pampered butler at a BDSM convention. It reminded me of the gag that'd been forced between Drake's lips by Och.

What the hell was happening to Drake in the Reformation Room? Although, at least he wasn't strung up with us. *Then why did I miss him?*

Drool dribbled from the corners of Angel Titan's lips, dripping onto his posh collar. He didn't notice, however, because his gaze had focused on Rebel, who shuddered, even though he couldn't recoil in his bonds.

"You know the rules I gave you?" Ash's voice was tight, as he flexed his numb fingers. "Follow them."

How did Ash know so much about being held by witches?

If he'd been at their tender mercy, why didn't he have the same wagging tail as Blaze and Spark? The ancient powers surged in terrified swells at the thought of losing Ash...*that I might still lose him*...yet I also had the urge to stroke imaginary fox Ash.

*Yeah, I'm screwed-up.*

Rebel was as transfixed with the new Addict, as Angel Titan was with Rebel. "General Lamechial, I'm mortified so I am to see you like this, after we fought such a number of battles together. But idiot as I am, you're after wanting to listen: this is our princess. *Queen*. She's—"

*Crack* — Lamechial backhanded Rebel.

Rebel's lip split; I retched at the sight and scent of his candy blood, transported back to the Bailey and *swish* — *thud* of the cat o'nine tails.

"Why do I have a feeling you haven't won us an ally?" Mischief sighed.

"We'll help you, General," Rebel insisted. "We'll take on these battle-axes and free you. I know what it's like to think this is how it should be. That fam has to hurt but it doesn't."

*Slosh* — Lamechial banged down the water bucket.

I winced, as water slopped over the edges, and Lamechial slammed the hard ladle against Rebel's teeth.

Rebel turned his head to the side.

No drinking in a coven: I'd learnt that rule back in the House of Rose, Wolf, and Fox. Rebel had kidnapped me to keep me safe with his adopted family of witches, except one of them had poisoned me and all she'd needed had been a glass of water.

Lamechial narrowed his eyes, before throwing down the ladle and clutching Rebel's small head between his massive hands.

"Keep your hands to yourself." I growled. "All heads are nondetachable."

Rebel whimpered. "The General here's also known as the Truth-seeker because—"

"Let me guess? He forces you to tell the truth?" Mischief

scoffed.

"There's no more dangerous weapon," Ash yanked more urgently on his chains. "We'll be flayed."

"Sometimes I still think I'm lost in the dark," Rebel said, before his eyes opened comically large. If he'd been able to slap his hand over his mouth he would've done. Instead, the traitorous words continued to slither out, "And that Feathers never saved me because who saves bad angels? I was just mad as a box of frogs and *thought* she did. So, I'm still there, on Angel World, locked away in the birdhouse prison and I never got out...*never*...and I dream that because how is any of *this* more real? How could she love—"

"Stop it," I hissed. "Just bastard stop this."

Lamachial raised an eyebrow at me. But he didn't lift his hands away from Rebel.

"I've lost two families, and both times it was my fault; I bleeding miss them." Rebel's eyelashes were matted with tears; his mascara ran in thick spider tears down his cheeks, and he couldn't wipe them away. "But I'd die happy just to be blessed with a moment of my new family's love, even Drake's...and he can be a difficult git. I didn't choose to be Bonded or Marked, but I've loved my princess forever and—"

"Love, loss, *bored*." Ash gritted out, rattling his chains to drown out Rebel's agonising confession.

I didn't miss Rebel's hurt flinch, but I knew a distraction when I heard one.

Ash had warned that we'd be *flayed*. Yet it hadn't only been Rebel. I shook from the power of his words and love.

Honesty Tower: yeah, I got the point now. *I wished that I bastard didn't.*

Ash shrank back, as Lamechial stamped over to him, crouching down and offering the water.

Ash straightened his shoulders. "Unless that's vodka, I'll pass and get straight down to the agonising interrogation by truth."

"How about you pick on somebody your own size? OK, much smaller, but let's take off these cuffs and see if bigger is actually better?" I booted against the wall, but Lamechial

134

ignored me.

Instead, he touched Ash on the temple far more gently than he had Rebel.

"Dirty," Ash whispered. "Creature. Seducer. *Pet 52*." *What the hell was that?* Yet even as I battled against the spiralling rage and panic, I bastard knew: why Ash was no stranger to the spell casters. "I'm meant to be a soldier; I should be able to take...anything...without breaking. But I'm broken. The Wynter's pet familiar in training, I lured an apprentice witch into freeing me. Because that's all I'm good for: seduction. I deserved Lucifer's punishment to become the army's whore and my sisters' deaths... I don't deserve to touch Violet and desecrate the memory of real love. How could anyone love what I've become? Love this—"

"Is there no other truth than love?" Mischief tried for swag, but his face was as wet with tears as my own.

This is why we hid behind secrets, lies, and masks because our truths were our own. Our self-beliefs — not *the* truth but those we believed — were too raw to be spoken.

*Unless some bastard dragged them into the light.*

Lamechial held the water up to Mischief's lips, as his head was turned to the side against the floor; one hand was already pressed to the base of his skull.

"They made me hurt my little brother, Nathanael." Mischief's eyes gleamed with tears. "And he had to hurt me. They wished to break our sense of family, until there was nothing but the Legion and obedience. Yet I'm weak, feminine, wrong, and I couldn't inflict pain like the others, so I learnt instead the trick to take it upon myself. But now the beast who torments me both takes my pain and gives it to me in greater measure than I-I..." Mischief stared at me, his eyes widening. He took panicked breaths through his nostrils as if battling the Truth-Seeker's Angelic Power. "...Greater measure than..."

Mischief lapped at the water.

I gasped. "*Bastard no....*"

But it was too late. Lamechial gave a satisfied nod and

tipped the ladle.

Mischief swallowed.

Ash roared, rattling and clinking his chains, as Rebel called out to Mischief. But Mischief had already slipped into unconsciousness...*not dead, please hell, not dead*...on the cold floor.

The world was blurred by my tears, as I hung, helpless. What truth had so terrified Mischief that he'd risked drinking the water? Or had it been me? Was it what he'd reveal about *me*?

Suddenly, I was shrouded in the winter scent of cranberries. I blinked through the haze, only to recoil from two crimson fingernails, which had shimmered into existence on the end of bony fingers. They poised like snakes about to strike over my eyes.

I froze; my heart thundered.

"Those who don't recognise the truth, child," the same simpering voice that had haunted me in the stable murmured into my ear, "are blind."

The talons twitched forward to poke out my eyes.

# 15

If I could've bleached away the view of Wynter Sister the First slowly pulling down Rebel's red bondage pants and batting at the silver skull chained to it like it was a kitty toy, whilst Rebel stood trapped on his pedestal, then I would've done.

But I wouldn't have plucked out my eyes. *A bitch wasn't crazy.*

Wynter Sister the Second's talons were still poised over my eyeballs like a threat. My eyes felt dry and itchy; the air stung them, until tears collected in their edges.

I'd never known your eyes could be held to ransom.

I could still summon up, however, the death glare. "Oh look, it's the Enchantress."

Wynter Sister the Second's grey eyes narrowed. There wasn't a mark on her from Ash's shot to her guts. With her wavy black hair and porcelain skin, she looked like a china doll that was desperate to star in *Chucky*. Her sister was a study in opposites: fair hair and sky-blue eyes. Their outfits were identical: crimson lace dresses. Except, the sister who had her claws out was also power dressing in a black wolf fur coat, just as I'd joked to Rahab.

*Yeah, maybe I should be the one who was gagged.*

They both could've been Jade's age, except if you caught them just right, their masks wavered: they were as powerful as Mischief and as old as Ash.

*We were screwed.*

Hadn't Rahab said no one had completed the Mage's Challenge? How many Mages had he sent here to suffer — die — at the hands of the Wynter sisters?

I glanced at the clothes all around the tower, which were like the soft lining of a coffin. Wynter Sister the First blinked her reptilian eyes, rubbing Rebel's trousers down her cheek, before folding and adding them to the closest pile on top of his leather jacket.

I drew in my breath. We were buried in the clothes of the transformed familiars and the dead.

*And we were next.*

Mischief still lay unmoving and silent. I couldn't let myself think...*that*...about him.

*Please, hell, let him not be poisoned.*

Mischief had to be OK because anything else tore my insides, as the silver stormed in a savage sea, brutal and raging even at the thought.

When had Mischief become so essential to me? His connection wasn't the same as my one with Rebel, Ash, or even Drake. It ran deeper: a part of me like my new magic.

I didn't understand it, and as the truth he'd spoken had made clear: neither did he. Yet we needed each other. He didn't treat me as a queen, but when I didn't yet know *what* he was to have such power, I didn't hate him for that. Instead, I loved him.

*Hell, I loved him.*

Panting, I clenched my fists. "Before you have your fun with my eyeballs, tell me what was in that water?"

Wynter Sister the Second raised her eyebrow. "The monster loves the mage." I flushed. "Fear not, child, he only sleeps. The water was a test, and what deliciously agonising truths your slaves spilled. Except for the mage, who hid his secrets because all nasty mages do, you know."

"They're not my slaves."

"Sweets, they are."

When Wynter Sister the First, who I was starting to think was mute or telepathic because she *spoke* to her sister only

138

through darting glances, reached for Rebel's collar, he whined. "By all the saints, if you're to kill me, at least let me die as—"

"A bad angel?" Wynter Sister the Second smiled at me, as if I was in on the joke; I scowled back. "Elinor, leave the collar. Even runaways can be saved. Let no one say Sibyl Wynter can't break an Addict of his wickedness. Even Lamechial's a good boy now, and he was such a challenge. If our new acquisition misbehaves, we'll replace his collar with our own."

*I knew I hated spell lobbers.*

How did they know Rebel...? Had he been unlucky enough to be *saved* by them, when he'd been a captive himself of his own adopted witch family?

Elinor sniffed Rebel's neck in long, jerky *snorts*, before licking around his collar. Rebel screwed closed his eyes, shuddering.

Sibyl glanced at Ash, even as she leaned closer; her coiled black hair swept across my cheeks. "Pet 52 knows what it is to be blinded. He pretends to be a brave little solider, but if you put him in the dark, he breaks the same as the delectable Addict."

Cold tingled across my skin; the rush of the witches' red wine scent made me want to hurl.

Ash had lain in the alley in Hackney beneath hunters, who'd later tipped bleach in his eyes, taking blindness as his due *for loving me.*

*Yet these witches had already blinded him.*

Did Ash think that's what love was? That he had to prove his courage? Lack of cowardice in the face of pain? Sacrifice?

That I'd demand it of him?

*Had I?*

Sibyl's lips curled. "The monster child finally perceives. Maybe not so blind...?"

"Retract your bitch claws." At least my voice didn't waver: I'd take small victories. "Because here's a truth train and it's thundering towards your tied to the tracks arse: you're going for the Morgan le Fey vibe but you're coming across Worst

Witch. These are my fam, and I'd sacrifice myself for them, just as much as they would for me. They're not my slaves: they're legends."

Ash barked with laughter, but I didn't miss how intently both Rebel and he had been watching me.

*Listening.*

I stiffened, waiting for the *squelch* and shrieking pain of nails into eyes.

Instead, Sibyl giggled, twirling away. "The monster has bite! Shadows, silver, and spark. I like this one: she'll be years of fun."

Elinor nodded, nibbling on Rebel's earlobe.

"Hmmm, and you brought back our children. My sister has taken quite a liking to Zachriel," Sibyl pondered. "She thinks up horribly imaginative games. They'll play very well together."

Rebel's startled gaze met mine.

"Stick it, bitch, your freaky sister's banned from play dates." I wrenched my wrists against the shackles; scarlet snaked down my arm.

Sibyl merely *clucked* her tongue as she raked her nails down Rebel's chest; he gasped. Yet he didn't tremble, until he studied her wolf fur coat. Had he known a wolf familiar? By his sudden, panted breathing like he was holding back sobs, I'd go with a big fat, *hell yeah*. "My sweet pudding angel doesn't need to fear little me." Sibyl preened. "We'll be such friends."

Elinor's hands splayed across Rebel's arse.

*Growls*: I realised they came from both Ash and me.

"You'll be friends with Elinor too, won't you?" Sibyl crooned, whilst Elinor blinked up at Rebel like she was a saint and wasn't kneading his naked buttocks. "I get angry when our angels hurt her feelings. You should be the happiest little sinner because you've upgraded from mutt to thoroughbred."

*The cheeky bitch.*

Yet why was there the smallest part of me that feared Rebel wanted this? The safety of a witch family like he'd had before I'd torn it away from him by causing his family's deaths. Even though he was an Addict, he was still an angel. He wasn't a vampire or a mage: the witches' enemies. *He could have a home here.*

Would it truly be so much worse than the nightmare of Rahab's Legion?

*What if he chose the Wynter sisters over me?*

"It's like this," when Rebel smiled at Sibyl, I stiffened, "not only do you talk shite but you both have heads like busted cabbages. Wait now, I didn't hurt your feelings, did I?"

Sibyl stared at Rebel in shock. Then she hissed, clawing her nails down his cheek.

I grinned, even as I flinched at the bloody lines scored down Rebel's face. He grinned back at me over the witch's shoulder.

"Rule Number Three," Ash bit out, "no heroics."

"Worth it," Rebel and I answered in unison.

Sibyl snatched Rebel by the chin so hard that her nails bit crescents. "Don't grieve for your lost family anymore, Zachriel. You have us now. The Deadmans were always so greedy; they refused to share you. I wonder, did your *Da* ever tell you how delightfully he screamed in *his* training?"

"Dry up! Don't be after talking about my Da," Rebel's eyes sparked. "He was hardly more than a babby—"

"He was a male witch." When Sibyl scowled down at Mischief, who was defenceless on the wooden floor, I swallowed, holding back the howl to *not touch him*...because the more the Wynter's knew I cared, the more they'd hurt him. "A mage, misfit, and *monster*..." She spun to me, pulling her fur coat more firmly around her shoulders. "Just like our latest acquisition in our collection of the bizarre: our monstrous zoo." I flinched. "What strange sensitivity. You are a monster, are you not?"

"You better believe it, wicked witch of the buttugly."

*What had she said about hurt feelings...?*

Sibyl's grey eyes flashed with silver lightning; it streaked through her hair, crackling in electric waves. She rose up, levitating off the floor. Her mask of youth dropped away, until

141

all that was left was an ancient power. I quaked, chained before it.

Elinor slinked behind Rebel, glaring at me as she slid her hand down his bare arm.

"I need not be kind." Sibyl's soft voice had deepened, sizzling with power. Hell, that had been her being *kind*? "Shall I show you the second path?"

"Don't bother with the demonstration. I'm not a visual learner..."

Rebel hollered.

Where Elinor had rubbed over his arm, scarlet glowing words had risen up out of the skin, as if they'd always been there: **BAD ANGELS ARE PUNISHED**.

Rebel whimpered, sweating like the words were *burning* him. When he gritted his teeth, Sibyl *tssked*. "Say it."

Rebel shook his head.

The words glowed brighter, and Rebel wailed.

"I told you enough heroics," Ash barked. "Say what they want. It doesn't change you. They can't—"

"They can," Rebel whispered. "They have."

How did they both know what was going on? Had those words always been carved there?

*Bad angels are punished*: it'd always been Rebel's mantra, or maybe one that his adopted witch family had forced on him.

The words throbbed again. At last, Rebel screamed, "Bad angels are punished."

Finally, the agonizing words bled back into his forearm.

Rebel stared down at the ground, avoiding my gaze. His *shame* booted me in the gut through the bond.

Sibyl glided closer, stroking over Rebel's arm where the words had been. "My, you don't remember your daily lessons, pudding candy? So sad. I shall have to increase it to hourly until you do. Am I still talking *shite*?"

When Rebel shook his head, she gripped him by the base of his neck, and his eyes widened. "The game is to answer with words, and we call our kind new adopted mama: Mama Wynter."

Rebel bit his lip. "Yes, Mama Wynter."

142

Rebel couldn't have *hidden* that daily ritual from me, could he? Made to recite his shame...badness...every day to take away the pain? To see it carved in his own flesh?

Yet I'd heard him say it — mutter it — and I'd merely thought...

Rebel had been tortured every day, and I hadn't seen it.

*I couldn't stop it.*

"Sparkles, levitating, and schoolboy lines," Ash rolled his eyes. "I've been Lucifer's personal whipping boy, so let's just say you gave this whole Evil Dead thing your best shot, and we'll be on our way."

"What happened to Rule Number Three?" I demanded.

Ash shrugged. "Who says Rebel should hog all the glory?"

Sibyl floated to Ash, whilst Elinor couched over him, clasping her arms around his shoulders and sucking purple bruises along his bowed neck.

"Charming that a Seducer can still imagine *glory* for himself: how self-deceiving." When Sibyl scrutinized Ash, a storm built around her; the static spat and jumped. "The apprentice you deceived to free you, wailed your name, whilst we burnt her. Do you think she truly believed that you loved her?" Ash blanched. "One more added to your list of sacrifices, dark Brigadier." She bent down, sniffing him, just as her sister snuffled along his throat. "*Death*. I haven't supped on such darkness for centuries. You shall make the fiercest familiar, Pet 52. Although..."

The lightning died, and Sibyl landed back on the floor.

*Clap* — at the clap of her hands, a fluffy white cat with sapphire eyes fell through the ceiling and into her arms.

Sibyl cradled the cat like a baby. "Pet 19, sweetums," she cooed. The cat lay unnaturally still like it'd been trained. I was no cat expert, but surely even their tails twitched. Then its gaze met mine, and I realised that it was a familiar. *And it was bastard terrified.* "I've always liked the idea of my sister owning a black cat. You'll be as pretty as Pet 19."

Elinor nodded eagerly, winding around Ash to lie her head

143

in his lap like she was the cat.

Ash's expression darkened, until I thought *he'd* spit lightning. The way his gaze lingered — anxious and guilty on Pet 19 — yeah, he knew the furball. "Sorry, but kinky pet play just doesn't do it for me."

"Silly, Pet 52." Sibyl dropped Pet 19 at her feet, before running her nails through Ash's hair, scraping his scalp. "What does it for *you* no longer matters."

"That's where we have what I call a *conflict*, bitches." I waggled my hands in their shackles.

Sibyl barely even glanced at me. "Then maybe you shouldn't watch...? Pet 52 had such awkward notions of *control*, the first time he delighted us with his rebellious presence. Do you know how to curb a defiant child?"

"Chocolate and computer games...?"

"Tough love. You take away what's precious to them." Sibyl tilted her head in thought. "Lamechial so hates to have his words stilled. But you...? I believe you fear the loss of sight."

I stared at her. Was she threatening to pluck out my eyes again? Yet she hadn't moved towards me...

Instead, there was a sudden pressure on the back of my eyeballs. I whined, my breath hitching, as black pressed down.

"Please, I'll obey," Ash urged, low and intense. "I'll do your tricks, perform for you, become your kitty. Just don't do the same to Violet as you did to me."

*Pop* — the pressure burst like a bubble, and I hollered.

*And everything became black.*

I blinked desperately, but my vision didn't clear. My eyes were open, but I couldn't see. *How couldn't I bastard see...?*

"I stole Pet 52's sight for two weeks to train him," Sibyl's voice sliced across the dark with a smug slyness. "By the end, he was a broken doll, rocking and weeping. Not much of a soldier. You know, maybe I should change him into a mouse, rather than a cat. Pet 19 could hunt him. What splendid games we could have!"

I growled, but it echoed too loudly in my head, like my breathing, pulse, and the *clinking* of the chains above my head.

When cold lips explored my neck, inhaling deeply along my

144

skin, and a hand grabbed my hair, wrenching my head to the side to give them better access, I startled. Lost in the dark, everything was more intense: every caress and blow. Only by the cranberry scent did I know it was the sisters.

Until Sibyl whispered into my ear, "Little monsters shouldn't wander uninvited into a witch's house. Not unless they want to be played with."

Tears pricked my eyes. How could I battle these ancient spell casters, when I'd been blinded?

# 16

*Black, black, black...*

I gasped, blinking rapidly, but it didn't clear the night pressing on my eyes.

Chained in Honesty Tower, how many hours had passed since my sight had been stolen?

The backs of my wrists itched, as if the dried blood was burrowing its way back in, I could taste sickeningly rich berries, and I choked on my own saliva.

*Too much, make it stop, make it—*

**Are you asking, girl?**

*J...?*

**Do you know any other fabulous bitches who've raised you and taught you to hold your own against the world's freaks and floozies?**

*They're the Head Coven. No one's ever—*

**You're not *no one*: you're the Bitch of Utopia.**

**If you hadn't shied like a shy virgin from the magic gift that the Fae Underserving gave you, then you wouldn't be the one hanging in darkness.**

**You'd be the Queen of Chaos and Shadows.**

*The Silver Queen.*

My magic curled at the name, stroking me in reassurance. I sighed, brought down from my panic. For the first time, the silver didn't feel alien but *part of me*, twining with the shadows.

Until I started at the sound of footsteps and a gasp. "And there I was feeling quite left out."

*Mischief:* raspy and low.

I grinned, flooded with such joy that I forgot I couldn't see and blinked hard, as if that would clear my vision and I'd see him: *alive* and punking the spell casters.

*Wait, punking the spell casters...?* What was it with my fam and *heroics*?

"Let's call it an epic fail on following your rules, Brigadier." I booted the wall.

"Don't worry, monster, we shall help you learn to love rules. And you, prickly but pretty mage? We brand male witches with the letter of our house," Sibyl's taunting voice dripped with sadistic pleasure.

"You wouldn't dare... T-that's sacrilege...to inflict on a magic user... Your own magic would cry out to denounce you. B-better to take my h-hands or my head..."

My heart ached at Mischief's tears. I'd never heard such devastation: he'd been broken at a threat.

*Sacrilege?*

What the hell were the bitches going to do to him? *Brand him?*

"Allow it," I growled. "The pretty prickly one is *my* fam and not into branding or any other type of witchy freakery."

"How rude of us to allow you round to play, then stop you watching the fun." I jumped at the soft stroke to my cheek. Sibyl's lips mouthed against mine. "So, *watch.*"

There was a sudden pressure on the back of my eyeballs; grey bled into the black.

*Pop* — when the pressure burst, I whined.

Light streamed in an agonising burst. I screwed closed my eyes, panting. At last, I cautiously opened them again, as the lights haloed.

Rebel and Ash, paler than before, studied me anxiously. Mischief, still tied facedown on the wooden floor, writhed —

not asleep, poisoned, or dead. He was horror-struck, however, as Elinor straddled his back, pulling aside his hair to reveal the base of his neck.

Sibyl's porcelain doll face smirked, close to mine; I craved to shatter it. "My busy, busy brain has been pondering all night, why do you fight on the side of nasty mages?" She tilted her head like she truly wanted an answer. "Hide as you like behind your childish insults, but we're not the wicked witches, or haven't you worked that out yet?" Her tongue darted to wet her lips, lizard-like. "We battle vampires, save Addict angels from themselves, and fight mages who resurrect angels from the dead. Now then, who sounds evil? Maybe it's *you* who's on the wrong side?"

"There's nothing as simple as *sides*." I met her intent stare. "Or *evil*." I smiled at Rebel, softly. "There's only righteousness, and you, bitch...? You're not righteous."

*And that's how to shatter a mask.*

Sibyl's eyes lightning flashed. She snarled, backing towards Mischief. Only then did I notice the small silver wand in her hand, which was topped with a white-hot brand: **M** in coiled snakes.

"Men possessing magic is *unnatural*." Sibyl crouched over Mischief. When he tried to pull away, Elinor held him tighter. "**M** for male, mage, misfit, *monster*... I'll lock away your magic, pretty, where you'll never harm a witch or use your perverted powers again."

The brand sizzled as it pressed into Mischief's flesh, flashing silver.

Mischief howled, drumming his legs — *thump, thump, thump* — on the floor.

At last, the brand was lifted, although the flesh beneath throbbed red and blistered. Elinor slid off Mischief, carding her fingers through his hair, whilst he sobbed.

Sibyl knelt over him, running her thumb through his tears. "Hurts, doesn't it? Your magic there but...out of reach." Mischief whimpered, convulsing. "Only if you're a truly good boy will you ever play with it again." She smiled, coldly cruel. "Maybe we'll never let you out of your magical chastity."

Mischief quivered, torn apart between two witches. Elinor licked down his ear. "Maybe we enjoy you *frustrated*."

A sacrilege, which one magic user should never do to another. I got it now: the darkness of their binding. Ripping away part of your soul, no different to taking someone's mind or memories because the magic *was* Mischief. He hadn't learnt to access it, like me. Instead, like Rahab, he'd known the truth of his magic from the moment he was born, and now suddenly it'd been torn from him.

He'd been blinded. Except, his mental powers made him *who* he was. *And the witches wanted to punish him for that?*

The slivers of Mischief's magic, which he'd transferred inside me, howled at the assault on their kin; they rose in fury, surging through me, until I trembled, breathless. They whipped the shadows and violet fire into an equal spiralling rage: I was the Queen of Chaos and Shadows.

*I was the Silver Queen.*

With a roar, I snapped the cuffs that shackled me.

The Wynter sisters' looks of surprise that their caged zoo exhibit had broken free would've been comical, except my shadows had already reached out and caught Elinor, pinning her against the waves of clothes and smothering her, until there was nothing left but a tarred witch.

Then Sibyl's expression flickered between fear, grief, and rage.

High on the silver, whilst the shadows whispered *revenge* on the sacrilege, Sibyl looked tiny. A doll. Even as she crackled with fire, I merely grasped her by the throat.

Sibyl choked, as I rammed her against the wall. Her youth withered, and she became as ugly as Rebel had said.

Sibyl wheezed, shoving at me with wizened hands. "There *are* sides, monstrous child." Her cracked lips burnt; her words sounded as ancient as a prophecy. "Magic frees us to rise or Fall. The mages have those confused, as do you."

Shivers trembled down my spine, but I tightened my hand around her throat. "We voted for a burning." Silver flames

149

flickered from my lips. "I don't let down my fam."

A bolt burst from me in roiling waves, which was followed by a shriek and the stink of roasted witch.

I staggered backwards, staring down at the pile of ash. The silver inside me lapped in satisfied swells. The shadows quietened, as both sides of my natures bellowed in victory.

Yet when I turned back to my fam, I flushed, expecting them to cower back like they had when I'd gone nuclear at the Pure fanatics in Hackney.

Instead, my blokes were grinning at me, as if they'd been watching the most epic *Game of Thrones* finale.

"That was brilliant!" Rebel glanced at Ash. "Do you think that counts as heroics?"

"It counts as hot," Ash waggled his eyebrows.

"Perhaps once you've finished performing your victory dance, you could untie us?" Mischief's voice was hoarse, but his eyes still twinkled.

I knelt next to Mischief, pushing his hair back on his forehead. "What about your magic?"

He flinched. "The infernal brand will always be with me, but the witches' deaths have freed my magic." He met my gaze, levelly. "I may not kneel for you, but you have my eternal gratitude for unbinding me. For a magic user that means I'm coupled to you in ancient customs, which are stronger than any oath. In every way, I am yours, queen."

I stared at him, shaking at his intensity and the way my silver reached to his, stroking and intimate.

*Yours...*

When had Mischief called me *queen*? It hadn't felt as if he'd been calling me *his* queen but acknowledging I was *worthy* of the title. And why should that matter so much that my eyes burned with tears?

At last, Mischief knocked his forehead gently against mine. "Come now, let us return to trading insults and blows or we'll spook your faithful lovers. Do you imagine these chains will fall from us by fairy wishes?"

I smirked. "You're rusty. You'll have to up your Snark-O-Meter."

His eyes glinted. "I do so love a challenge."

Suddenly, a moan echoed from the far side of the tower, and a wave of clothes undulated. There was something large burrowing underneath them and peeking out at us with sapphire eyes.

Still flaring with silver, I stormed past the tarred witch, throwing Rebel's leather jacket and pants off the cowering head of...

*A vampire.*

Nope, not a vampire. Unless, I'd been slurping on the crazy juice. Because the creature who was cowering...naked...in the clothes and gazing up at me in blinking innocence had soft cat ears poking out of his shaggy white hair, as well as a fluffy tail.

"How flexible were you on the whole *pet play*?" Mischief smirked at Ash.

"I'm sure I can work another branding," Ash's eyes narrowed. "How are *you* with leashes?"

"What? He's adorable. Can we keep him?" Mischief's gaze darted to mine.

The silver faded away, soothed by Mischief's gossamer soft strands, which sang *calm* and *safe*. I sat cross-legged in front of the Cat Vampire; he shied away, curling his tail around himself to shield his modesty.

"I'm not adorable," the Cat Vampire hissed, "I'm Tiger." He nuzzled his chin against the studs in Rebel's jacket, scenting them. He peeked at Mischief. "And I'm not the one with sparkly hair, angel."

Mischief arched a brow. "*Meow*, the cat has claws. I hope he knows that I scratch back?"

"Dry up, muppet." Rebel's gaze was serious. "Do you think Pet 19 needs your blathering? The Head Coven is dead, now for the first time the familiars are free or...the Halfings are..."

Ash grimaced. "They're not hobbits."

I stared at the *Halfling,* who'd hunched back amongst the clothes.

Pet 19: *Tiger.*

Tiger's sapphire eyes peeped out at me, as his ears twitched, and a shamed flush spread down his neck. Even though he struggled not to drop his gaze, his hands clenched in Rebel's jacket like I'd burn him the same as the witches.

*Tiger*: where had I heard that before?

My eyes widened, and I snatched Tiger by the scruff of the neck, dragging him closer. His wings beat frantically; his heels kicked.

"You're Misrule's boy," I breathed. "His missing Blood Lover."

Hell, the leader of the Under World's first Blood Lover, before he'd taken Harahel to be his, hadn't gone *missing* as Misrule had thought: he'd been here, stolen as a Blood Familiar.

All along, he'd been the Head Coven's slave.

"You know Misrule?" Tiger's hope was painful.

I nodded.

"But you're..." He glanced between us, his brow furrowing.

"As I told the psycho witches, everything's not about sides anymore. The Underworld's changing."

"Figured," Tiger muttered. "But it's not like I'm going back." He thrashed his tail. "I'm a...*Halfling*. A disgrace. *Nothing*."

"Hey, hold the shame bus, this is our stop." I tilted up Tiger's chin; brimming blue eyes met mine. Mischief was right: he was *adorable*. "You're not the same bitch you were, but then neither am I. I've already birthed one species — Blood Angels — and they're epic. Whatever you are now, it doesn't matter because you can be and do whatever you choose..."

"Look out of the window, Violet," Ash said, quietly.

I leapt up, staring down at the stable below and the Halflings breaking out into the golden dawn, which kissed across the horizon. Vampires with the ears, claws, or tails of squirrels, red pandas, ring-tailed lemurs, chimps, badgers, and wolves escaped into the light. A new species born of Blood Familiars and freed from the witches.

My mouth ached with my grin: joy tingled through my wings, as the Halflings spread over the lawns, beating and pulsing in the thrill of united liberty.

"There's not a chance we're giving them up to the Legion," Rebel's voice was low, vibrating with a remembered grief that ghosted across the bond. "I won't be after making them slaves again."

I twirled to where he hung, still in bondage, tracing down his cheek with my knuckles.

How in the ecstasy of my magic or the buzz of discovering a new species could I've forgotten the stakes? That losing the Mage's Challenge meant losing Rebel and Ash?

How could I've saved my fam from the witches, only to sacrifice them to the mages?

"You'll die," I whispered.

"Then I'll die," Rebel's gaze was soft, yet laced with steel when it met mine.

"And I'll play at being a good pet," Ash added.

I hugged myself, staring at the Halfings emerging into the dawn.

*You can't save everybody...*

Yet why did the birth pangs of a new species have to be so agonising?

*Why did it have to cost my fam?*

I lurched at a sudden pull, which tugged at the shadows inside. Startled, I fell towards Tiger, wrapping him in my arms, as the room shook.

"*Naive, little apprentice, did you imagine I wouldn't feel the breaking of my spell? The death of the Head Coven? The creation of new creatures, almost as if you believe yourself to be my equal...?*" Rahab's fury burst telepathically into my mind.

I flinched. "*They're not Blood Familiars now, so there's no souvenirs left to bring back from our trip. The Mage's Challenge is broken, rather than failed. Let's call it even,*" I shot back at him.

*Please, please, please...*

Rahab's chuckle was dark and not indulgent. "*I allow no*

153

*disobedience, yet still you rebel as if there'll be no consequences. I shall stop one punishment only for overcoming the Wynters. Yet the other you'll face. You demanded a chance to free your brother. You requested to take the Challenge. And you accepted the cost. Who truly is to blame here?"*

I bit back bitter tears, as the room darkened and was sucked towards Castle Drake. Tiger squirmed in my arms, yowling. I'd failed the Mage's Challenge, and now my fam faced the retribution.

# 17

What do you do or say on the last hour before your lover's execution? A death that you've caused by playing with your fam's lives in the same twisted way your mum and dad always had? As if there were no *consequences*?

*How do you say goodbye to the first bloke you've ever loved?*

I shivered, clutching Rebel close in the quiet of the Mirror Lodge. We lay entangled in each other's wings on my Sleeping Beauty bed. I rubbed my cheek against the sheets, as if that could make any of this feel more real — one hour before the dawn execution in the Bailey — whilst the violet fire orb flared, casting its spectre glow, repeating endlessly cloned across the glass walls.

When I'd been dragged back to the Legion with Tiger quivering in my arms, Rahab had kept his promise: Ash had been turned over to the Undeserving, rather than the mages.

*And that'd been the signing of Rebel's death warrant.*

Tonight, alone in my chambers, Rebel and I spent our last night together.

Rahab hadn't softened his tough love parenting towards me, but he'd caved to Rebel's quiet request.

Rebel had knelt before Rahab. "Please, grant me some time with the queen before everything I am — Zachriel and Rebel — is gone. I know I'm saying it all arseway but...you're murdering me." *Why had Rahab flinched?* "Don't you owe me this favour?"

Rahab had cupped Rebel's cheek, before nodding. "Tonight only. By the light, Zachriel, what I do is for your own good."

I laid my head on Rebel's chest. His heart beat, slow and steady; it was as *right* as his copper candy scent that shrouded me.

*How could it be stopped in less than an hour?*

Both ancient powers inside me screamed in tribal despair at the threat to my bonded and Marked Blood Lover: a protectiveness that burrowed to my core, fogging the world to nothing but a whining chant of *Rebel, Rebel, Rebel...*

When Rebel and I had first burst into these chambers, with me storming whirlwind ahead, I'd raged, promising to sacrifice the *world* to save him.

Yet Rebel had simply shaken his head. "For ages, I've made a woeful number of bad choices; now let me make a good one. Can't tonight just be you and me, Feathers, bollocks to the rest?"

So, even though I'd thundered inside, craving to smash the glass and rip the ropes from the roof, I'd buried the grief and pain instead. I'd laid down with Rebel, hugging him in silence, on his last night alive.

At dawn, he became nothing but a number: A Phoenix slave.

I blinked away the tears pooling in the corners of my eyes, winding my arms tighter around Rebel's waist like I could hold onto him forever that way, stroking along his wings.

Rebel's ornate emerald shift brushed stiffly against my skin. Intricate gold gilt was woven into its sleeves, and a phoenix blazed on the front.

Expensive. Formal. Ceremonial.

*His bastard burial clothes.*

It'd booted me in the gut the way Rebel had first picked the shift off the covers, where it'd been left out for him. Then how, without a word, he'd stripped off his leather jacket, folding it neatly on the floor, each item joining the first with a final loving stroke. Until he'd only hesitated at his collar. The sorrow had torn through our bond, when he'd unbuckled it, placing it carefully on top of his clothes.

Naked, Rebel had met my gaze. And I'd known then: the ritual had prepared him to die.

He'd been ready. *It'd been me who hadn't been ready to let go.*

When Rebel had pulled on the emerald shift, I'd hungered to snatch it by the collar and *rip* the screwed-up death robe to shreds.

Rebel had chosen this, however, so I didn't have to make the choice: *sacrifice him, or sacrifice...everything.* At last, I'd got how agonising it was to watch powerlessly, whilst someone else took the lead.

I traced upwards, clasping a handful of Rebel's feathers: warm and soft.

*Hell, I couldn't bastard do this.*

In an hour's time...less...*less* than an hour now... How could Rebel simply no longer *be* here? At my back, willingly kneeling, shadowing me with feelings...

It was sacrilege, the same as the binding of Mischief's magic. And as devastating.

"Talk to me, Feathers." Rebel's breath was warm, as he nuzzled into my hair.

I fought to stop my voice wavering, "What, bro?"

"A story," he whispered. "My ma...when I was nothing but a cub...before she died, she'd tell us tales. She wasn't like my da; she was a good woman and she'd sit with Briathos, Haman, and me and weave these stories from *your* world. About *humans*. Here's the thing, I don't know how much was true — things she'd seen or heard — and how much imagined or legends. But I never forgot." He laughed, soft and fond in a way I'd never heard before. "Sweet Jesus, I haven't remembered that since... Maybe *Addict* runs in the family, so it does. But I'd like..." He kissed the top of my head. "It's been so long, see, since someone held me, and I knew I was safe."

I bit my lip; blood beaded. My throat swelled up, as I

157

battled not to sob. I forced out, "I can't..."

*How could I pretend?* Just spin tales like I always had in the children's home, creating fantasies to hide the reality: Jerusalem's Jinn. But no number of wishes would save Rebel.

He'd been a kid on his ma's knee listening to stories of the human world: a curiosity that'd led to his shame and punishment as an Addict. Yet bitter jealousy shook me because he'd lived all those centuries without me. Other angels had known him — loved him — whilst I hadn't even been alive.

*We could've grown up together.*

I gripped Rebel's wing tighter, as the fantasy deepened, weaving into a multi-colour, all singing and dancing musical production. I could've known him before his forty years in the bird cage prison. He'd only been mine for less than a year: *it wasn't bastard enough.*

Both sides inside me sang that Rebel's blood belonged to me, but Rahab planned to shed it for the Legion, whilst resurrecting Rebel as a shadow of himself. And he'd never remember his ma again.

*My Rebel would be dead.*

I couldn't even trick myself with the lie that the angel I loved would be raised again.

Rebel stiffened. "I'm mortified I asked like some babby—"

"There was once a foundling. No one knew who'd left her in the human world. But she was powerful and swore one day, when she was all grown up, she'd take her rightful place in the magical world and take her vengeance..."

"And did she?"

"She went medieval on the bastards who hurt her and her fam. She curbed stamped every single supernatural prick who'd messed with them."

Rebel's mouth curved into a smile against the crown of my head. "I'm blessed to be avenged by such a bloodthirsty foundling."

"It's just a story, bro."

When he nipped my ear, I yelped. "And I'm just a fellah with wings." He settled back, gazing at me intently. "Will you look after Eclipse for me? If...when you free Haman, he'll be after needing our da's sword."

"Screw it, why would you even have to ask?"

"Do you think...?" Rebel tore at his lower lip with his teeth, worrying at the tender flesh. "Do you think it'll hurt much?"

My stomach lurched.

Rahab, Mr Sadist in Shiny Packaging, had detailed how Rebel would be killed, of course: hung by the neck until dead. The raised platform, wooden gibbet, and electrified noose for the modern touch.

I swallowed. "The psycho says he doesn't want to cause you pain. It's not torture. He'll just..."

*Snap your neck quickly.*

Rebel's breath quickened; the steady thud of his heart sped up. But he shook his head. "Not the being hung." He wet his torn lips. "Death. *After.*"

It was my turn for my pulse to thunder, alive and alien in my ears — *boom, boom, boom* — because how did I answer that?

Ash's sisters had walked to their deaths in Lucifer's Light. And they'd gone joyful and filled with hope based on the lie, which *I'd* told them because hope had been the only way I could save them.

It'd sliced me to ribbons, but I'd survived. The living had to take on the guilt and suffering, because to die in fear and despair was too cruel.

*No way I'd let it happen to Rebel.*

"I think," I said, gently, "you'll be *safe*, after."

Rebel's breath hitched. "But where do you go?" Centuries older than me, he suddenly sounded so young and already lost. "What if it's dark? An eternity of being alone in the dark?"

"Listen, my Irish bondage angel," I bit my tongue to stop the tears, "you'll fly in the light. The Legion say *rise* in it. So, dying here on their island, you'll never be in the dark again."

At last, Rebel sobbed, sagging against me. "Thank you," he murmured, like a blessing.

I slipped an iPod out of my skirt's pocket, which Mischief

had smuggled to me, before he'd been dragged away. It'd been my sister's iPod. When she'd gone missing, it'd united Rebel and me in her search. I'd thought Jade had taken it from me as another way to kick my arse for daring to believe we'd still been sisters, even if we'd landed on different sides of the war's divide. Yet Mischief must've stolen it back.

Why had he been holding onto *my* music like a relic?

Yet the desperate glance, which Mischief had cast Rebel, had told me that he understood how much the iPod meant to Rebel. Even if to share the music with my punk angel again, knowing that it'd be the last time, would be agonising.

I plugged one earbud into Rebel's ear and one into my own. Eel's grungy "Novocaine for the Soul" — our dark misfit anthem — wove its spell. We'd rescued the Broken slaves in the Hollow to this song, whilst I'd held him and soared up through the shafts on my newly birthed wings.

Just for a moment, we'd been united in joy and *freedom*.

Even though tears glistened in Rebel's eyes, he linked our pinkies as he kissed me: a sweet revelation, which was also a goodbye.


I shivered, scoring my nails down the whipping post like at least that'd mark a memory of this: a private execution in the Bailey.

The sun glinted off the cobblestones: the world ablaze. The noose on the scaffold sizzled with emerald fire; the gibbet rose from a raised platform next to the cannon. Rebel marched to it with a steely dignity, even in bare feet and his shameful gilt-edged shift. Then he hesitated, scanning the Bailey. "Where's the Brigadier, Blaze, Spark, Mischief, Commander Drake…"

Rebel's sudden trembling desperation shot adrenaline through my limbs, which had been numb with shock or denial.

Rahab, who'd been lounging next to the three steps up to the scaffold, huffed, "Enough. Do not make a scene." Yet he tapped his fingers against his palm in agitation.

"You mean like this, bro?" I snatched Star out of its sheath, but Rahab blasted me to paralysis with a casual flick of his wrist.

I hung, reduced to one of the Legion's statues, whilst Rebel placed his foot on the first step. "All I want," Rebel whispered, "is to say my goodbyes."

"Why?" When Rahab leant forward, Rebel raised his head: this time, his expression was darkly righteous: it thrilled me with its terrible grace. It was Rahab who flinched back. "You shan't even remember your companions...afterwards. Hangings aren't the same as corporal punishments: spectacles as examples. Do you imagine I gain satisfaction from killing those I teach?"

"Then bastard stop this," I hissed.

Rahab didn't even glance at me. "Silence. Do you not think your presence a mercy? Or are you blind to all but your own suffering?"

"For the love of Christ, woman, stop grousing; I need you here with me." Rebel cast me a troubled glance, only to be swung back to face Rahab.

"I've indulged you," Rahab's thumb stroked down Rebel's neck. *If he bastard touched the Mark...* "But as my Phoenix, you'll learn your place."

"Cop on! My body's not even cold yet," Rebel snarled, wrenching himself free.

Then Rebel turned back to the platform, scaffold, and the fizzing noose. He squared his shoulders as he faced his execution.

# 18

The first time I'd slipped a shank between the soft skin of another kid's ribs in Hackney, a part of me had died, just as another had arisen phoenix-like. I'd spent my life, dying and rising again, simply to survive.

Now, Rebel would truly die on this scaffold in the Bailey, whilst pale dawn awoke, and be resurrected as a Phoenix. Yet he wouldn't be the angel I'd known: the one who'd fallen into my lap. And the hunter he'd awakened who could trust and love — who believed in fam — I trembled that she'd die too.

Rebel took a step — *one* — up the stairs to the platform.

My pulse fluttered in my neck, but I was still paralysed by Rahab. Tears leaked from my eyes at my bastard helplessness.

Rebel's bare feet shuffled up onto the second step.

*Two.*

How could I stop time? *Where was the bastard pause button?*

Rahab crossed his arms, watching Rebel's ascent to the scaffold with an assessing gaze.

Rebel didn't even pause on the third step...*three.*

Where was my last-minute miracle? The posse riding in to save the innocent from being lynched?

*J, he's almost... You have to help him... Do something.*

**Sorry, Miss Eleganza is not at home. The Big Bad Mage is here, so unless you want him rooting around your head like it's chockful of fabulous prizes, we're on silent running, girl.**

162

*I don't care. Screw the visions, world saving, and crowns. This is my bloke, and I won't watch him die for me.*

**Then close your eyes because that's the next feature.**

*When did you become such a bitch?*

**I've always been a bitch, and so have you. I know the choices are impossible, but they're still yours to make.**

**Sugar-coating and sparkles sure are pretty and they make the world easier to swallow. But they still don't change the truth.**

*Then I'll have to step-up and kick truth's arse.*

**Haven't you learnt the Consequences Song yet? Because it's playing now.**

Rebel drifted to the noose in the centre of the platform; his eyes were dazed.

I quested through the bond: *loss, anguish,* and *dread.* Yet also lapping beneath those, as the noose lowered over Rebel's head at a twitch of Rahab's fingers: *acceptance, calm,* and *peace.* Because I'd lied to Rebel, and he believed that in moments he'd fly towards an eternity of light.

I bit back on the tears that threatened to choke me. *Not now.*

*After...*

I could let out the wails locked in my chest...*after.*

Instead, I forced myself to smile at Rebel, even as the electrified rope began to tighten. The corners of his mouth curved into a smile. Then he gave a strangled gasp, as the trapdoor sprang open beneath him and the hangman's knot jerked shut. His feet kicked, whilst he struggled against the agony.

*I'd bastard promised it wouldn't hurt...*

And that was it: the moment I broke. When I knew I couldn't give up Rebel or let him suffer for me.

"Anything," I pleaded. Rahab raised his eyebrow. "Punish me in any psycho way. Make me march to your fascist tune. Do anything. But not this."

Rebel gurgled; his neck blackened. He swung back and forth more slowly, as his struggling weakened.

Rahab glanced between Rebel and me. "When we first met, I *saw* you, hiding behind your sunglasses. Yet you still hide. Desires mistaken for pain, lessons for punishment. You don't even know who you are."

"I'm yours," I breathed, "if you let Rebel go."

Rahab grinned, wide and feral. He clicked his fingers. "Done."

The rope snapped. Rebel yelped as he slammed through the trapdoor.

*But he was alive...*

I sobbed at the relief tearing through both sides of my nature.

*Yet why did I feel like I'd been outfoxed?*

Rahab sauntered closer, stroking his fingers through my hair. "You don't belong to the unnatural witch magics, which have infested you. You're *ours*: The Brotherhood's. In return for Zachriel's life and slavery, I take your loyalty and servitude." I stiffened: J had told me about the *Consequences Song*, and it was splitting my head now with death core metal. "How about I show you the Bleeding Chamber? By nightfall, you shall be in no doubt that you're our Phoenix Queen."

I shuddered even in my paralysis. Rebel was *alive*, and I quaked with joy that I'd be able to touch, kiss, and *love* my punk angel again. Yet I'd sacrificed myself, along with everything that I'd promised Mischief.

Instead, I'd be moulded into the Legion's Phoenix Queen.


Gold arteries whirled from the sides of the Bleeding Chamber, which pulsed like a bronze heart, wrapping around my arms and slamming me against the wall.

*Crack* — my head crashed against the metal.

I groaned; my toes wriggled, dangling above the rust-stained floor. I gagged, choking on the coppery stench that mingled with a tang of sour lime; I half-expected the walls to be sticky with tequila rather than blood.

Rahab scrutinized me in full-out Blofeld mode from his metallic throne across the chamber; he even stroked his own *pussy* on his lap. Tiger curled awkwardly on Rahab's knee; his humiliated gaze met mine, whilst Rahab petted his ears. He flushed, wrapping his twitching tail more closely around himself.

Yet Rebel was alive... My breath hitched. *Hell, he was alive.*

Still, I'd promised loyalty, not to transform into a grovelling house-elf. Rahab wanted a queen? *Then he could bastard have one.*

"I'm not digging the kinky coronation gear." I swung backwards and forwards from my wrists, which were bound by the slippery pipes. "What would the Queen of England say?"

Rahab tossed his curls. "Luckily for us, Her Majesty's not here, and you're not yet crowned." His fingers tightened in Tiger's snowy-white hair; Tiger's back arched. "When you are, the darkness will lift, and you'll Lazarus Rise. I wonder, did you hope I was ignorant to this abnormal Fallen's status as Blood Lover to the leader of the Under World?" He shook Tiger.

"Why? Does the whole Cat Man look do it for you?"

To my surprise, Rahab gave a low laugh. "I believe humans call that *projection*. Isn't the better question: whether the look does it for *you*?" I pinked, squirming in the pipes' hold. "Because to me, appetizing or not," he ran his thumb down Tiger's back; Tiger stilled, tremoring, "he's still a dirty Fallen."

I stiffened. "Why this outing? Why here?"

Rahab leaned forward, gesturing around the lime and copper stench of the Bleeding Chamber. I gazed around at the trenches, which ran into an angel-sized turquoise bowl in the central hollow. When he pointed at the gore slicked bowl, Rahab's shirt fell open over his creamy chest. "Everything's about blood. This is the heart of the Brotherhood. Do you remember how it felt the moment *your* Blood Lover swung on

165

that noose...?"

I swallowed, tears burning the back of my eyes. I cocooned myself in Rebel's emotions, which were seeping through the bond: *exhaustion*, *concern*, but *love* too.

*Please let him be safe.*

"The bond of *blood* will break Misrule, the Under World, and *worlds*. Then, having used the *blood* of Phoenix's son to raise my personal army of angel slaves — the weapons of my devoted Lazarus Mages — I'll wipe the contaminated *blood* of the Fallen away forever."

Tiger hissed; his steel claws sprang from his nails, raking down Rahab's chest.

Rahab bellowed, clouting Tiger to the floor and towering over him. Scarlet oozed down Rahab's skin, dribbling to stain the golden perfection of his trousers.

"Looks like the Fallen have drawn first *blood*," I smirked.

Rahab fastidiously wiped at the scratches with the edges of his shirt, whilst Tiger watched him from a crouch. "Except this won't be war. *This'll be an extermination.*"

Suddenly, my mouth was too dry because this was *vampire genocide*: The reason that I'd refused to back the Legion on Angel World.

Had Rahab known Tiger had been held as the Wynter's familiar all along? In which case, had the Mage's Challenge been about bringing down the Under World and forcing me to become his bitch, whilst I'd thought that I'd been saving my brother?

*Crack* — the golden arteries rammed me into the pulsing wall again.

I yelped, then screamed, as the arteries released me into the air, hurling me over the bowl.

I flapped frantically but too late, landing with a *crunch* on my knees. I winced, shuffling backwards towards the vibrating wall behind me. "You have more chance of tiny warlocks whammying rainbows out of your arse."

Rahab's wings flared in flaming arcs. "Why do you defy me?"

"Why do you have a hard-on for dictator impersonations?"

166

"Hush. Does your wagging tongue never stop? Truly, I am intrigued."

I curled my fingers along the wall. "You bought yourself a new monarch, but not my silence."

When Rahab snatched for Tiger, I dragged Tiger — *yowling* — by his tail towards me, winding my arms around his waist and shooting Rahab my best challenging raised eyebrow.

Rahab only shook his head. "Long ago, I bought your brother. Except, your mother was in fact disposing of him, rather than selling. Much like my own." Rahab pulled at his cuffs, for once fighting to hide his flare for the dramatic. But I caught it anyway: *cast out, abandoned, and left to die...* Why the hell had our mother done that to my brother? The shadows stirred inside me, blackening my eyes. "She considered her experiment with Phoenix, who she'd been most insistent to try out, a failure." Only Tiger's tongue licking my cheek, brought me down from the quivering rage: The Matriarch had forced Phoenix, just like she'd forced my dad, Lucifer, to conceive *me.* "She bore a boy, rather than a girl. Instead of allowing the child to be putdown, however, merely because he wasn't a Glory..." *Hell, were those tears wetting the corners of Rahab's eyes?* "I raised him here alongside my own son. Duma loves him like a brother."

Why did both Drake and my brother get to know each other — *love each other* — whilst once again I was the outsider?

*Was Drake's love for my brother the only reason that Drake had ever helped me?*

Yet my guts twisted sickly too because my brother had been rejected for being a boy, whilst my mum had gone on to have me as her heir. And I'd rejected *her*, the Crown, and the entire Angel World.

*That had to be a boot to my brother's balls.*

"Maybe it's all the time you spend in despot mode, but on Planet Sane dads don't usually *bleed out their sons*. They protect them, just like sisters do."

"You mean sacrifice for them?"

I drew in a breath. Tiger rested his chin on my shoulder, nuzzling me with his nose. "Always."

Rahab stalked towards me. "Remarkable how alike you sound to Duma: the things he's sacrificed for the prince..." I hungered to let out the monster raging inside and rip away Rahab's smirk. Despite centuries of abuse, Commander Drake had fought to protect his kid army on Angel World, and now I knew he'd done the same for my brother. *How could Rahab miss the worth in his own son?* "Duma's greatest use has always been as whipping boy to the prince." Rahab spread his arms with a smile, as if I'd join in the joke. "In fact, it's Duma who's the slave."

I growled, letting go of Tiger. Before I could launch myself up, however, Rahab struck the wall behind me.

*A jarring screech.*

I grimaced, falling back. The aroma of sour lime flooded me, more powerfully than before. The back wall parted: a spiked flower unfurling. And Drake collapsed out of its insides.

Startled, I caught Drake, lowering him to the ground. My shaky hand hovered over him. *Where could I even touch...?*

Almost every inch of Drake's skin was seared with burns or purpled with bruises — courtesy of the Reformation Room. Yet even that was veiled under blood, which seeped from the holes through his chest.

I stared up, transfixed, at the chamber that Drake had been trapped inside: an iron maiden attached to the pipes, which had been wrapped around me, sucking Drake's blood.

*Bleeding* him.

I guess these angels weren't big on the whole *like bastard vampires* irony.

Rahab steepled his fingers. "Just helping the physical learner."

"I am to be your whipping boy as well, am I not?" When Drake coughed, scarlet spotted his dry lips. Its aroma of

168

frankincense wove through me, battling against the tang of lime; I drew my fingers through his curls.

Tiger peeked over my shoulder at Drake, who lifted an eyebrow at him.

I lifted Drake's chin. "You're fam." I licked the blood from his lips, before gently kissing him. His brow furrowed in confusion. He shuddered with pain. "And I love my fam."

His eyes widened in shock, even as his fingers curled into mine.

"My son's fondness for you has ever been amusing and an embarrassment." When Rahab's shadow fell over us, Drake blushed, moving as if to try and stand or at least to kneel. *Not happening in a month of drunken cupids.* "And *your* use of it almost as Machiavellian as my own." Why did Rahab have to use long words when what he meant was: *devious?* Except, he thought it was a compliment, and I thought it made us both the Big Bads. "Yet *your* fondness for my son is unexpected, since no one has ever shown such an interest in him before. Although, he's not missed experience of a certain sort as the Matriarch's Marked Wing."

Way to turn up the cringe factor, and now Drake looked like he'd rather be squaring off against an army of vampires on the battleground, rather than here with his dad telling me how *no one had ever loved him*, but *not to worry he wouldn't know how to shag because he'd been used as a bed slave...*

I kissed Drake again. "My love," I whispered.

"First," Rahab wound his hand in my hair, and I yelped at the burn to my scalp, "you're *my* Phoenix Queen."

Rahab dragged me backwards away from Drake and Tiger, flinging me into the turquoise bowl like I was a giant's supper.

*Clunk, burble, clunk...*

I peered upwards at the hole in the roof, which was opening like a winking eye.

*Or the spurting end of a cut artery.*

169

My eyes widened, before crimson gushed down: lime, copper, and *life*. Then I was lost in my brother's blood.

# 19

Yesterday, my brother's blood had anointed me as Phoenix Queen. Today, I'd rise to the rank of Lazarus Mage by raising my own slave.

I twisted the gold angel ring on my left hand: the ring of an angelmancer.

*The final test.*

My eyelid twitched, but otherwise I stood motionless.

The trestle tables had been pushed back to the sides of Phoenix Hall. A plinth rose out of the centre; a golden statue of an angel perched on it like it was poised to escape. The sun caught the red in the stained-glass windows, until the phoenixes blazed, and their fire seared across my cheeks.

I breathed out, burning with the power of the Legion.

*Let me walk in the Code and join the Brotherhood!*

Joy sang through me, whilst the nobility of the Code wound around me: comforting and warming like I'd known it since birth.

Yet at the same time, a numbness had settled across my skin where the blood had soaked in from the Bleeding Chamber. It was a coating that blocked out everything but the truth — *nope, not truth: propaganda, conditioning, brainwashing...battle to remember that* — which Rahab had murmured telepathically into my mind, whilst he'd held me against his chest, rocking and petting my hair.

*Why had I fought against my true father: the liberator of the Legion?*

When Rahab swooped over my head, circling eagle-like, I smiled.

*He'd set me free.*

A nagging awareness that I'd forgotten something...*someone*...prickled the base of my neck, as if fam who weren't Brothers could matter. *Feelings* floated just out of my grasp, brushing against me, until I flinched at their disapproval: *unease, disgust,* and *rage.* Like resurrecting your own slave wasn't a glorious gift from Rahab, as well as the ultimate celebration for finally becoming a mage.

*I'd earnt it.*

So, why the flicker of smarting *shame*, despite the flames that flared to burn it out?

I prowled closer to the plinth, raising my hands to its hinged back.

"Do you not see the dangerous line, which you're marching towards?" I glared at the Undeserving with long silver hair, who'd dared call out to me. He sat on the bench by the wall, encircling his knees with his arms. That niggling sense again itched at me like I *knew him.* "I once swore not to allow you to become the beast you truly fear. If you raise a Phoenix, stealing all that he was, then I care not if you call me traitor because *you're* the villain."

I drew back my shoulders, frostily studying him. "Do not address your queen, Undeserving."

His mouth gaped open.

Maybe he was the court jester. Then why was he at my ceremony? I shifted uneasily from foot to foot.

"My apologies." The Underserving turned his head, dropping his gaze. "There are clearly *two* slaves raised here today."

I stroked over the angel ring again.

Rahab landed softly, clasping my hands between his. "One last task to prove your worth, and you shall be a Lazarus Mage. *Mine.* You wish only that, remember?"

Whispered words drowned in blood: *light, love, and*

172

*Lazarus...*

I nodded. *By the blood, I'd hold to the truth of the Brotherhood and obey.*

Yet, why did violet and black squirm in my guts? Why did silver howl?

"Hush," Rahab held his finger to my lips. "How loud your thoughts are, Phoenix Queen."

*Silence.*

I forced myself to look away from the intensity of Rahab's stare. Apart from the pretty Underserving, Phoenix Hall was empty: no mages crowded to witness my special day. Instead, only the eyes of the shadow witches, vampires, and angels swivelled to watch from the tapestries, ready to weave in my story.

*Was this real?*

"Why the dirty secret treatment?" I muttered.

Rahab smiled. "Believe me when I say you have all the audience you need for your coronation."

He slipped out a curved blade, carving it down the centre of my palm.

I gasped, crushing my hand into a fist, as the blood dripped. I smeared it over my ring.

The ring glowed a sudden ruby, and I ached at the rush.

Then Rahab swung open the statue along its hinged back, and I juddered at the aroma of candyfloss blood: magic and power. In a deep well inside the statue, pooled the original Phoenix's blood: not scented with lime, but sweet like...

*Who?*

Who the hell made me shudder with such excitement that I craved to lick the sugary copper, even though I couldn't remember his name...?

*Bonded, Marked, Blood Lover...*

I swayed, but Rahab steadied me; his warm hand didn't leave the dip between my shoulder blades, as he plunged his

173

fingers into Phoenix's blood with his other hand and anointed my ring. "*Call him*," his command echoed in my mind: it left no space for other thoughts, names, or memories. "Feel, control, resurrect. He is your Chosen."

In a bed of blood, Rahab had repeated one name, until I'd been unable to hold onto anything apart from the slave who would be mine: *Nat*.

"Unleash that infamous monster of yours," the silver-haired Underserving howled, leaping up. I frowned: *he'd be for the Reformation Room*... And why did my stomach roil at the thought? "Break out the bitch, destroyer or... Bring your beastly self back to me."

I hesitated.

*Monster*...?

Wait, what in the Nine Realms of Zombie Angels was bastard going on...? Why was I about to raise my very own mind-wiped angel, whilst...*Mischief, hell that was his name*...ganked me with his death glare?

Rahab's grip on my back became firmer. "Call him."

I hesitated.

"*Nat*," Rahab's reminder was a telepathic kick up the arse.

I flinched; the fire inside sought to burn higher again, even as I fought against it.

I shook: *Mischief, Mischief, Mischief*...

"Nat," Rahab repeated, out loud this time; his jaw clenched. Then he coaxed, "Don't you wish to become a mage and see your brother? *Save* him? Just say the name once."

I blinked, yet the world bled to scarlet. My blood bubbled, even as the blood fizzed on the ring, snaking in shadowy coils back into my palm through the gash.

My knees buckled, whilst my shoulders shook at the Phoenix blood surging through my body and bonding with mine.

It was too late: Rahab had created a hidden world where everything rested on purity of powers and blood. An angel had already been called back to life. If *I* didn't call for him — claim him — now, I'd leave him in limbo.

I knew myself that the only thing worse than bad parents,

174

was to be abandoned and unwanted.

*No way my Phoenix would start that way.*

"Nat," I whispered.

"You truly are a monster," Mischief growled.

I jumped at the sudden burning flash and shock like the strike of lightning to the side of the hall. When the stink of ash and burning bonfires assaulted my nostrils, I lurched.

I imagined Lucifer dead. Resurrected. My own slave.

*Please, hell, not my own dad...*

But why then had I been calling for *Nat...?*

*Whimpering.*

I startled, crouching down to stare at the naked angel, who was huddled in a terrified ball underneath the plinth. His golden wings were wrapped around himself, and he peeked from beneath his feathers at me with leonine eyes, which were framed by long black lashes.

*My Phoenix.*

The blood still surging through me screamed that I'd birthed this angel, and I tremored with the desire to protect him, even though I'd betrayed him already.

*Gift...?* Yeah, but only if a child was a gift because he was part of me. I dropped to my knees, reaching out my hand.

I'd expected him to flinch, but instead he edged towards me, allowing his wings to fall away from his face: he was a teenager with sharp cheekbones and short silver hair.

I remembered then: Rebel, Ash, Drake, Mischief...*all of it.*

Also, how I'd freed Barakiel, who'd lightning fried Mischief's younger brother: the brat member of the Legion who'd tormented Drake and ambushed me.

*Nathanael.*

The slave angel whose memories had now been wiped, and I'd resurrected. Who was staring at me with awe like I was a bastard god. "Mother?"

My breath hitched. "Call me Feathers, yeah?" *Mistress*

175

might've been cruel, but why had I given the Phoenix my nickname? I'd hated the weasly arsed mage back on Angel World, yet now Nathanael had no memories and gazed at me with such innocence, I didn't know how I felt apart from it was big on the conflicted. "We're fam, and you're safe now."

"Brother...?" Mischief keened.

*How had I forgotten Mischief? Or that he didn't know his brother was even dead?*

When I glanced at Rahab, his slow smile was predatory. *He* hadn't bastard forgotten; there'd been a reason this was a coronation ceremony for only us four. "I imagine like all boys, Zophia, you think your perversions hidden. I have academies throughout the human world; my apprentices wank to fantasies of witches sweaty in their desires, as if they're secret. So, play as much as you will with your unnatural magic, but when you infect the Legion's queen with it...?" He trailed his hand along my shoulder, and my skin rose in goose bumps. "Let me offer in return a reminder of how I saved you, Och, and your little brother: Phoenix 28."

Mischief roughly wiped away the tears tumbling down his cheeks. Then in a sizzling spray of sparkles, he transformed into a tiny silver unicorn.

Tears still wept from Mischief's eyes, wetting his fluffy face, as his pink muzzle mewled. Then he trotted across the hall, dwarfed by its gloom, towards Phoenix 28.

*Because Phoenixes weren't allowed a name, only a number.*

Against my side, 28 stiffened, curling his much smaller hand into mine like the unicorn was the threat. I didn't pull away.

Mischief nuzzled against his brother, however, resting his warm head on his lap, and I was flooded with an unexpected image of them both when they were younger: Nathanael had suffered a nightmare, and this had been how Mischief had comforted him. Mischief would've been a live soft toy to make up for the Victorian workhouse bleakness of the Iron Barracks. As a kid, I'd have sold every computing minute owed to me in the children's home for Mischief to have cuddled *me* at night.

And no way was I admitting that to Mischief...ever.

Only, when Mischief tried to crawl further onto his brother's lap, 28's brow furrowed, and he quivered.

*Because 28 didn't bastard remember.*

28 sneaked a glance at me, before swiping the unicorn skittering across the straw-covered floor with a shy smile at me like I'd be proud.

When 28's tentative smile wavered, I hurriedly grinned back at him.

Mischief lay, dazed, before shaking his mane with a soft *squeal.* Then he stared back at us in shock.

Rahab soared up to the arching roof of the hall. "You made her your queen, yet she's mine, Zophia. The destroyer who'll always put her brother before yours. Look what she'll sacrifice to save him, yet we both know how little my cunning monster needs saving. She even freed her brother's Tainted lover, Barakiel, who murdered 28. Now 28 is her slave. Tell me, do you love your brother more, or your queen...?"

Mischief's eyes sparked silver, as his gaze met mine.

Hell, Rahab had set us up against each other. *This* was the final test. And Mr Reason had taken a vacation because here was Mischief's brother, not simply dead but raised as a slave.

Yeah, I understood because Rahab had walked me through the dress rehearsal with Rebel.

So, when Mischief shifted from toy to killer unicorn, growing as large as a war horse, I knew I was screwed.

I either tamed a unicorn, or I died beneath his hooves. Mischief lowered his horn and charged.

# 20

A flare of metallic light, like liquid mercury, shot from the killer unicorn's twisted horn. I threw myself to the side, but it singed my wing; I howled. I'd seen Mischief decapitate a vampire with the move before, but I'd never thought he'd turn his unicorn god-out on me.

Yet Mischief and I had both been incited to monstrous rage over brothers. I was battling to save mine, and Mischief to avenge the Phoenix who now cowered, mind wiped and terrified, underneath the plinth, looking to *me* for comfort.

"Stay there," I ordered, wincing at the puppy dog command and knowing that if 28 had remembered who he truly was, he'd have shanked me. "Feathers has a naughty unicorn to go...spank."

28's eyes widened, and his lip trembled, even as he nodded dutifully.

Hell, he bastard thought I meant it. From now on, dialling down the Violet-o-Metre.

"No spanking, just a calm little chat." I glanced across Phoenix Hall: our *calm chats* had already splintered the trestle tables to fire wood, burnt the benches, and shattered the stained-glass windows.

We'd messed up Phoenix Hall legendary style: let the tapestry shadows weave *that* into the bastard story.

Yet Rahab still only hovered above us, coolly watching.

I stumbled, for a moment imagining that I was back in the Under World's Cages, forced to fight as *their* Champion.

*That I'd never escaped...*

I blinked down at the golden angel. 28 cocooned his wings around himself as he peered at me uncertainly.

In the Under World, I'd fought to defeat my opponents, yet here I fought to save mine.

When Mischief shook his mane, spittle flew from his foaming mouth. He pawed at the stone ground. He was both hot and *terrifying*. Because despite the stakes, I knew I couldn't return to the beast of the Cages. I'd fought Mischief there too, when he'd hidden his magic and had his arse kicked: I'd plucked a feather from his defeated wing, wearing it in my hair.

*Never again.*

Then Mischief lowered his head to charge at me once more.

*A roar of rage.*

I shivered at Mischief's furious scream, as he thundered towards me, striking out with his front legs.

I soared up, swinging around at the last minute to land on Mischief's back. Startled, Mischief reared to throw me off, but I snatched his horn, wrapping my wings around his flanks like a saddle. He *squealed*; his eyes were wild, as his nostrils flared.

Then I rode the untamed bastard, whilst he bit, kicked, and galloped around the hall in circles, holding onto his mane.

High on the thrill, I laughed; magic vibrated through me, boiling away the last of Phoenix's blood.

*The Bitch of Utopia was back.*

I turned my head to the side, catching Rahab's eye, before leaning over Mischief's neck and sniffing at his scent of sweat, horsehair, and sweet popcorn.

Then I bit.

Mischief stilled, quivering under my soothing hands, whilst his pain-trembling blood — his silver magic questing out and

179

stroking mine — burst onto my tongue.

Taking him down had been a hunt. Just as my dad had hunted Mischief with me.

*How had Rahab known to tempt me with this?*

"Stop trying to gank my arse, My Little Psycho Unicorn," I whispered to Mischief, whilst making a show of licking over the bite. "I'm just putting on a show. You were the one who told me to lead. Maybe you can hide in the shadows, but I'm the Champion of Light. You know we can't talk about any of this here, but I can't lead, whilst I'm hidden away; I have to be in the light. I'm still your Silver Queen, though. <u>Trust me</u>."

I held my breath. I didn't want Mischief tamed: I just wanted him at my side, trusting me. Why should he, however, now that his brother was my slave?

Yet, at last, Mischief lowered his tail, blowing gently out of his nostrils. I stroked down his heaving flanks.

*Clap, clap, clap.*

I forced myself to look up into the smug face of Rahab, who applauded the conquered Mischief.

*Newbie mistake to see the puppet and not the strings.*

"Brotherly love has its uses." Rahab's smile was too wide: my insides fluttered with fear. "You'll discover this when you train 28 in the arena. Phoenixes are not our children but our weapons; we simply need to know how to sharpen them."

"You promised that when I became a Lazarus Mage, you'd free my brother. Pay up, bro." I peered around Phoenix Hall, as if the glass box would appear any moment with my brother still trapped inside.

Rahab's smile widened even further. "If he could only hear your devotion... I've been father to innumerable mages, yet I've loved every one. Work with your Phoenix and you have my word, your brother will come to you."

Mischief trembled, shaking his head.

Why had Rahab's words sounded less of a promise and more of a threat?

I peered over the ledge of the stone gallery, which ran high above Neptune's Courtyard. The stone crumbled under my fingers, painting my palms chalky. Above, the bronze-faced disc of the sun beat down through the open roof. Beneath me, weathered wooden masks of the forbidding god of the sea grew out of craggy walls. Their mouths hung open as if about to unleash the Kraken.

28's amber eyes peeked back at me from the gloom. He knelt on the courtyard floor, shivering. He was dressed in gold silk harem trousers and his silver hair had been shorn into the same buzz cut as all Phoenixes sported. I'd hated forcing him to stay in *kneel*, whilst the only thing he'd had left from his past life — his appearance — had been stolen. When I'd abandoned him at the bottom of the courtyard and flown to the top of the gallery, he'd trembled.

But what could I tell him? All the god faces freaked me out too.

Mischief stood on one side of me, his hands smartly behind his back. He was as stiff and fragile as glass; he'd shatter if he moved. Drake stood on my other side, his arms across the healing wounds in his stomach, eyeing Mischief warily.

"Do begin," Mischief sounded as if he was munching on glass as well, "after all, you're an angelmancer: not merely a slaveowner but bonded to your slave. The ultimate control over life and death. Why not savour it?"

"Be silent," Drake's command was ice-cold.

Mischief blinked but didn't reply. Hell, I didn't need a gag; I only needed Drake in Commander mode.

"Good. Now, I propose you remember that you're talking to our queen. And she's important, whereas our feelings are irrelevant. It appears the stories about you are true: An Undeserving who doesn't know his place."

Mischief's hands clenched behind his back. "Now what was it I always believed about the golden son of the Mage...? Arrogant, spoiled, and entitled." He cocked his head as if in

181

thought. "*Check, check,* and *check.*"

When Drake paled, I hurriedly rested a hand on each of their chests like a posh kid had been dropped into my school in Hackney, and I'd suddenly become the one separating him from the Jerusalem orphan.

Except, I wasn't certain it'd be the posh kid getting shanked.

I didn't miss the way Mischief had attempted to close his tunic to hide my purpling bite on his neck, nor the way Drake's gaze was drawn to it with more longing than concern.

"Snarky and spoiled: you're both brats, Undeserving, and my fam. Plus, we're here to train my new Phoenix who's in the courtyard, alone." Both angels had the decency to look down, chastened. "So, how do I start boot camp? Push ups or...?"

"Was I not clear?" Mischief bit his lip. "It's a bond: you control my brother. That's what I meant..." He shook his head. "He shall never be closer to anyone than you."

I understood Mischief's sadness then: what had been wrenched from him, only to be gifted to me. His brotherly bond had been erased, and now I held something even deeper. Yet I couldn't help the thrill, which ran fizzing through my blood at Mischief's words (and I knew he'd seen it), because 28 felt like he belonged to me, even as I belonged to him.

I nodded down at 28 in the arena, and he rose to his feet with feline grace. His delicate golden wings spread.

I concentrated on our connection. I mapped it, as it spread in crimson tendrils between us and in the blood we shared.

"*Are you picking up my frequency?*" I sang telepathically, lifted on the joy of the bond, before pinking. Maybe I should've rapped something more hardcore?

But when 28 grinned, blushing too...? It was worth it.

"*I can hear you in my mind, my Feathers,*" 28's voice — so much softer than I remembered it and heartbreakingly similar to Mischief's now that I knew they were brothers — lit up my brain like it'd always been meant to be there. "*Are you safe with those creatures beside you? One with the melancholy gaze and the other so cold?*"

"*They're called angels. Fam: your fam. How about you*
182

*have some fun and show me what a badass you are?"*

28 frowned. *"I don't believe my ass is bad. Do you wish it to be? Or will you spank me if it is?"*

Yeah, dialling down on the Violet…

*"You and your arse are both good. We're just going to test out our powers."*

He straightened his shoulders. *"I shall make you proud, my Feathers."*

I couldn't hold 28's serious, sincere gaze. How many times had I been desperate for someone to be proud of me? Yet no one ever had been. I'd have given anything for someone to say those words. Yet I didn't want my slave to earn my approval through pain and sacrifice on the battlefield.

The mages took the Phoenixes' innocence and warped their trusting loyalty. No way on his bristly silver head was I doing that to Mischief's brother.

*"I'm already proud of you."* I shot warmth through the bond, winding my Firebird (because he wouldn't merely be a number to me, even if that was breaking the Code and I couldn't call him by his real name), even closer. He grinned, spreading his wings further, as if basking in the sun. *"You're my epic Firebird. Let's see your moves."*

I reached through the bond, spinning Firebird up into the air. I gasped: he was fast.

*Thunder* — all of a sudden, water spat out of the Neptunes' mouths in gushing torrents.

Firebird laughed in delight, even as the power of the waterfalls drove him downwards, soaking him. Trenches opened in the floor, sluicing away the floods. I sniggered too, leaning further over the rocky ledge and shooting more power through the bond.

Firebird dived side to side, splashing through the foaming spittle like a kid at bath time.

I staggered back from the ledge: *hell, he was a kid.* Firebird had only been a teenage assassin under Rahab's control, who Barakiel had killed, and I'd resurrected.

Drake caught my elbow, pulling me close into his side. "My Queen, calm yourself."

"You see now?" Mischief said, gazing at his brother, who was fluttering in between the streams of water. Firebird's wet wings glistened like he was a fairy slave. "His only reason for existence is to battle, hurt, and die for you. Then he'll be raised again, so it can all be repeated."

"Not a chance," I snarled. "What happened to the Trust Train?"

"It left the station, unlike your obsession with the Butcher." Mischief gave a shaky laugh, raising his hand, as if in apology. "You're working to release an ideal that doesn't exist. If only you'd—"

"I thought I'd already warned you to silence?" Drake's eyes flashed predatory fury and hurt.

Rahab had told me that Drake had been raised with the prince like brothers, but it was only hearing Drake's immediate defence of him, as harsh as any he'd spoken for me, that I believed it.

I lost my focus on Firebird, jittering with anticipation. *Soon, I'd see my brother...*

Yet Mischief's expression still held that pleading wary edge, which I'd seen so often on the faces of the carers at Jerusalem's. When I'd been handed over to my adopted parents, they'd worn it: a caution *not to hope*. As my adopted mother had carried me back, unwanted, I'd realised they'd been right.

"Do you truly wish your brother to be free?" I jumped at Rahab's honey-like question, as he stalked from the shadows of the gallery with Tiger at his heels, who was dressed now in golden silks that were slashed to reveal his tail and wings.

My stomach clenched: *this was it.*

"What do you think I've been battling for? Free parking spaces for everyone who knows the lyrics to "Bohemian Rhapsody"?"

Rahab grimaced. "Your brother to be unhurt and saved from the glass box. But not everyone should be *free*." He smiled; his sandalwood scent wafted through the gallery in creamy waves. Tiger shrank against Mischief. "The prince is the only mage with the strength to challenge you for the title of Champion of Light. Are you so eager to help him now?"

I rapped my boot *tap — tap — tap* on the stone. "Stick your title and stick your light. Where's my brother?"

Rahab waved his fingers lazily in the air. "It's time you met the Invisible Prince. Then perhaps you'll discover why I'd never free the true monster in this castle."

A dark silhouette blotted out the bronzed sun.

The water spouting from the Neptunes' mouths sputtered out in shock. Firebird drifted to the floor, kicking his bare feet in the puddles.

I shielded my eyes, squinting up at the angel — my older brother, no longer a baby but a masterful prince — who was plummeting towards Firebird with a predator's savagery. The true monster had been unleashed, and whilst I'd always been terrified it was me, it'd been my brother all along: The Butcher.

# 21

When my half-brother plunged from the sky, wreathed in wild flames — my dark reflection — my shadows whipped out towards him. They strained to meld with his because he was safe and *alive*, just as I'd first felt when I'd seen his snowy shoulder in the mirror room. They also froze me, holding me back from battling him, whilst he turned his blazing gaze on Firebird.

I knew that look... I'd *given* that look myself, just before I'd hacked some poor bastard into a fine red mist.

I battled to focus on Firebird, who was still at the bottom of Neptune's Courtyard booting through the shallow waters below the masks. He was grinning like I'd allowed him a treat: a trip to a waterpark, rather than an imminent arse kicking.

I shot magic through the bond, forcing Firebird to look up. He gasped, stepping back.

*Crunch* — the prince landed on Firebird, knocking him onto his back.

Firebird yelped, scrabbling to wriggle out from underneath my brother. The prince only stared down at him, like a hunter over his felled trophy with one bare foot on Firebird's bruised ribs.

"I don't imagine anyone has told our beloved Invisible Prince that attacking an untrained Phoenix is cowardly?" Mischief hollered, shaking from the effort of holding back his magic.

Why hadn't I yelled that? *Why had I allowed Mischief to risk himself?*

Yet I knew it was because I couldn't look away from the prince, who towered over Firebird — freed because of me. Here was my brother all grown up: imposing, proud, and with an air of sparkling superiority that sparked burning jealousy. What the hell did I know about being a princess...or queen?

*My brother, on the other hand, looked born to royalty.*

"No showing off for your sister," Rahab laughed, as if the prince had merely taken roughhousing a little far. "Join us, Anael."

*Anael*: my brother's true name.

It thrilled through me like love and life. I soared on the connection, as my shadows rushed back inside, thrumming.

When I leant on the ledge, eagerly gazing down at the courtyard, Anael ground his heel once more into Firebird's ribs. I winced on Firebird's *whimper*.

Firebird's leonine eyes met mine in blinking confusion: *why wasn't his fam keeping him safe?*

My chest tight, I leant further over the ledge, but Drake snatched my shoulder. I remembered our unspoken body language:

**Hold on, don't do anything crazy, bitch.**

I shrugged him off:

**My choice, bro.**

Anael raised his head, tossing his brunet tresses casually out of his eyes, before meeting my gaze. I'd expected relief, joy, or excitement...*something*. After everything I'd risked to save my brother from the glass box, as well as his wailed distress, which pricked my eyes with tears even now, how could he look at me with such studied indifference? Then he shoved away from Firebird, swooping up towards the gallery and landing next to Rahab.

I shuddered, desperate to reach out to Anael: there was no mirror or glass between us anymore. He was no longer hidden from me. When the sour tang of lime caught in my nostrils, I swallowed with difficulty. It'd been *Anael's* scent that'd coated the Bleeding Chamber, and it'd been *his* — rather than Phoenix's — blood that'd bathed me.

*His magic was inside me.*

Yet Anael ignored me, prowling to Rahab and draping himself around him; Rahab relaxed against Anael with a contented sigh.

I stiffened. *What in the freakverse was up with this picture?*

With a *click* of his fingers, Anael summoned Drake.

Drake squeezed my shoulder, before sauntering to Anael with a smile that curled *both* sides of his mouth; he didn't even try to cover it. Anael ghosted his fingers up Drake's injured chest with a frown, before tenderly pushing a stray curl behind his ear. Then he glanced over Drake's shoulder at me, and Drake gave a short shake of his head.

They had a language of their own, the same as Drake and I did: Anael thought *I'd* been the one to hurt Drake. And why did that bastard shank *me*? The same as the happy families pose of Rahab with his son and my brother?

Where did I fit in, standing on the edges, whilst Anael's insolent gaze swept over me?

At last, I couldn't take the silence. "I'm Violet," I stuck out my hand because we weren't at the hugging stage, "your new annoying little sis."

Anael's lips quirked mockingly, whilst he ignored my hand that hung between us like a gooseberry on a date. "Annoying? Surely not." Then he glanced away, as if bored. *Why was his indifference more painful than hate?* His gaze settled on Mischief, who'd shrunk back against the ledge. "Clearly you don't discipline your Underserving thoroughly enough. Would you like lessons?"

Rage roared through me: black and twisting. I dropped my hand, stepping in front of Mischief. "I haven't applied to Brainwashing College. Look, we could—"

"Bored." Anael wound closer around Rahab. "You promised meeting her would be fun, father."

"Patience, my pampered monster. She's earned this, after all." When Rahab grinned, Anael laughed: a wicked Prince Charming.

*And I wasn't being let in on the joke.*

What had been done to my brother that he could lounge next to his captor like he hadn't been deaged before the entire Legion?

Gritting my teeth, I stormed towards Rahab. "Why's my brother tripping? Doesn't he remember the glass box?" I sneaked a glance at Anael, even as I stabbed a finger against Rahab's chest. "This is the sick bastard who played cage the baby with you, and I'm the brave sister who risked my fam to save you."

Anael gave a lazy smile. "Who do you think came up with that touching tableaux?"

My breath hitched, as my head jerked back. Horror and grief spiralled through me: *Anael had planned the whole scene at my celebratory feast...?* He hadn't been the prey but the cunning predator all along...?

*The Butcher.*

I shook my head. "No bastard way..."

"All I had to do was imagine what would burn me and make me perform doggy tricks, if I discovered I had a brother and couldn't help him." For the first time, Anael's expression softened, yet I hadn't missed his emphasis on *brother*, rather than *sister*. "I'm touched by your concern." He flicked imaginary lint off his muscled shoulder. Had the bruises been from Rahab's abuse or nothing more than training injuries? "That is, I would be...if you weren't a loathsome Glory."

Tiger's eyes narrowed; his tail lashed. "She's not just some Glory. She took out the *Wynter sisters*. Show some respect, angel."

I stiffened, as Anael's interest ignited fully for the first time. He looked over Tiger like a new chew toy. He let go of Rahab, sliding closer to Tiger, who didn't back down. Instead, he bristled. Until Anael snatched Tiger's tail, stroking its tip

189

snake-like over Tiger's nipples.

Tiger shoved against Anael's shoulders, beating his grey wings in furious gusts. "Figured you Legion sorts would be deviants."

*Smack* — Anael slapped Tiger across the cheek.

Yet the blow was a delicate caress, compared to the savagery Anael had used to tear into Firebird.

"Hold your tongue, moggy." Anael traced the light pink that shaded Tiger's cheek. "Or I shall bite it off."

*This was my brother?* The innocent trapped on the opposite side of the mirror? In the glass box? Except, they'd both been illusions. Traps to play me and make me dance.

*Yet was this the truth?*

Rahab laughed high with delighted surprise. "Something new has caught your eye? A pretty pet to play with in your lodge? Well, when have I denied my favourite?"

My guts clenched not only at Anael's twisted smile, but also at the way Drake's gaze dropped to the ground. It hadn't been just at the reminder that Anael was the *favourite* son (and I'd never seen Rahab act daddy indulgence like this towards Drake), but as if Drake recognised Anael's *play* and it wouldn't be chasing after balls of string.

Drake had been Rebel's gaoler and torturer for forty years, even if he had been forced into the role by my mother. He knew about pain and pleasure. If Drake had on The Grimace, then Tiger wasn't in for cuddles and milk.

It seemed Tiger thought so too.

"I'm no one's pet anymore." Tiger's fangs shot out, as he whipped his tail away from Anael's hold.

Yet the moment Tiger crouched and leapt with a beat of his wings onto the crumbling ledge, I saw his mistake in the excited flash of Anael's eyes. Because I buzzed with the same pulse pounding call to the *hunt*, even if Angel World's training on self-discipline held me back.

Yet when Anael licked his lips, blowing Tiger a taunting kiss, Rahab *didn't* hold him back. Instead, he nodded. "Good boy."

I'd never been so grateful that Rebel had warned me

against becoming nothing but a monster, and that Mischief battled against that side of me now.

I growled, snatching Anael's ankle, as he soared over my head. He twirled, booting me onto my arse. When spinning discs began to grow on Mischief's palms, however, I shook my head, hiding my gasp behind a cough.

The discs faded.

All those years of hiding his powers, yet Mischief had been about to reveal himself...?

By the time I'd pushed myself back up, Anael had plucked Tiger off the ledge.

Tiger howled, slashing his claws through the air.

"It's lonely in my tower; I promise, it'll not be as bad as you fear to be mine." Anael sank his blunt teeth into Tiger's neck, just as I had Mischief's when I'd been taming him as a unicorn shifter.

I shuddered to see my own weaknesses — or power — acted out in front of me.

Tiger stilled, tremoring: what happened to a Blood Lover if another drank from them?

Anael didn't suck from the wound, however, only dragging Tiger after him like *he* in fact was the cat. He spat Tiger out at Rahab's feet. "I've done the meet and greet thing." He rubbed his head against Rahab's chin, who smiled at him, fondly. "May I take my treat back to my room?"

"Is this how you treat your Halfling *guests*?" I glared at Rahab. "Rehabilitation by mauling?"

Anael waved his hand at me. "Why is this Glory still talking?"

I bit hard on my tongue, sucking at the tangy copper. "You're my brother, whether that means anything to you or not. I know you've been raised on this freaky island with no one to...but I'm here now. And I'm asking you not to drag Tiger away with you."

"Why on earth should I do anything for you, *sister*?"

I recoiled; Anael's sudden scorn broke through the

indifference like a slap.

Drake sidled to Anael, reaching up to tip his head, until their gazes met. Drake ran the fingers of his other hand along Anael's feathers, even though my brother loomed over Drake's slight frame: it was a mouse taming a lion. At last, the tension bled away, and Anael started to purr.

Drake had spent his childhood taming *my* brother; he knew the tricks. Finally, Drake murmured, "Calm yourself. If you won't release the...Halfling...for your sister, then how about for me?"

Anael reared back, but Drake stood his ground. Anael tilted his head with a calculating look. "Why, cherub?"

I sniggered: Barakiel had used the same nickname for Drake on Angel World, and I still hadn't been able to call Drake on being the Angel of Love.

Anael glared at me. "*She's* the one you speak of like she's different to the others?"

*Yeah, not the time for name calling.*

Instead, I painted on my holiest expression, peeking up at him through my lashes. Nope, he wasn't tooting the belief horn.

Drake snorted. "The queen is foolish, reckless, and hotblooded." *One, two, and three points in Drake's ass kicking pot...* "But so are you." Now Anael was growling too. Did Drake enjoy having his wings broken? "Plus, she's *your* sister. I apologise if I've not made it clear enough, but for that reason alone, I'd protect her as I would you. And you're not petty enough to harm her over me."

Anael's growl died. He stroked his knuckles down Drake's cheek. "Am I not, cherub? I've always found it bewildering how easily you forgive those who hurt and humiliate you." I flushed at Anael's hard stare. "Yet this Glory believes herself better than us."

"This Glory can talk for herself. If there's one bastard belief I've never bought into, it's that I'm better than anyone else." I stepped closer, my hands shaking. "Look, I didn't even know I had a bro, until I was dragged to this castle. But I *am* your sister and I'm psyched about that, even if you never want to see me again. I just wanted to know you were OK."

Anael's face flickered with confusion, whilst he glanced between Rahab and me. He turned away, then faltered, turning back again. "Maybe I will see you again," his voice was gentler, as if the bravado had been stripped away. "Keep your moggy; I have no wish to catch fleas."

Tiger hissed.

When I stroked Anael's wing, he didn't flinch away. "Cheers, bro."

"He's *my* Invisible Prince." Rahab's fists clenched, as he flapped his wings, flustered. Our meeting wasn't going down like he'd hoped. Had he wanted my brother to rip out my heart? For us to remain rivals? For me to be the misfit on the outside of his happy family? *Screw that.* "Don't mistake my indulgence for weakness. Raised amongst humans, I imagine you have little idea of true devotion or dedication." He swept his wings up in a flaring arc, before barking, "Brothers of the Legion!"

Instantly, his two sons — Drake and Anael — snapped to attention like they were on the drill ground.

My shoulder blades and gums tingled with the same creeping warning that wormed across skin that was suddenly too tight.

Rahab met my gaze; his lips were thinned into a grim line. "My darling monster, kill yourself."

I gasped, and Drake flinched. But Anael didn't even hesitate: he placed his hands on either side of his head.

*Crack.*

I jumped, as my brother snapped his own neck.

## 22

Grief is a devourer: it hollows you out. Unless you let in the darkness and let out the demons.

Once, when Rebel had hunched on the concrete floor of the cellar in the House of Rose, Fox, and Wolf, clutching his dead witch family like he could bring them to life, I hadn't understood the intensity of his grief. Only now that I rocked, cradling my own brother's corpse in my arms on the stony ledge above Neptune's Courtyard, did I get it.

Ash had also sacrificed his sisters. *How the hell had he done that?*

When I sobbed, shadows blasted out of my chest, expanding over Anael's body and mine like I could keep him safe.

*Like it wasn't too late.*

I stroked my fingers through Anael's cooling feathers, then down his cheek. He looked like he could be asleep, but I'd seen enough dead bodies both on Utopia Estate and in battles since to know the difference.

Anael had killed himself on Rahab's order. If Rahab had wanted to show me his control, I was convinced. Yet he'd severed any control he'd had over me as Phoenix Queen because my connection in blood to my brother screamed *vengeance.*

Maybe it wasn't righteous but it was another side to me:

primal, ferocious, and protective of my fam.

I shook, glaring through the veil of tears at Drake, who still stood at attention next to his dad. To my surprise, Tiger had pulled himself up and wound himself around Drake in comfort, rubbing his ears and mop of hair under Drake's chin. Drake remained motionless, even if a single tear traced from the corner of his eye.

*The cold bastard*: Anael had been raised as Drake's own brother but he was only worth *one tear*...?

Shadows howled through me, banshee wailing that Drake had no right to stand there, like stone, whilst I alone clutched Anael's corpse. "I thought you loved the prince as a true brother?"

I bit my lip. *I didn't mean it... Why was my blood burning with such outrage...?*

"And I thought you stronger than the shadows, *Phoenix Queen*, than to allow them to use your words as whips." I jumped at Mischief's rebuke.

Mischief didn't crouch next to me, but instead, skirted the shroud of shadows, slipping his arm around Drake.

Drake blinked in confusion but didn't move away.

I flushed, winding the darkness closer, whilst it fogged ever denser.

**Cool it, Feathery-darkness. Call off the wailing mourners, million dollars' worth of lilies, and unicorn drawn hearse.**

*Hell, J, I've missed you. I need you—*

**Who wouldn't miss this level of fabulousness? But the Sorcerer of Shadiness, who'd not only bleed the prince but demand he break his own neck, would do much worse to *my* neck. So, excuse me for not putting it on the block.**

**This is a *now you see my sweet ass, now you don't* kind of visit. Because you've forgotten that you're on the island of illusions.**

*It's kind of hard to forget the magic.*

**Not magic: *what's real*. What's *ever* been real.**

*The noose around Rebel's neck felt bastard real.*

**You promised *anything* to save your angel in eyeliner. Even if you hiss and spit, Rahab thinks he has you by the throat. Just like your brother.**

*Help me...he's dead...and I can't...*

**You can. This sorcerer has moulded his own world for so long, he's forgotten that others can shape stories too.**

**Pull an illusion on him. Then show him what a true monster looks like.**

I straightened my shoulders, dragging the shadows back inside with a shudder. They settled with a reluctant shrug.

I forced myself to study Anael's face: he had the same cheekbones and chin as me...*as the Matriarch*. His brunet hair, however, he'd inherited from Phoenix.

If I'd been raised by the Legion, held in the Mirror Lodge with nobody but *pets* to torment and Drake as my whipping boy, what the hell would I've been like...?

The Matriarch would've killed Anael simply for being a boy, however, so was Rahab these boys' saviour or their oppressor?

*A choked breath.*

Suddenly, Anael's eyes snapped open, his wings fluttered, and he gasped back to life.

I squealed, clutching Anael closer; my pulse drove a deafening beat, as my fingernails cut into his upper arms. No way in a wizarding white winter was I letting go.

Anael's dazed gaze met mine; my breath hitched at the intense connection. This wasn't indifference or hate. My blood called to his in a genuine sibling bond; it made laughter bubble up my throat, just as tears streaked down my cheeks again.

Anael's brow furrowed, as he swiped a finger beneath my eye. "You would weep for me?"

I wiped my own scarf across the tears, as I grinned. "Yeah, bro. If you're into this resurrection trick, get used to it. That's what it means to have a sister."

Anael cocked his head, before tentatively smiling back. Then he caught Drake's eye and gave a tight nod, which made the tears trembling on Drake's eyelashes fall.

*Drake had known his brother would rise again.*

How many times had Drake been forced to witness Anael's self-murder? How many times had he welcomed him back to life?

"My clever monster." Rahab rapped one hand on the palm of the other, prowling closer; I gripped Anael tighter. "Such a good boy." Anael's smile slipped into something vicious; Rahab faltered. Then Anael's insolent mask was raised again. "Your sweet father hated forced resurrections too, even if, unlike the Phoenixes, he lost no memories."

"Your zombie angels are unnatural parasites who steal *my* life." Anael uncurled from my lap. He had some swag talking back to the bloke who'd just had him kill himself. "Why would you expect them to come back whole?"

"Now, now," Rahab wagged his finger at him, "I can offer either a hug or a spank, don't push me to worse."

"I would advise you not to touch me." Anael's eyes were wild, as he pushed himself into a crouch. I wet my lips, hunkering next to him.

Rahab stared between us; his wings flamed behind him. Then he gritted out, "Brothers in the Legion."

"Bastard, no..." I launched myself at Rahab, but he blasted me back with his invisible magic that had paralysed me before.

Anael caught me, before laying me down; my muscles juddered. "My resurrection trick did not amuse you?" His lips curled up at one side of his mouth, yet his gaze was still dark and savage.

This time, he lounged to his feet, impudently raising an eyebrow at Rahab.

Killing Anael might've taught me a lesson, but it'd also taught Anael one: that he had a sister who loved him. It'd loosened Rahab's hold over him. Maybe each resurrection reset something, until he'd been reconditioned again...

"You both think I'm a harsh father." *Was that wet glistening in Rahab's eyes?* "But you've been sheltered from the harsh truths. There are creatures, realms, and universes, which I hope you never discover. Do you believe I'm doing anything more than preparing you for leadership of our Brotherhood? As if I'd..." Anael broke position, snaking his arms around Rahab's neck and massaging his back; Rahab stiffened, before softening under the caresses. "You are *my* prince, Anael."

"Sorry to hurl all over your bonding moment, but you're the prick who told him to break his own neck." I stared at Rahab. "In the book of Sick Parenting Techniques, that's Number One."

Rahab shrugged. "You're a child of Lucifer who was raised amongst humans. A Glory. I'd be shocked if you *did* understand." I paled, glowering at the way my brother's head rested on Rahab's shoulder. "Have you not learnt, with all your spying and plotting, that there's a faction within the Legion who think a Glory has no place in the Brotherhood? They call you the *False Pretender*."

I forced myself not to glance at either Drake or Mischief: *spying and plotting*? Just how much did Rahab know?

"How amusing," Anael chuckled, "do I get to play with their insides?"

At least when he'd been dead, I hadn't shivered at my brother's *Dexter* vibes

Rahab *tutted*, like Anael was the bright kid in class who'd missed the point of the lesson. "Don't you see it? I raised you to be the Phoenix King: Champion of Light. But your sister stole that from you."

Anael shoved away from Rahab, tremoring. "Is this a new game, father?"

"Game?" Rahab soared into the air, pointing down into the courtyard, where Firebird slumped against the wall. "Only the one we've trained towards your entire life. The battle for your birthright. You always needed a monster who was your equal to prove your worth against and look...I've found you one. If you lose now, your sister will take your place in the story. Rise, my savage prince, do not Fall."

Hell, the crazy bastard had dragged me back here to lay before Anael's feet, in the same way Anael had hunted Tiger. He'd needed me to grow into a worthy opponent for his own prince. Like with everything else on this island, Rahab had created a narrative of opposition: siblings battling to outdo each other: Rising or Falling.

All along, I'd only been needed as my brother's shadow.

I bit hard on my lip, resting my hand reflexively on Star's handle. I'd never be reduced to someone's shadow again.

*Invisible, misfit, freakshow.*

I was the bitch of Utopia; I was the *Silver Queen.*

When Anael twisted to me, his eyes blazing, I didn't need to read his thoughts by telepathy because I was the only thing standing between him and his birthright. Then he'd be *king.*

*A rumbling roar.*

Anael spread out his wings and howled. He rushed towards me, scooping me in his arms, as he tumbled us both over the railing.

I thrashed in his lime-scented hold, but his arms bound me like iron.

*Crunch* — I landed underneath Anael in a feathered heap of bruises and fractured bones.

I hollered, booting my heels in the puddles.

"Unhand my Feathers, brute." Firebird launched himself at Anael: a kid scrabbling on a giant's back.

Anael almost smiled, before he rammed his elbow into Firebird's gut. Then he leapt off me, hauling Firebird by his neck to slam him against the wall.

*Crack* — when Firebird's head smashed on the rock, he whimpered.

"You don't discipline your Undeserving, and your slave dares to address me...?" Anael ran his hand over Firebird's soft head of silver bristles, before whispering, "To think of the pride you used to have in your pretty hair..."

I'd forgotten Anael must've known Nathanael. Yet he still treated him with such savagery, compared to the gentleness of the slap he'd given Tiger.

"Don't worry, you'll always be the fairest of them all." I drew Flight in one hand, who hummed her joy and agreement in the fight, and Star in the other: because a bitch could never have too many blades. "But according to Daddy Nero, only one of us is getting out of here with the title Champion of Light. Would you believe me if I said that I'd learnt my lesson on the hollowness of the Phoenix Crown, so take the bastard?"

Anael's grin was fierce. "Sister, the *Crown* is mine; every world will kneel before me when I rise." *So, that's what it feels like to have every hair on your body stand up at the same time...* "And weapons aren't sporting when I'm unarmed."

"What can I say?" I weaved the blades through the air as I stalked closer. "A bitch fights dirty."

Anael examined his nails, whilst spinning and pinning Firebird to his chest. "Surely not? Pity for you, I play without weapons at all."

The water around me heaved. Distracted, I glanced down, only to attempt — unsuccessfully — to tug away my feet from puddles, which had solidified to rock around my boots. I swayed, struggling not to fall over. Anael raised his eyebrow, jerking his head behind me. I twisted around, just as water gushed from the mouths of the masks at high pressure. I closed my eyes against the assault, which washed away my weapons.

*Water, water, water...*

I held my breath, as my skin felt scoured clean away from my muscles.

At last, the jets petered out, and I gulped for air. When I opened my eyes, I found myself staring directly into my brother's face. I bit back the scream.

I was on Anael's turf: his training ground. He could manipulate the castle like Rahab, and I stood between him and his deepest desire.

I'd mourned his death, when I should've been mourning my own.

Anael still held Firebird by the scruff of the neck.

Firebird studied me; his gaze was desperate and aching with love that I didn't deserve. "Tell me what to do, my Feathers. W-what should I do?"

"Come, give orders to your slave. Are you not a queen?" Anael's mocking smile didn't reach his eyes.

"Stick it," I snarled, before meeting Firebird's lost gaze and saying, softly, "You look to Rebel after—"

"What?" Anael whispered, his fingers tracing my chin, as he tipped it up, bringing our faces together like he was mapping our family similarities, just as I had done. "After you die? After I kill you?" When I shuddered, he pressed even closer. "Yet I find I have no desire to hurt my little sister."

I reached through my Blood Bond to Rebel, pulling his power into me, even as I hunched my shoulders like I was defeated. To my shock, Ash tugged on me as well: an outline of vampiric power. It fed into my own.

"I love you, Anael, messed up as you are," I murmured. "But I promised to save the world, even if that makes me the villain who *does* hurt you."

Anael's confused gaze met mine. Then I seized the back of Anael's neck, before I tore into his throat.

# 23

It was dangerous to shatter someone's glass world, just as I'd brought down my brother's by defeating him in Neptune's Courtyard. The lies, pretenses, and dreams of their lives fell around *both* of you, slicing you to ribbons.

Lime-tinted copper — my brother's stolen blood and birthright — still coated my mouth, as I huddled on my bed in the Mirror Lodge. The violet ball of light crackled, dimming. I licked my tongue along my teeth, seeking out the taste of my brother: the connection. As if I could chase away the look of betrayal in his eyes the moment my blunt canines had worried through his neck.

Rebel and Ash knelt next to me on the covers, dipping silk cloths into a bowl of water and drawing them over my scraped elbows, cleaning out the dirt like they could wash away how I'd violated Anael: the rush of his power between us, whilst I'd sucked his life into mine.

How did Ash stop himself when he drank? How did any vampire become more than a killer? Yet Lucifer had taught them a way.

Hell, kudos to the bastards because in that moment, with no one to hold me back, I'd buzzed on Anael's magic and I'd risen on the magnificent call of Code and Brotherhood: to see the world *kneel*.

Except, I'd fought against both my mum and dad forcing

any world to their knees. I'd never be the same as them: a tyrant.

I'd struggled to let go of Anael, stumbling back. Then *he'd* gracefully fallen to one knee in front of me.

*Why had he done that?*

My fingers bit grooves through the velvet cover. I'd hunted my brother, and by his twisted rules, I'd won. Then why did I have the feeling that Anael had *done a Drake* and thrown the fight?

**Let's throw the *whys* in the trash and ride straight into celebration town.**

**You beat the Butcher, Violet-fire. The crown sits on your queenly head.**

*Then why does my bro's desperation, despair, and darkness shift through me? It's like hot ash in my bastard arteries.*

**You played the game by his hunters' rules.**

**Plus, if you put your mouth on something nasty, you'll catch something, hooker.**

*And you've just upped the Star Wars brother and sister cringe fest.*

**Half-brother.**

*It still counts, and never going there. Look, the Midas Mage bleeds Anael, then resurrects Phoenixes using <u>his</u> stolen life. And I just took Anael's blood like...*

**You were the same?**

*Like I had a right to it.*

**You're wrong, girl. You took a walk on the vampiric side because *you're* the true champion and queen, whereas your *I could ride him into battle* gladiator of a brother was never meant to be more than a prince.**

**Don't you feel it...?**

*You're scaring me and what's worse...you're tempting me.*

**What's to tempt? Your regal arse already knows it's true. The only question is: now you've become the**

203

**highest rank in the Brotherhood, how far will you go to bring this screwed-up cult crashing down?**

**After all, we both know winning a place here as honoured queen is your deepest wish come true...**

I snarled — alive to myself once again — diving off the bed. The water bowl tipped over; rusty coils spilled out, staining the covers. Ash snatched Rebel's hands like he didn't dare let go in case Rebel vanished; purple that deepened to black still noosed Rebel's neck.

Rebel wasn't dressed in the shift anymore, at least. I shuddered to see him wearing his spiked collar and leather coat again. Yet the reality was overwhelming. Rebel was alive, *but I'd almost lost him.*

I shook my fuzzy head, focusing instead on an attempt to remember. *After the heady drink of blood, followed by Anael kneeling...what'd happened...?*

I clenched my fists, but the buzz of borrowed magic and victory had blurred the memory.

When I stared around the chamber, I noticed Firebird's bowed head. He knelt in the far corner next to the mirror; his small body was mottled with bruises. Ceri knelt next to him, rubbing into the skin over his ribs a lavender paste, which I hoped was for healing because my brother had kicked Firebird's arse epic style.

Yet I sprawled on a bed, whilst Firebird knelt on the floor because he was a slave.

*Not in the world of the Silver Queen.*

When I prowled towards Firebird, he quivered, bowing his head lower.

Ceri set aside the bowl of paste, wiping his finger sensually clean of it down the centre of Firebird's curved back; Firebird whimpered. "There's a lush sight: our sexy champion, just like I knew you'd become, see." He kissed the back of Firebird's neck with a tenderness that shook me. Nathanael had been a *Discipliner*: the bastards who'd trained, beaten, and stolen Ceri's wings. Yet Ceri handled Firebird now that he'd been raised a Phoenix, as gently as woven glass...*like his death had absolved him.* Ceri sighed dramatically. "Will my queen still not play with me?"

"I thought we were done playing?" I dropped to my knees in front of Firebird, pulling him onto my lap.

Whoever Firebird been before, now he was mine.

Firebird peeked up at me through thick lashes, resting his head on my shoulder. "I'm sorry, my Feathers," he muttered, "for failing you. Please punish me."

My guts twisted. "You could never fail me." My gaze met with Ceri's; Ceri leant forward, massaging Firebird's shoulder, even as he furrowed his own brow in concern. "You're my fam and..." *Hell, I hoped Ash and Rebel were listening too.* "...that means I'll always have your back. It doesn't matter what you do, I'll love you because that's what fam means."

"I'm getting a piece of this loving." Ceri *whooped*, swooping in to nip light kisses down my neck. I squirmed, shifting Firebird to one side, although he clasped onto my hand. I glimpsed his smirk, however, when Ceri dug his thumbs into my feathers, and my breath hitched. "Do you know the torture you've put me through with only my hand — and this whole fantasy with you in kinky Domme mode — to get me through?"

"We tried that fantasy in the Under World: it sucked." Ash soared across the chamber, enveloping my other side with his wings. "Although, Violet in kinky bondage wear was hot."

Rebel sniggered, diving after Ash to wrap his legs around me from behind, tracing patterns down my back. "Feathers is always hot, so she is." His voice was raspy and sore. "And she's ours."

I shivered, relaxing into their embrace.

*Hot ginger, sweet copper candy, citrus orange, and warm bonfires...*the scents mingled and wove around me, spiralling me higher: building me stronger.

How had I ever survived without my fam? *Please, never let me have to again.*

Except: two scents were missing. Drake's frankincense and Mischief's sweet popcorn.

*Where were my Undeserving?*

"Is there a chore or ritual going on?" I asked, pushing down on the waves of panic.

"Not the most romantic way my love making's been described." Ceri licked my earlobe. "But once I get started, the poets will be lining up to write sonnets to this shag, see."

"Sonnets to your muppet arse." Rebel grinned, nuzzling my back.

Ceri cocked his head; his brunet mane tumbled into his eyes. "It is a fine arse."

"I mean, some big job that Mischief and the Commander are working busy bee at, almost like they're servants..." I gripped Ceri's hair, dragging him up to meet my gaze; his eyes were suddenly serious. "Do you think...?"

"Still you engage in such dishonourable depravity." Och's frosty voice cut across the warm tinglies building in my shoulder blades.

I stared up at Och, who stood with his hands smartly behind him, as sombre as the ghost at the feast. He towered over my vampire and angel fam like I'd broken every taboo.

*Which I had.*

Ceri had instantly drawn back, falling with his forehead to the floor and his wings out; he'd dragged Firebird with him, who'd yelped at the jolt to his ribs. Both quivered before the Discipliner: Firebird's own brother.

I glowered at Och. "Door, meet hand." I *rapped* on the floor. "It's a depraved thing the dishonourable kids invented called *knocking*."

Och drew himself up to his full patrician height. "I wish to speak to you...away from your slaves and creatures."

Ash growled, but I hadn't missed the way Och's gaze flickered to Firebird.

I nodded, disentangling myself from the web of blokes and following Och to the far side of the room. Then I rammed him against the glass.

*Crack* — the back of Och's head smacked against the glass, but he didn't even wince.

I gestured for Rebel and Ash to stay back, even as they

leapt up. Och's inscrutable mask had fractured, and all I saw now was a brother who'd learnt that his younger brother had been raised from the dead.

Rahab's trick had been against Och as much as Mischief.

"Mage Drake hid my brother's death from me," Och whispered, not even attempting to wriggle free of my arm, which pinned him to the glass. "I was unaware Nat...that my brother had been...I was unaware, until Mage Drake told me of his resurrection..." His gaze swung again, as if magnetized, to Firebird's kneeling form. "He doesn't remember me. *He fears me.*"

"Why could that be? The toys, hugs, and fun with Santa Och? Wait, you're more like sticks, slaps, and stolen wings with Grinch Och."

Och clenched his fists. "I never take joy in discipline, but everyone has their place."

"Then your brother's is now as a slave."

Och narrowed his eyes. "I suggest you don't—"

"Treat him like one? What are you going to do? Report me for following Rahab's orders?"

Och hissed, finally shoving me back. "At least, let me say... I wished to say goodbye, but now I realise..." Och's laugh was hollow, "...I'm nothing but a stranger and I'd only scare him."

"Touching, bro. Do you care when the other Phoenixes cry in terror? Or do you flog them, until they know *their place*?" Och turned away his head, but I snatched his chin, twisting him back to face me. He'd wanted to see his brother and the truth: so, *let him bastard face it*. "What about the Broken, when you steal their wings? Or Fynchan? Do you even know his name?"

"I've been blind. Is that what you wish to hear?" Och broke away from me; his cold eyes gleamed in the light. His shoulders shook, as he punched the glass. "I've thought over every possible way to release myself and my brothers since we were brought here. Yet it's never been possible to save all three of us, and I'd never leave the others behind. Mage Drake does that...uses one sibling against the other. Now *you*, our Queen, have my brother as your slave, I can never be disloyal or even hesitate in my duties again, don't you see? What can one blind angel do?"

"Not as much as an army of them." Ceri slunk towards us; he wasn't cowering any longer, but was as untamed as he'd been in the Ghost Caves.

I thrilled at the transformation.

Ceri lounged next to Och: like they were equals. I traced my finger down Ceri's caramel shoulder. "This is my Lion Boy. You know him as a Broken, but in my army, he's a General. And he outranks *you*."

I don't know which of the bloke's eyes widened more. Then Ceri pushed out his chest, standing straighter. He raised his eyebrow at Och.

*And that took bastard courage.*

Och glanced over my shoulder at Firebird, who'd lifted his head to watch us with interest. Then Och gave a curt nod to Ceri. "Then this fool is at your disposal, sir."

Ceri flushed, even as his smile brightened.

Hell, even I hadn't thought we'd get a *sir* out of Och. There was no way to miss the irony of a Head Discipliner who was prepared to take orders from a Broken slave.

"And my other brother?" Och asked, carefully.

My magic snapped in alarm and rage; flames sizzled down my skin in an uncontrollable wave. I gripped Och by the back of his neck, slamming our foreheads together. "The one you've tormented all his life for *not* being blind?"

Och gave a superior smile. "The very one."

When Ceri tapped my shoulder, I flinched. "My cariad, he's...there. *Please, please, please...*"

I glanced away from Och, behind him at the wall. Only the mirror no longer reflected back the chamber but through into my brother's side of the lodge.

I let out a wail, stumbling past Och to hammer my fist *clanging* against the glass.

Mischief knelt in the Looking Glass room, swaying as if he'd been whammied with magic or mind control. Anael stood over him with his fist wrapped around Mischief's long hair.

Mischief had never knelt for me; he'd never have knelt willingly for Anael.

Silver licked out of me on the wings of shadows, pressing against the mirror to break it. My ancient powers roared at the wrongness of Mischief being forced to kneel.

Mischief glanced at the glass wall, biting his lip. He knew I could be watching, and it fractured him, as much as the binding of his magic. *And Anael knew it too* because when my brother had knelt for me in Neptune's Courtyard, it'd been the tribute of a conquered warlord: I should've known he'd find a way to hurt me back.

Anael had learnt his tricks from his daddy Mage. How to Control 101: Hurt someone through the person they love. And Mischief had been the Undeserving who Anael had seen at my side.

Yet what Anael couldn't have known was the way Mischief's magic boiled within me at the sight of Anael's casual dominance, driving my pulse higher, until I pounded the mirror — *clang, clang, clang* — howling.

Voices called out to me; hands tugged at me.

When Anael leant down to bite Mischief's neck, however, silver flared from my fingertips, the wall shattered in a scream of murdered glass, and the Mirror Lodge came tumbling down.

# 24

Two days, twelve hours, and three minutes: that's the longest I'd ever gone missing from Jerusalem's Children Home.

It hadn't been a game but to escape retribution; I'd smashed the glasses of Mr Sandy Hair. But then he'd touched me and not in the caring way; he'd been lucky it'd only been a headbutt. I'd already had enough street smarts, however, to know who'd be believed.

I hadn't even had the words to tell what he'd tried to do to me.

*What he'd done so many nights after that...*

When J had screamed at me to *run and hide*, I'd dashed out into the cold dark and found myself a hidey-hole behind the playground under the cardboard boxes. I'd freaked with the sensation that only now had my life become *real*.

Eventually, the feds, along with Mr Sandy Hair shaking his head in disappointment, had dragged me out of my cardboard home and back to the light of Jerusalem's. I hadn't been fooled by the carers' fake smiles of relief or concern, but their anger had been real.

I'd returned the *bad runaway*. I could never escape from that label again.

Yet I'd learnt my lesson: when you shatter your world, you can't run or hide because the true bad bastards will always find you.

My eyes fluttered open, even as my eyelids were heavy like rising from deep sleep. I shook my head, wetting my lips. A thought skittered, just out of reach, as fire sizzled underneath my skin.

*What the hell happened?*

I forced myself up onto my elbows. Then I stared at the nicks that stung along my forearms and the backs of my hands.

*Shattering glass, as I exploded the wall between my chamber and my brother's...*

I was death. End. Destroyer. And *I* happened.

I sat up, even as my head spun.

**Don't freak out, but we're not in Kansas, Feathery-slayer.**

*You're not making headline news, J.*

**Focus, girl. You're in your brother's land now, and he could either be the Legion's Terminator or your own.**

**Believe me, we want this crazy bitch on our side.**

I clutched my thumping head with a groan, forcing my eyes to focus.

*Hell...*

A forest of twisted iron trees surrounded me; their branches tangled up to a steel sky, which swirled in constant motion. When I shuffled backwards, breathing hard, my hands brushed over the rough ground that was made of coiled rope. I scrambled to my knees, only to slip on the pebbles beside a gushing blood-red stream. Dark shapes darted underneath the water: bronze mechanical fish.

"Isn't it beautiful?" Anael sauntered towards me, as I twisted back to him. He appeared different here: more relaxed, younger, and *wilder*. "A Hidden Land for an Invisible Prince."

"Mischief and the others," I choked out, desperate for the answer, even as I quaked to know it because *what if I'd killed them...*? "Are they waking up somewhere in this fairyland too?"

211

Anael waved a haughty hand. "Your Underserving teleported them away. He tried to take you too, but I wanted to bring you here." His gaze sharpened. "What's your Underserving concealing?"

I launched myself up, grabbing Anael by the throat. He didn't struggle, only studied me curiously. "No one hurts my fam."

"How droll," he raised his eyebrow, "you steal my birthright, take all I've trained for from childhood, including the attention of my father, and destroy my home...even now have your hand around my throat...and yet you claim not to hurt fam." I flinched. "I believe we truly are related."

I snatched my hand away from him, stumbling backwards.

"Yet you wept for me." Anael's eyes darkened; his mouth twisted downwards. "Who would weep for the Butcher?"

"Who would weep for a misfit, runaway, bitch, orphan, freak like me?" I crossed my arms. "Turns out, I'm also epic. Who knew?" When Anael grinned, for the first time, I believed it was genuine. "But I thought Rahab had you locked up in that tower? Looks to me like you've come down with a healthy dose of the free."

Anael's grin died, as he reddened like a kid before a tantrum. "My father believes I'm trapped but then he's...*stupid*."

*Crack.*

I jumped at the thunderclap. The steel sky flashed with lightning, whilst the deep roll of thunder echoed. Twisters roared in howling mouths.

I shivered, as rain pelted from the sky.

*When my brother had a tantrum, he bastard went for it.*

"Can the all-nosey Mage hear you disrespecting him? Because I've already smashed more than a window and—"

"Father only hears what I want him to hear." Anael shrugged one elegant shoulder with a flick of his hair. "Bored now."

The storm shutoff like it'd never been tearing down.

I wrung the water out of my hair. "Why this freakshow world?"

Anael's princely mask dropped, and his gaze became uncertain. He tugged at his bottom lip, before huffing. "Is this not...right?"

I swallowed. This island was all he'd ever known. He had no idea what true trees, fish, or grass were made of, only what he'd heard from the others who were allowed in the world. He might think he was free, but this was no different to hiding in a cardboard box. "Yeah, it's legendary. How'd you magic it up?"

Anael blinked, and a black rainbow burst over the iron forest in sparkling splendour. Now *that* was bitching.

"I've lived my entire life in the Mirror Lodge, do you not think I've learnt how to reshape it like father? This is my playground." Anael slunk to a tree, winding around it.

Slowly, under his caress, the tree reformed into an angel.

I gasped, as the iron angel's eyes blinked open, staring at Anael in adoration; Anael tenderly kissed the angel.

"These are my friends. As I'm a prince, father never let me mix with the riffraff, only Drake. Well, there was also once Barakiel, father's favourite." I stiffened: The Lightning Angel, who'd been imprisoned on Angel world. Anael forced himself to take a deep breath. "Then Barakiel was taken from me. My...love...offended father."

I remembered Barakiel's emaciated form curled in a cell with his wings strapped down to his back...*all because he'd been the prince's lover*. Yet now I understood Drake's caring dedication to the beautiful prisoner; Drake's loyalty to my brother warmed me with a trust that I rarely experienced.

"After father disappeared Barakiel, even though Drake promised to help him if ever he could, it's been...lonely." Anael stroked the iron angel's wing. "But I'm hidden here...safe."

My throat was tight; I couldn't swallow. I rubbed my foot through the rope grass, even as the friction warmed to heat. This was my brother's childhood fairy tale, which he'd escaped to, warped to darkness because he'd known no light. And now

213

it was his adult fantasy. How could I blame him, when in the real world of the Brotherhood he faced the control of Rahab, who made him kill himself to order?

Now there was no hiding, however, and I had to shatter his fairy tale, as I'd shattered his home. *And that shattered me.*

I'd only wanted to keep Anael safe, but that'd been as much my fantasy, as this was his. Anael was as powerful as me: I shouldn't have been protecting him, I should've been enlisting him to fight at my side because I was a leader, and leaders made those choices.

*Crowns are heavier than they bastard look.*

"The thing about being locked in a tower...or hiding here with your statues...is you haven't seen the true suffering of the *riffraff*." I paced closer. "Your daddy dearest chops off wings, flogs bloody, and executes his own boys. Or didn't you know?" I'd noticed Anael's flinch at each word; his gaze was downcast. "Whatever he's told you about Glories and vampires are lies. Your little stunt, tricking me in the glass box...?" He had the grace to pink. "Not bastard cool. But if you turn that cunning to work for my side, we'll free you, and I'm not talking out of your room but off this island."

Anael's head shot up. "You jest."

"Often but not now."

Anael gave a final stroke down the naked side of the iron angel, before it slid back into the form of a tree again. Then Anael prowled towards me in full out regal mode. "You'll free my brother as well, or I'll transform you into a weeping willow to adorn my riverside."

I jolted: it wrenched to hear him call Drake *brother* and with such fierce protectiveness. I craved to hear him call me *sister* in such a way and mean it.

"Wow, look at you, Mr Precise. Have you been hankering after one of those willows, since a mage got all excited about his trip to a gardening centre?" When Anael raised his hand, I backed away. "*Of course* we're freeing the Ice Commander; he's *my* fam too. And I'm not talking running away, but taking down Rahab and liberating the Broken and Phoenixes." When Anael growled, I sighed. "I get you have a problem with the

214

Phoenixes, but they never asked to be dragged back to life. How about you take out that anger on the puppet master, rather than the puppets?"

Anael's expression clouded, before he suddenly disappeared.

I spun in a circle, searching for him. "What's with the Houdini act?"

Then Anael's voice whispered in my ear, "Do you like my trick? Hidden...invisible...that's my power. I taught it to Drake, although he can't use it on himself, only others. I've eavesdropped secrets I never wished to know. You think me in the dark to the cruelty of the Legion? Perhaps, but I've always saved those I can, even if it's as pets."

Anael hadn't been hunting Tiger to abuse, although it was a charade he'd played out for Rahab. He'd been claiming Tiger to *save* him, as Misrule had Harahel in the Under World.

When Anael appeared again by my side as unexpectedly as he'd vanished, I clutched my arms around him, breathing in the aroma of limes. I allowed myself to hug my brother because we'd never been the rivals and enemies Rahab had set us up to be. Instead, we were simply two kids abandoned by our parents and raised apart, who'd found each other at last.

Tentatively, Anael raised his arms to embrace me back. "I rescued the others too, when they transformed in your chambers. Father wanted to experiment on them, but I begged to have them for playmates. He's indulgent of my little *weakness*, as long as it doesn't corrupt his boys."

"You lost me."

"Blaze and Spark. Would you like to see them?"

My grip tightened; my steel claws lengthened, slicing into Anael's back, but still he didn't shove me away. Finally, I managed to force my nails to retract, before spinning around.

Two vampires emerged from the iron forest dressed in olive leather: one athletic and the other graceful. Both had untamed waves of red hair down to their waists (although the graceful vampire's tousled locks were brighter), which

215

matched their pointed ears and lustrous fox tails, which swung side-to-side through their slashed trousers.

My fox brothers — *Blaze and Spark*— had been freed from the witches' magic because I'd killed the Wynter sisters.

*Halflings.*

Black arose in me, thrilling with hallelujahing joy, until I dashed towards the brothers, splashing across the river.

Behind me, Anael hollered, "My sister, the drama queen..."

Then the waters parted with a thrum of magic, which I knew had been Anael's, and I grinned as I jumped to the other side, shaking the crimson droplets from me like a dog.

Blaze caught me around the waist, as Spark settled his head under my chin, peeking up at me. I buried my hand in Spark's hair, which was as silky as his fur had been. When I brushed over his fox ears, he purred.

"Are you trying to drown yourself, Keeper?" Blaze chided. "I know we look like numpties with these tails and such but at least we can fight for you now. We're warriors: we protect what's ours."

*Yeah, there was no doubting this was my fierce Blaze.*

"It's a hot look on you." I tweaked the tip of Blaze's tail.

Blaze smirked. "Aye, but it's *this* idiot who's been pining after you..."

Spark's betrayed gaze shot to his brother. When Blaze pinched Spark's arse, Spark yelped, before settling closer to me. "I'm yours, yours, yours," he whispered against my neck.

I shuddered, stroking Spark's hair. *Mine*, both sides of my nature called, *mine...*

"I swear that I had no idea you were vampires trapped as familiars. I'd have done anything to free you."

Blaze huffed. "Will you take me for daft? Rebel taught you to hunt — *kill* — Fallen like us. And how many fangs hung around your neck in the Under World?"

I flinched, but Spark nipped soft kisses along my jawline. "I believe her." He peeped up at me through long lashes. "She looks out for us, whilst Ash—"

"You wouldn't be about to finish that sentence...? Because otherwise my fangs..." Blaze's canines shot out, as he wrenched

Spark's long neck back by his hair. "...will be taking a trip to your backside."

"...Abandoned us to the witches," Spark hissed, flaring his wings to flames.

*Sizzle* — Blaze's eyes widened, before he stumbled away, wildly patting at his seared skin.

I grinned with the pride of a mum whose geek kid had stood up to his jock older brother. Yet the way Blaze had blushed on *Ash* made me realise that Spark wasn't the only one *pining*: two brothers fighting over their love's honour would be romantic, if we weren't standing in a dark fairy tale about to save the world or get our arses kicked.

I snorted. "Shake hands." Two pairs of eyes blinked at me. "Or hug, manly pat on the back, rousing chorus of "He Ain't Heavy, He's My Brother"..."

Spark glanced from underneath his eyelashes at Blaze, as if regretting his pyro rebellion.

Then Blaze grinned, sweeping his brother up in his arms and crushing him. "Come here, you idiot."

"Sister," at Anael's call, I glanced across the river. Anael stared up at the dimming sky, shaking. "Perhaps I was arrogant to assume *hidden*..."

A freezing wind blasted from skies that rumbled once again with thunder. I drew closer to the lip of the river.

*One — two — three* bubbles broke the surface of the water. Then it erupted in boiling geysers, which blew high into the air. Spark dragged me backwards, away from the edge, as motionless mechanical fish rained down on us like we were living through End of Days. The earth shuddered and shook, whilst the iron trees started to melt and as they did, they changed back into angels, twisting in their agony and *screaming*...

My brother screamed too, falling onto the quaking ground, his arms outstretched to his dissolving angels in comfort or as if he could save them.

His world — fantasy — was being taken apart piece by

piece: the only safety he'd known.

*Because you couldn't hide from the true monsters of the world.*

"Father, I'm sorry," Anael wailed, clutching his fingers through rope grass that was liquifying.

A shadow soared above us in the cracking sky: Rahab in blazing fury. His violet wings lit the black, as he smote Anael's creation as surely as any god.

When Rahab swooped towards me, I shrank back. The true bad bastard had found me. What would he do to me for shattering his perfect prince?

# 25

Paralysed and pinned to the wall of the infamous Reformation Room: it wasn't my Number One favourite way to face the wrath of Rahab. At least Drake hung next to me, equally captive.

I stared around at the room, which freaked out hardened members of the Brotherhood, assessing the shining black floors, ceiling, and walls: a trendy dance club.

*Nope, the Reformation Room wasn't so tough.*

I smiled at Rahab, who lounged against the far wall, scrutinising me, as if I was a beetle who'd somehow transformed into a giant and stomped on his toys. Anael paced across the blackness; his wings flared trails in the dark. "Problem, bro?"

Drake sighed next to me, and Anael paused to cast me a scornful look.

But Rahab only returned my smile. "My Queen, what could the problem be...? Shall I count the ways...?" He tapped his palm, before counting out on his fingers, "One: you broke the Mirror Lodge. It intrigues me how you achieved that. Two: both you and your brother went *missing*." I hadn't expected the tremor in Rahab's voice, or the way he clutched his arms around himself. *He'd been worried?* No one had ever parental panicked over me before, and how could I twinge with guilt over that, even whilst my shoulders ached from being twisted above me?

Anael let out a dismayed gasp, diving to Rahab. He wound his arms around Rahab's neck, petting his wings. "Forgive me..."

"*Shhh*, my darling monster, calm yourself." Rahab kissed the top of Anael's head, before pushing him back. "I've spoilt you. You've forgotten who holds your leash."

Anael froze, before his eyes sparked. "How could I ever forget that, father?"

Rahab's look was dangerously knowing. "Be silent. Now is the time to choose."

He turned Anael by the shoulders towards us.

Anael shrugged, even though I didn't miss the anxious glance he exchanged with Drake. "If I've erred, I should suffer myself."

"You shall; it's why you're making the choice."

Anael glanced helplessly between us.

"I'm an Undeserving now, am I not?" Drake said, meeting Anael's eye. I was desperate for Drake to look at me, but paralysed, he couldn't turn his head. "The queen, however, is important. I propose you choose me, prince, and don't grieve over such a simple judgement."

"*You* are important, cherub," Anael hissed, marching to Drake and caressing his curls. "You're my brother."

"I'm not—"

"You *are* and ever shall be my brother." Anael tightened his hold in Drake's hair. "Plus, you're still recovering from your last trip to this...nightmare."

I glanced around the dark box of the Reformation Room: no whips, chains, brands, thumbscrews, or even fiendishly ticklish feathers...

*Nope, still not getting the horror vibe.*

"Allow me to do this. I can take it for both of you," Drake pleaded.

Anael shook his head. "When will it be enough?" Then he

stepped away, before muttering, "My sister."

Rahab arched a pale brow. "Your sister is the most infuriating Glory ever born...? Your sister is more disobedient than my human apprentices, even though they spend more time fantasizing about witches than learning how to kill them...? Or your sister....?"

"My sister is the one I choose to suffer the Reformation Room," Anael blurted.

Rahab's lips curled into a smile, as he steered Anael closer to me. I shuddered, despite the fact I couldn't force my muscles to *bastard move*. I'd guessed Anael would point the finger at me — he'd been raised with Drake, whereas we were hardly more than strangers still — yet that didn't mean it didn't feel like the torture hadn't already started.

Rahab fixed me with an intent stare, from which I couldn't squirm away. "You, Phoenix Queen, might have become Champion of Light but you haven't yet earnt the right to *rise*. I'd be a bad father if I didn't teach by example what happens to those who hide from me, allowing me to think..." He shook his head. "Anything could've happened to you. Vampires, witches, and supernatural creatures, which you haven't even dreamed are real, await in the dark. You need some time to think about your actions, about who you truly are, and how your brother isn't the only one who's leashed now. Because his blood can take, as well as give life."

Rahab snatched Anael's wing, hauling him until he hung close to me. Anael winced but didn't struggle. He glanced questioningly at Rahab, but Rahab's expression had shuttered. Then a flash of molten gold shot from Rahab's finger, slicing through Anael's wing.

Anael howled. His blood dripped from the gash onto my wing.

My world imploded, and I screamed.

Pain. Excruciating. Black and violet.

My wings, like raw nerve endings, sizzled in an agony that shot down my shoulder blades and spinal column, before blasting back up into my neck. Held motionless, I couldn't even arch, only shriek out the bubbling pain, which crackled along each feather. Dazed, I felt Anael's blood smeared onto my other wing.

Then the world exploded for a second time.

I drifted then, lost in the burning fog. Raised voices broke in waves, lost somewhere in the haze.

*Crack* — the paralysis broke, and my body hunched, dropping to the floor.

White...everything swirled in white-hot mists.

My wings wilted, withering.

*Dying*.

My eyes drooped closed against the brightness and the throbbing in my back. When they slowly opened again, I hissed.

*White*: a migraine-inducing white. Groaning, I raised my hand to shield my eyes as I shifted to sit up.

It was the same shaped room, but it'd transformed to blinding white floors, ceiling, and floor. It seared my retinas and drilled a headache deep within my temples.

And I was alone.

I stumbled to my feet, shaking my head to clear it.

*Silence*.

A quiet so deep you could drown in it.

I swallowed down the childish desire to scream. Then I shrugged my shoulder: something was off. My balance or...

*Where the hell were my wings?*

My panicked gasps sounded deafening in the hush. I twisted around, grasping at my own back like maybe my wings had only shrunk, and I'd be able to find them under my clothes.

*Rahab had taken my wings.*

The loss cut across me as keenly as a death. I sobbed, slamming against the wall.

*Thud* — I thrilled at both the solid sound and pain as my forehead hit the hardness.

A focus that wasn't my wings. Something real in all the white. A way to hurt.

*Thud — thud — thud.*

I collapsed to my knees, but my wings couldn't cradle me because they'd been stolen using my own brother's blood. I rolled onto my side, staring numbly at the blank wall: I'd tried to understand the Broken and now I did. Because it'd happened to me.

Tremors broke out across my skin, and I couldn't stop them, gasping for breath.

*Alone in all this white...*

I closed my eyes to escape it. Suddenly, the scent of cranberries overwhelmed me, as ghost kisses explored my neck. I kicked out, thrashing: *I'd been blinded again...*

Yet when my eyes snapped open, I was back in the white room.

*J, I need your sassy arse right now.*

My own voice in my head thundered loud enough to make me wince.

*Silence.*

*Not the time to play Hide from the Silver Queen. This white hell is driving me A Clockwork Orange psycho.*

*Silence.*

I pushed myself onto my elbows, trembling.

*He took my wings. J? He stole...*

*Silence. Total. Absolute.*

*I need you. Please!*

When J didn't answer, I howled in a savage explosion of frustration and fear, before falling back in shock, as it echoed off each wall, resounding back so loudly that I shoved my

223

hands over my ears and cowered.

*Yeah, I take it back, the Reformation Room was badass.*

Rahab had wanted to give me time alone to *face myself.*

*And that was the thing I feared the most.*

I backed against the wall, hugging my knees. I counted, recited, planned 99 Ways to Skin a Cult Leader. But my mind drifted on the white, lost in the silence. Terrified to close my eyes, I couldn't sleep. Sometimes I paced, just to remind myself the floor was real *and so was I.*

When the black and violet spun in tangled frenzies, I *bam — bam — bam* punched the wall; my knuckles split and spurted scarlet onto the white. Just for a moment, I buzzed on the adrenalin rush and the thrill of the red: it settled my mind back to reality. Then the wall shimmered, smoothing away the scarlet back to white.

I growled, before shuddering at the way the sound broke the silence; I sank down to my knees.

If I was on a leash, then I'd never have freedom, nor would Anael or any of the Brotherhood. A puppet couldn't be a true champion, even if I had influence, status, and a home. Rahab's power could break my fam and me apart, just like he had my brother's hidden world, but if we didn't risk the fight against him, we'd all be the slaves of his cult. Maybe Anael would still choose his father over me, as he had Drake, but he was still worth saving.

*Or I'd bastard die trying.*

I blinked.

A white paper cup of water and bowl of white rice had appeared next to me. I peered at it, before holding my breath and listening for *something*: the *footfalls* of my gaolers, *sniggers, shrieks...*

Yet there was nothing but the same unnatural quiet that was deeper than anything I'd ever experienced.

I peered at the rice. Rahab was going for Pennywise chuckles. I batted the rice over in a hot spray.

Later, I rocked backwards and forwards in front of the mess, biting on my nails. The whorls of rice floated in front of my eyes. Were they forming patterns or was I losing it?

*A low whining.*

Was I making that sound or was the rice?

I shook my head, as the rice paraded like tiny soldiers, before feathering out into six wings.

*It wasn't real.*

The whining broke into a desperate keen.

*Can't think... Can't think... Can't...*

I stared down at my fingers that were sticky with starch, then in shock at the word, which I'd spelled out across the floor in rice:

**SERAPHIM**.

The silver inside me coiled in rapturous delight at the word, whilst my vampiric and angelic sides recoiled in terror. I scrabbled back until I hit the wall; my heartbeat thrashed in my ears.

Facing myself hadn't unleashed me, it'd freed something dangerous.

This time, I risked closing my eyes because continuing to look at that word was worse. When soft hands caressed my cheek, however, I screamed, lashing out with my steel nails.

"I had imagined a *thank you, Mischief* would be beyond my beastly queen, but I'd hoped you wouldn't pull the Wolverine claws," Mischief's murmured snark broke into the silence, making me wince.

I opened my eyes.

Mischief's sparkling hair hung over his cheeks, as he crouched close to me; his tunic had been slashed.

*Hell, I'd done that.*

I retracted my claws, staring at him: silver was my new favourite colour.

*Please, let him be real.*

I tentatively reached out, tracing down his nose, then his

chin, throat, chest...

*He was real.*

I threw myself forward, clutching onto Mischief. Unexpectedly, another set of wings wrapped around me, followed by a fluffy tail...

Tiger purred, rubbing his head against mine.

Mischief sniggered. "The adamantly *not* adorable one was most insistent he helped in your rescue, since you're his *saviour*."

I flinched at the title, but Tiger only hugged me harder: I wasn't complaining.

I fought to keep my voice from wavering but lost the battle, "You have to leave me here. If Rahab—"

"We spoke together in the Ghost Caves, do you remember?" Mischief asked, picking his words with deliberate emphasis.

I nodded.

"You're now in the position we sought. But we cannot wait any longer. You should know Fychan's Ritual of the Wings occurs tomorrow."

I drew back, grimacing at the memory of the child sized guillotine and *thud* of wings as they fell into the basket.

I couldn't stop the tears spilling down my cheeks. "My wings..."

"I know," Mischief murmured; wiping my tears with his thumbs. "I once questioned your dedication to our cause. I should rather have questioned my own fear of Glories, amplified by my time spent in this hateful room." He waved his hand at the walls. "It projects your personal nightmare, just like the Lower Vault traps you with..." He shuddered. "Each angels' time spent here is uniquely horrifying. We can only be plucked apart by our own fears, doubts, and truths." He glanced around, before startling at the word marked out in rice: **SERAPHIM**.

"You know," I whispered, as the silver inside me surged to meet his own, "what it means."

Mischief glanced down, whilst sparks skittered along his skin. "Something more dangerous, deadly, and ancient than even Rahab."

Mischief clasped my hands. I shook at the shock, as our magic met in crashing waves. Tiger clasped around my neck; his ears tickled my throat.

Then everything broke from white to silver, and the Reformation Room vanished.

# 26

I stared at the deep well that led down to Harahel's Oubliette, which heaved with eel-like coral reef snakes. My guts squirmed, as much as the mass of writhing snakes. I glanced out of the corner of my eye at Mischief: he'd paled, leaning back as far as he could against the corridor's dank wall. Here was Mischief's personal nightmare, and after his punishment trapped in the Lower Vault, I didn't blame his hesitation.

To break this fear would be to break Rahab's hold.

"Why can't you simply do your teleport thing to Harahel?" I asked.

Mischief rolled his eyes. "I may not appear to wear a Compulsion Collar, but Mage Drake controls me just the same. He'd sense the use of my power, which would rather derail my plan to rescue Harahel now that I have you. Although the Mage imagines he watches every movement within his castle, however, he misses a magician's sleight of hand; Rebel is providing that distraction."

Still Mischief didn't edge any closer to the well.

Tiger glanced between us, before waggling his eyebrows. "Fun."

Then he lifted his tail and dived into the water.

Mischief gasped, rushing to the crumbling brick. He leaned over, shooting wisps of light down into the well, as if Tiger had only been pranking and would still be clinging by his claws to the sides.

Mischief snarled, banging the well in a shower of sparks.

*Outraged hissing.*

"Silence foul reptiles!" Mischief howled, stumbling back.

I raised an eyebrow. "Is this Harahel-sized tantrum because of the word I scrawled in rice?"

Mischief became motionless, trembling. "As if a thoughtless self-centred Glory—"

"Hold the flaying, I'm skinned already. Since when was I a *Glory* to you? You're my fam: *mine*."

Mischief crowded me against the wall, pressing his hands either side of my head, whilst his wings caught us in a violet cocoon. "I am *not* yours: we belong to each other." The breath caught in my chest at his sudden closeness; his lips ghosted against mine. "You raised my brother, but you brought me to life." His hair swept soft against my cheeks, as I lost myself in the magic explosion of his kiss: despair and passion, crackling with popcorn sweetness. My silver rose, spiralling with his in sparking crescendo. Until he drew back, just enough to whisper, "I'm the reason Nathanael died to be resurrected a slave, and Och was forced to become a Discipliner."

When I shook my head, Mischief hushed me gently.

"I'm their half-brother only and for my differences, my mother despised me. Her cruelty was such..." Mischief swallowed, looking down; I stroked his wing. "...She never touched my brothers, only me because my magic was *wrong*. My father attempted to shield me, but what could a Marked Wing do? You know the control a Glory holds, after all, you've Marked a Wing yourself." I flinched, but Mischief met my gaze challengingly.

"I didn't know..."

"I rather think you did. It's enjoyable to be the one with the power. Don't you relish your dominance over Rebel?"

"Only when he's willing."

Mischief stared at me searchingly, before nodding. "Perhaps, now." He shrugged, although his muscles were so stiff, he vibrated. "Do you know what happens when no one teaches you to control your magic? You see, I do. I teleported my father to London by mistake, where he was captured by the Pure." He leaned closer; his lips touched mine. "Did I ever thank you for the opportunity to assassinate their leader?" I shrank back, remembering Mischief's wild transformation into killer unicorn mode and his decapitation of the Pure's leader, Stephanie. "Here comes the reason I don't trust Glories, please do tell me that I'm overreacting: my mother petitioned for my execution. Pray, have a guess who the Matriarch decided would be added to her harem of Marked Poly-Wings as punishment?"

I grasped Mischief's neck, as if I could erase even the thought of him bearing my mum's Mark there, like Drake did. Hell, no wonder my Fae Angel freaked out about Glories...and me. And I'd asked him to *trust me*...?

Mischief's expression gentled, as he licked along the seam of my lips. "Mage Drake truly did save me. The price, however, was my two brothers. Please don't waste your rage on either one of them: they lost both parents, home, and freedom because of me. Yet they've always shown me love, despite what I am."

I frowned. "An Undeserving?"

Mischief stretched out his silvery-violet wings, just as his eyes gleamed to silver. "A Child of the Seraphim."

I gasped, reaching out to touch Mischief's cheek, but he backed away. Twisting to the well, he winked at me over his shoulder. "Why let the adorable fleabag have all the fun?"

Then he jumped headfirst down the well and into the snakes.

*Bastard dramatics...*

I edged closer to the well.

*My turn...*

I took a deep breath, before swinging myself over and into the black.

*Splash.*

The water hit me like a slap. I cringed at the brush of snakes against my face; coils wrapped around my legs, as I booted out, kicking further into the dark. I clenched my jaw against the pinprick smart of snake bites along my back and hands, feeling for the brick sides of the tunnel.

My lungs ached, struggling for air. My legs flailed. Then one final kick and I was out of the water, taking desperate gasps.

I hauled myself, shivering and dripping, onto the tiny grated ledge. Then I opened my eyes, only for them to widen at the Drama of the Week scene in the murk.

Tiger had Harahel pinned against the wall; Tiger's fangs were out, as he sniffed up and down Harahel's neck. Harahel's head was turned away; his arms were crossed against the attack, even if his gauntness made clear he couldn't defend it. Mischief lounged next to them, examining his nails, although his coiled litheness growled that he was ready to leap between them the moment Tiger moved to sink in his fangs.

Mischief might've let me take the lead in Castle Drake but in the Under World, he'd helped and plotted with Harahel, whilst I'd still been ripping out fangs for my leather necklace in the Cage. No way he'd let Harahel be hurt.

*I trusted Mischief to protect my fam like his own.*

Mischief raised an eyebrow. "It appears whilst we were chatting, our friends discovered that they were both Misrule's Blood Lovers." His lips pursed, before he singsonged, "*Kitties don't like to share.*"

Tiger hissed, jamming his tail like a finger against Harahel's chest. "You're not wanted. Why would *my* Misrule...?" Tiger sniffed Harahel's sweet apple aroma again; tears trembled on his cheeks. "How did you trick him, angel?"

"Misrule never forgot you." Harahel curled his hand around Tiger's waist.

"He replaced me with an angel," Tiger spat, scratching his

231

claws down Harahel's wings. I leapt up from my crouch, but Mischief held out his hand, holding me back. I gritted my teeth. "By the blood, trapped in that hell, I knew Misrule was looking for me because he was *my bonded*. He'd never just leave me there. He'd rescue me like your saviour liberated all of us." He stole a look at me. "And now she liberates you..." He shook Harahel. "Isn't that love?"

"Hey, Misrule loves you," Harahel murmured. "But you were missing, and he was alone."

Tiger deflated, slumping against Harahel; his forehead rested against Harahel's shoulder, as he now petted the wings that he'd gashed. "Selfish of me," he muttered, "to wish to be loved, as I love."

When I sidled closer, rubbing Harahel's shoulder, he smiled. "Rahab's big mistake: to think my legendary fam could ever be forgotten."

Harahel's smile widened. "At first, I reckoned I'd be buried under here forever, like the Bones."

"Your grin is creepily inappropriate, bro."

Harahel shrugged, transferring a now snuggling Tiger to one arm. "Then I remembered that almost my entire rebel gang was up there..." He smirked at Mischief. "...and I could be your pretty Trojan Horse with added BOOM!"

Mischief straightened. "Oh, I know now why Rebel wets his little panties whenever you enter the room."

Harahel flushed. "So, wiping *that* image from my mind...wiping images is where we start with your Legion. Your Phoenix Mage has built his power on a myth. *Himself*. The Gateways in my library groaned with his Legion's propaganda."

*The Mage's Challenge, Champion of Light, and Lazarus Rising...* I nodded: Rahab had been hyping me in order to blast my brother into the storybooks, except he hadn't bet on the power of sibling love.

*And wasn't that the true story?*

"Angel World both loathes and fears the Brotherhood." Mischief cocked his head. "But Mage Drake has always held too much power to be brought down, with his public decisions over the Broken and his Phoenix army."

"Then we kick his reputation's arse in a public duel." I glanced between them, as silver twined with shadows in a silky thrill at the thought of finally fighting Rahab. "I'm a part of his puppet play now: his queen and champion. He's set himself up for his own bastard fall. He turns his boys against each other in confessions, gauntlets, and duels... Let's see how he enjoys the disgrace."

Harahel's eyes gleamed. "So, he's into the divide and conquer game? Then we take out his points of power. See how loyal his followers are then."

I grinned, gripping Harahel's brunet curls, whilst I kissed him. "Hell, I missed you."

He sniggered. "I am awesome."

"Do you still have that freaky Breathing Underwater power that you stole from the witches?"

Harahel nodded. "We didn't make the return trip, so let's just say I managed to put it on ice."

Mischief *tutted*. "My, and you once threatened to spank me for attempting to steal your books..."

Harahel slipped into stern face, and Mischief paled. "*Attempting?*"

Mischief shuffled his feet. "What a shame we're in a life or death situation, else I'd love to explore my indiscretions. As it is... Why hasn't your beloved Misrule been hammering down these walls to rescue you?"

Harahel's gaze hardened. "I broke his rules to save the queen." He hunched his shoulders like a kid caught after curfew. "OK, so remember the Fallen who had a thing for me and followed me into battle? Colour me cynical, but they'd have betrayed me to save their own skins as soon as they swam back to the Under World. Misrule's not getting his crusade on because he knows better than to rush in without a signal from me, which I can give..." He patted Mischief's shoulder. "...as soon as I reach the ocean."

I grinned. "Then let's throw this catch back in."

233

I snatched Harahel's knee, attempting to overbalance him into the water; he laughed as he hopped.

"*By the light, you've broken the Code, as well as proven yourself unworthy of our sacred Brotherhood.*"

I backed away, gripping at my head, as Kunel's voice thundered. "Was it just me that tuned into Brainwash FM?"

Mischief's lips pinched into a thin line. "Mage Drake?"

"The First Reformer, and it sounds like I've been found guilty, *before* the trial."

"*Swim*: use the spell and take the secret tunnels that I taught you." Mischief thrust Tiger and Harahel into the water. "Find Ceri, you understand, cat?"

"I'm not the one incapable of remembering another's true species, *angel*." Tiger snatched Harahel by the hand and yanked him, protesting under the water.

"What the hell...?"

Mischief gripped my shoulder. "You'll not be alone in this, sailor doll. If you wish it, you shall never be alone again."

My breath hitched.

Why was Mischief offering all I'd ever wanted, just when my heart was pounding with enough fear to tell me I was screwed?

"*Phoenix knows, you've refused to confess or reform. You bring our whole order into disrepute by your degenerate actions. You won't cause us to rise but Fall,*" Kunel's voice continued to recite my crimes.

I grimaced. "But I have crazy mojo when I play "Overwatch"."

Kunel faltered, before ending with a flourish, "*You are the False Pretender. And we will carry out our duty to wipe your stain from the Legion.*"

Stain wiping not sounding good...

"Shall I assume sunshine and rainbows by your snort of derision or...?" Mischief rested his head on mine.

"Shadows," I whispered, as a black wave crept up from the waters. "Shadows and nightmares."

Mischief and I recoiled as far as we could on the grilled ledge, but Kunel's power — *living fear* — slithered in a

234

horrifying mass towards us.

My pulse pounded; my palms sweated. My breath rasped too loudly in the Oubliette. I couldn't tell if the tremoring was Mischief or me. When the first nightmare shadows touched my feet, before creeping up my leg, I cringed, squeezing shut my eyes. Dizzy, I clutched at Mischief, before I sank into the terror.

# 27

My head bobbed above the seagrass and algae skin of the pool in the cavern underneath the Invisible Bridge. Beneath the briny seawater that stung my nostrils and lips, jewelled fish brushed against my hands. I shivered, drawing my legs closer, as I doggy paddled. When sea snakes slithered across the unnatural emerald glow of the pool's surface, Mischief shuddered, swimming closer to wrap his wings around me.

Like two sinners at a freaky baptism waiting to be reborn into the light, Mischief and I floated in the centre of the pool, whilst black shadowed nightmares crouched on the filthy walls of the cave and a small congregation of adult mages watched us from the edge.

I narrowed my eyes at Kunel, who headed the smug Avengers: a zealous Captain America. "Get with the smiting; we're freezing our balls off."

*Horrified gasps.*

Mischief sniggered; his sparkling seaweed hair trailed around him. "And the famous last words of the Phoenix Queen were truly unexpected..."

I grinned, despite the twist of fear, which was still twining in my guts from Kunel's shadows and the knowledge that this False Pretender Faction didn't intend my baptism but my funeral. "Never be predictable."

"Also excellent last words." Mischief kissed the tip of my nose. "As are... *I love you, my maddening beast.*"

I blinked. "Could you try it again without the *maddening beast* part?"

"In the name of the Brotherhood," Kunel pointed at me with his brawny hand, "even now you mock our Code. I've tried to reform and purge you through both love and fear. But a Glory should never have been allowed into the ranks of our Legion. You, False Pretender, contaminate us with your—"

"*Blah, blah,* womanly bits, *blah, blah,* mansplaining, *blah, blah,* secret jealousy because my magic is stronger than your magic."

"By the Phoenix, your brother is our prince and he'll Lazarus lead us to wipe out the Fallen, the Children of the Fallen, and every Addict. Confess before we drown you like witches." Kunel soared into the air in golden glory.

*Unworthy, unworthy, unworthy.*

I flinched at the mages' chant, as they rose behind their leader. Except, I wasn't Drake being chastised after my forced confession. There'd been a time that Kunel's smile or frown could've made or broken me.

*But not now.*

*Unworthy?* I was the Bitch of Utopia. *What the hell did I care about <u>worthy</u>?*

"I'm an angel, vampire, monster and mage, but I'm not a witch. Even lost in your Crusader Land, gank a bitch for the right reason."

Kunel swooped closer.

**Don't go poking the fanatics, they're not messing around. If you swim, you're a witch, and if you drown...you're still a witch. You've been tried, sentenced, and this is your execution.**

*Then help me battle Kunel's terror shadows.*

**The Malfoy jackass can shape living nightmares. No one but the Mage can control his ass; it's why he's First Reformer.**

*Then where's Rahab?*

**Isn't that an interesting question...?**

Both vampiric and angelic sides seethed within me, contained by Kunel's terrors and his faction. Mischief settled closer against me.

"Your deaths shall honour the memory of Mage Drake's original abandonment." Kunel's eyes flashed with fervour. "Instead of the water taking his life, it shall take yours."

*Unworthy, unworthy, unworthy.*

I slapped the surface of the pool, catching my palm on a spiked starfish. I hissed at the sharp gash.

Mischief *tutted*, raising an eyebrow. "*Now* is the time you choose to throw a tantrum...?"

"Your deaths...? As in multiple?" I snarled up at Kunel.

Kunel's smile broadened. "The day will never be born that your Underserving rises. His magic is too...*feminine.*"

Mischief stiffened next to me, becoming dangerously still. I winced, glaring at Kunel. The bastard understood nothing about the ancient power of the silver, but he'd already judged it...and Mischief.

*How had Mischief lived with this prejudice all his life?*

"Mischief's in charge of the other Underserving like a butler or steward: you need him," I argued.

"A charming view of my importance," Mischief muttered.

Kunel jutted out his chin. "He dares to declare his *love* for a Lazarus Mage. Such an unfit wretch has no right to love."

*Jeers and hoots.*

Still Mischief held himself motionless in the water like a crocodile, only moving enough to stop himself sinking.

Kunel's nostrils flared, as he rested his feet on our heads, ready to push us under. "On the light itself, this Undeserving won't even kneel before you. Do you think it's gone unnoticed? His disobedience and disrespect?"

I winced, as Kunel's toes dug into my scalp. "He's a moody, scheming rebel, with a streak of dry wit and sass. He's also my fam, equal, and never has to bastard kneel for me. And if these are my last words: *I love him too.*"

Mischief drew in his breath; he reached out to touch my cheek, like he was memorising every detail.

Kunel huffed. "He's no better than a Glory with his womanly weak magic. Only when you're both dead, shall our Legion be able to *rise.*"

Mischief flinched, before his eyes gleamed and his expression darkened. Finally, he wrapped his wings tighter around me, as he raised one hand out of the water: silver danced in fairy twinkles on the tips of his fingers. "Perhaps I missed the part where Glories are weak, since they've dominated Angel World?" He tilted his head. "But then, my own magic *is* little more than pretty lights and tricks."

*Chuckles and catcalls.*

The silver inside me roared in winding ribbons, pulled out to Mischief's. His sparkles became spinning discs — *one, two, three* — that howled.

"What is the meaning of this outrage?" Kunel bellowed, shoving our heads under the water.

I spluttered, gagging on brackish mouthfuls. My pulse pounded, whilst living nightmares darkened the green to black, darting through the murk towards us.

Silver burst around me, dragging me to the surface, even as the black shrieked and burnt, shrivelling away. Blinded by the sizzling light, I flailed, until cool arms looped around me, hauling me to the edge of the pool.

*Screams and wails.*

239

Spinning discs, grown to giant size, blazed through the cavern, *smiting* the mages' heads from their shoulders, and for once, *I* hadn't been the one to go nuclear. Mischief stood on the fringe of the pool, dripping with seaweed and salt water: a pissed off Poseidon. Amidst the charred carnage, he vibrated with the unleashing of his true magic.

*Hell, he truly was my equal.*

He stalked to Kunel — who'd tormented Drake and me in the Initiation, breaking apprentices like Mischief's brother, Nathanael, to become mages and brainwash them into the Brotherhood — but now cowered against the cavern's wall. "Tell me again, pray, how *weak* is my *womanly* magic?"

Mischief casually spun another disc on the palm of his hand.

Kunel glowered up at him, before clawing at the wall, as he recoiled from the disc.

Then Mischief's expression hardened. "On second thoughts, don't."

He blasted his magic at Kunel, slicing his head from his shoulders.

I started, even as my magic sang rejoicing. Kunel had wanted a sacrifice to honour Rahab in this *place of his abandonment*. I gazed around at the blackened walls and feathered corpses.

*Be careful what you wish for.*

I reached for Mischief, but he backed away from me; his gaze was downcast. I frowned, trying again, but he dodged back.

"I apologise," he whispered.

"What for? Saving our arses?"

"I preach to you about controlling the beast, then I..." He waved at Kunel's headless body. "My magic is as terrible as your own."

"The Seraphim fruity extra?"

Mischief arched his brow. "You have no idea what that means or how terrible it can be."

"Then stop with the mysterious and tell me."

Mischief blew out his breath, fighting for control. *How bad was it to be fathered by one of those things?* "Our world believes it has a thousand reasons to subjugate descendants of the Seraphim, even though most inherit little of their magic, because the Seraphim are disgraced. The highest ranking and most powerful of angels, the Seraphim rejected their role to elevate themselves to *gods*."

I blinked. "It sounded like you just said you're a child of a god...? And I've been channelling—"

Mischief waved his hand testily. "Quite. I inherited the *weak* magic so mocked by our now so *dead* First Reformer from my true father."

"You better not bastard say Darth Vader."

"Close." Mischief hesitated, before finally answering, "His name is Jahael. I've spent a lifetime caught between wishing I was with him so he could teach me to control my magic — free me — and wishing just as vehemently that I'm never captured by him."

I grasped Mischief's hands, and this time he didn't pull away. "Are we talking the Odin of gods?"

**That's dangerous talk.**

**Seraphim are burning, glorious, terrifying angels with asses that are quite literally for the gods.**

**Not one-eyed Norse fashion victims.**

*What's got your panties in a twist?*

*More to the point, why didn't you tell me about these psycho...?*

**Their godly asses are in an entirely different realm. The only way that they could drag you to them, would be if your blood mixed with that of the Emperor's son: The Archduke.**

*There's a bastard Archduke...?*

When Mischief laughed, high and bright, I started.

"How very much I wish Jahael was listening. He's renowned for his vanity, as well as his ruthlessness. When I was tiny, my mother would call me nothing but *Sly Imp*." I squeezed Mischief's hand because hell if I didn't know how

241

that felt: growing up with people who couldn't understand the powers inside you. "The horror when she realised she should've been calling me *Sly God* all along."

"Then why doesn't this *Sly God* and *Silver Queen* rebel together and show the Brotherhood's father how high we can rise?"

Mischief squeezed my hand back, as his grin met mine.

Tonight, I'd duel Rahab to save Fynchan's wings, stop the genocide of the vampires, and free every angel under the control of the Legion of the Phoenix. I'd suffered through the Initiation and Mage's Challenge, so that I'd have the chance to shatter Rahab's false world, just as he'd melted Anael's. Yet once it started, there'd be no way out: this battle would be to the death.

# 28

The moon's ghost light gleamed off the gold wings of the Phoenixes who knelt before the mages, the bronze silk trousers of the anxiously shuffling apprentices, and the bronze cannon in the centre of the Bailey.

I patted the cannon's muzzle, before grinning at Och.

*Time to summon the jinn to the end of the story.*

Och gave me a soldierly nod, which might as well have been a salute. "Attention, Brothers of the Legion! Your Champion and Phoenix Queen..." he hesitated, before adding, "...as well as my brother, were attacked tonight by traitors within our ranks."

*Shocked gasps and whispers.*

I noted the mages who straightened, resting their hands on their Phoenixes' shoulders in attack mode. The apprentices, no longer under the watchful eye of the First Reformer, nudged each other and glanced around.

"Yet they're here to free us! Our true saviours." Och's haunted gaze met mine, as he dropped to one knee, bowing his head.

I swallowed at the sudden silence.

Then the apprentices *whooped*, bounced on their toes, or swept each other around like kids at a Bieber concert.

*Lazarus rises! Rises! Rises! And we will rise!*

I shook, when they chanted in ecstatic unison; they'd been whipped up by our counter propaganda, and now I had to whip Rahab's arse to create the real hope.

"Time to go BOOM!" I muttered to Och.

Och sprang up, aiming the cannon into the night sky and pulling out the rope on the cannon's friction primer.

*Bang.*

I jumped; my ears rang, as I choked on the smoke. The cannon's blast echoed around the walls of the castle, shocking the apprentices to silence. The mages were caught between crouching in battle stance and staring at their leader — Och — and wondering if they should be kneeling before me too.

**You're taking on the Big Daddy of the wizarding world, Feathery-fairy.**

*I've already schooled my own dad, so I'm up for schooling my false dad. This whole island's a fantasy, and I'm pulling it down.*

I glanced over my shoulder at my ragtag army, rebel fighters, and fam: two Halflings, a Phoenix, a Marked Wing, an Addict, a vampire, a Child of the Seraphim, and my monstrous brother.

*Hell, I loved them.*

I sauntered across the Bailey because whilst I still had life on this island of death and resurrection, I'd have swag.

Rebel caught me around the waist. He feathered kisses across my cheeks. "Kick the muppet's arse," he murmured. "Then by all the blessed saints, come back into the light with me."

I shuddered, gripping hard onto his arms. "Always."

I yelped as I was swung around: feathers, tails, and kisses. Candy sweetness, citrus orange, and rich frankincense...

I sank into my fam's embraces, until I *yipped* at a sudden nip.

Ash sucked at my lower lip, as his eyes sparked charcoal. "We have your back, Violet. Don't go all Saruman vs Gandalf on us. Danger, no retreat, need help...? You call."

"I just scream out *Violetbusters* in the place of *ghosts*?"

Ash nibbled harder on my lip, before releasing it again. "How about hollering *fam*? You taught it to my sisters and maybe you weren't wrong." I flushed, gaping at him because I was the reason his sisters had been turned to ash by Lucifer's Light. Yet his gaze was serious, before he turned me firmly back to the Bailey. "We're not perfect but we are family. Mage Drake *thinks* he has the same with his boys. Let's show him that he's wrong."

When Ash shoved me forward, Anael and Drake caught me on either side, clasping my hands.

Then the Bailey lurched, before rain drove down in a blustery storm. The stinging raindrops scoured my face; I battled to keep my eyes open against the torrent. The Brotherhood hollered and howled, cowering back against the walls.

*Summoned by the cannon, daddy was home and he was pissed...*

Rahab soared down in a crackling bubble of golden fire, which hissed along his vast wings and veiled him from the downpour; his shirt swung open revealing his chest that glowed as emerald as the shirt itself.

I'd thought he looked like a god before: *I'd been wrong*.

Hovering above the cobbles, which streamed now with rivulets, he scanned across the storm-swept Bailey, then over his two sons, before settling his glare on me. "*I set you a hard lesson in the Reformation Room: to face yourself.*" Even Rahab's telepathic voice seethed. "*Yet here you are, as rebellious as—*"

"Kunel and his merry band? Don't even pull the innocent face. You *let* them drown rat us...." I shielded my head with my arms against the pounding rain.

Rahab hovered closer, answering out loud this time. "I allowed them to *try*. A father was never so proud of a child's victory."

I gritted my teeth, even as I couldn't help the instinctive thrill at his *pride*. When Drake stiffened, I rubbed my thumb soothingly across the back of his hand. When had Rahab ever told Drake that he was *proud* of *his* victories? "You're not my dad. Are you still confused on this? Do I need to post it on my social media status? Write an angsty rap? Hang it on a banner around the castle?"

When the rain drummed down even harder from the star sharp sky, I flinched.

Rahab raised one hand, gesturing to his sons to walk to him. "Hush, my Queen. You merely have to believe it yourself."

My shoulders slumped. Why was this suddenly so difficult? I understood why Rahab had created this *refuge*: the craving to be in control and *safe*. Had I any right to destroy his world? To take this shelter away from the rest of the boys of the Legion...?

*Splash — crack. Splash — crack.*

I winced, as Drake and Anael's kneecaps hit the puddled floor.

In a flurry of *splashes*, followed by the gasps of the Legion, my fam knelt behind me. I peeked around: only Mischief stood proudly to the side with his hands clasped behind his back.

Rahab's hand still hung in the air like the awkward guest at the party. I glanced around at our audience: The Brotherhood were hooked.

Rahab's arm shook, as he slowly lowered it. "You would choose *her*?" The golden bubble spat in furious waves; his emerald skin vibrated even brighter. "You belong to me. You will obey. *I am your father.*"

"And I am nothing but a *disappointment*, am I not?" Drake shrugged his slender shoulders. "Yet extraordinary as it may seem to you, the queen loves me." His neck pinked, blushing down to his chest. "Yet even if she viewed me as no more than a sacrifice or a pawn, I'd still kneel for her and the prince."

Anael smiled, leaning forward to push a wet curl behind Drake's ear. "And I am your beautiful leashed monster, father. Would you ever have freed me? But now I have a sister to play with me instead."

Rahab roared, shooting out a golden whip, which lassoed Mischief around his neck. I dived forward, but Mischief held out his hand, holding me back, whilst Rahab reeled him closer.

"I should burn off Zophia's scheming head." I grimaced at the fizzing burn, as Mischief's neck blistered. "My sons kneel for you, but this Undeserving traitor imagines himself too important? Shall he stay on his feet because he readies himself to fetch us drinks or scrub the floor?"

Mischief glanced at Ceri and Tiger, who were ushering in the tiny bundles of Broken kids like we'd planned; Fynchan gripped Ceri's hand. I swallowed hard: Fynchan still had his small — beautiful — wings. Ceri's courage had brought me to the Broken Nursery, and everything I'd suffered and risked afterwards would be worth it if those kids kept their wings.

The Undeserving clasped the youngest Broken in their arms, as they trembled to see Rahab disciplining one of their own.

I grinned: *it'd blow their minds when they saw what happened next.*

Mischief panted, but his smile was shark-like. "I rather thought I'd fight."

Silver struck in spinning discs from Mischief's palms, slicing through the gold, before he twirled free from Rahab, firing at him.

I'd never even seen Rahab approach gaping before, but his eyes widened, as too shocked to even do more than raise his forearms against the blast, the silver exploded him backwards into a charred pile.

*Silence, apart from the drumming of the rain.*

Drake and Anael nodded at each other, before prowling across the Bailey.

Drake in maximum Commander mode, strode in front of the young apprentices, taking control of them in their confusion.

Anael sauntered to the mages, slipping between them, whispering threats and promises that had them paling and falling in behind him.

*Yeah, plausible deniability had its place with my brother.*

Then I screamed, juddering with the pain of an invisible shock, which held me paralysed. My pulse thundered, as Rahab dragged himself up: soaking, blackened, and *furious*.

Rahab shook with rage and humiliation. "Enough! Zophia, you are truly a *sly traitor*." Mischief vibrated with a fury as great as Rahab's at the insult. "Do you imagine hiding your talents all these years somehow makes you less unworthy? Fight it all you like, but we both know *what you've done*." He stared around wildly, suddenly childlike in his devastation. "I saved you."

"And you condemned and enslaved my brothers," Mischief snarled. "Excuse me, what am I thinking, you've enslaved our entire race through *fear*, where the only safety is your Legion. Your hope is false." He glanced across at the other Undeserving. "And tonight, our hope shall be real."

Rahab smoothed down his singed shirt. "The moment you disobeyed the Code by attacking me here in the Bailey, you had no hope."

Sentences that rate high on the *Bad Guys Freak You Out with One Line List*.

Mischief shook his head. "We're merely playing by *your* rules: this is a Battle of the Bailey."

Rahab's wings blazed, as he charged at Mischief.

Mischief twisted to the side, but Rahab side swept his legs out from underneath him; Mischief landed hard on the streaming cobbles.

Rain drove into my eyes, as I battled against the paralysis. Rebel and Ash hung at my shoulders, waiting for the signal to dive in and help, but this was about the *story*: breaking Rahab's brainwashed narrative of the Phoenix. I'd started this battle with Mischief, and we needed to end it together, even if the silver inside me screamed at the *crunch* of shattered bones, as Rahab stomped on Mischief's ankle. Mischief hollered, hauling himself away along the cobbles, but Rahab grabbed him by the scruff of the neck, pinning him facedown like he intended to drown him in the puddles.

"For the love of Christ, *please...*" Rebel shifted from foot to foot; his wings beat violently.

Even though I couldn't move, I shot *restraint* through both Mark and Bond, holding Rebel back. I hated to leash Rebel, as Rahab had my brother. Yet Rebel traced his pinkie over mine in understanding.

Mischief gasped, before Rahab shoved his head back into the water. Suddenly, I caught sight of Och marching towards them with a steely resolve: I'd been able to stop Rebel but I couldn't control Mischief's brother. Maybe after all these years, Och's eyes had been fully opened, and now he wouldn't stand by and watch his brother's abuse.

*Even if it destroyed our chance to take down Rabab.*

I clenched my jaw, wrestling against the paralysis, as a migraine pounded behind my eyes. Shadows were building inside me in tarry waves.

Mischief's legs kicked against the cobbles, as Rahab drowned him.

Then the roof of the castle darkened with crawling creatures like feathery winged bats, and the vampires attacked.

# 29

I shook as I struggled against the paralysis pinning me, whilst the vampire army swooped in grey tides from the roof into the Bailey.

Firebird snarled at the attackers, slinking to kneel in front of me. He blinked up at me uncertainly through the tempest. Blaze and Spark stalked either side of Rebel protectively with a growl.

Yet the two leaders of the Under World, Harahel and the Master of Misrule, strolled at the head of their army not like conquerors — as the Glories had blasted into the Under World — but as liberators. Their arms were slung around each other's waists, and Misrule swung his bone topped cane.

Like a punk god, Misrule swaggered in a PVC catsuit, with bones threaded through his afro. His anarchy scented the air; black plumes of chaos bled through the ordered ranks of the Legion, breaking down a society that was based on codes, regimented chivalry, and shame.

I thrilled inside, as my vampiric side roared, inflaming shadows and silver on a wave of violet, until I drowned in the frenzy.

Tiger rushed forward, leaping onto Misrule and winding his legs around his waist. Misrule ran his hands over Tiger's ears, then he was kissing them and dragging Harahel closer, until all three were caught in the safety of his wings.

"You see, my boys, why we train? The Fallen attack even our home." Rahab raised Mischief's head from the puddle; Mischief took one desperate gasp for air, before Rahab plunged him back under. "Defend the Legion!"

*Whispers, shuffled feet, and ruffled wings.*

Anael raised his hand with a smirk. "Father, bad boy." Rahab flinched like he'd been struck. "Don't make a fuss. They never truly were *your* boys."

Rahab paled, clenching his fists.

Tiger turned back to the Broken kids, bending down to pick up Fynchan, who cuddled against Tiger's shoulder. Ceri grinned, ushering the other kids out after him, towards Neptune's Courtyard, whilst the vampires paired up with them and the Underserving. Drake eyed his enemies warily, but at the same time gestured at the apprentices to follow them. Och led the cautious Brotherhood towards their freedom.

The war between the vampires and angels had been waging for centuries. The Legion had been conditioned to annihilate vampires. But what did I care about bastard rules or traditions? Misrule and Harahel — a vampire and an angel — had already rebelled against the old intolerance. Now they'd agreed to offer sanctuary to the Brotherhood, including the Broken kids, Underserving, and the Phoenixes.

It didn't stop the war with the angels, but it was still something new and exciting. And I didn't miss the irony that a witches' spell that allowed you to breathe underwater, would lead to the rescue of their enemy mages.

"You'll Fall!" Rahab shoved his foot against Mischief's neck. "Enough of this nonsense. This Glory is damning you."

The shadows inside me joined with the silver; wings beat in majesty, furious at being caged by Rahab's spell. Suddenly, they broke out of my chest. The phoenix wings shattered the paralysis as they flamed through the cold night air and scorched Rahab's feathers. Rahab howled, stumbling away

251

from Mischief.

Mischief forced himself up to his elbows, before shakily raising to his knees; scarlet snaked from his split lip.

I shook off the tingling remains of the paralysis, prowling towards Rahab. Shadows rippled around me; I blazed on righteousness.

*And vengeance.*

Rahab was right: in the Under World, the angels would Fall eventually, unless they returned to Angel World. But I knew one thing: at least by then, they'd be able to make their own choice, and my fam and I would have a shot at taking down the Matriarch.

Rahab panted, struggling to stand upright.

When I seized Rahab by his golden curls, his eyes glistened with tears. "How'd your like *your* personal nightmare?"

"I believed you exceptional and I was right," he whispered. "I mistook just how monstrous you are, even compared to your brother." I flinched, but didn't let go of his hair. "Do you imagine it a surprise to me that a Glory can't be trusted? But for the sake of my...son...I raised you up, gave you family, and *life*. It's a hard lesson, but you're nothing more than a *destroyer*."

Emerald tendrils forced themselves into my mind.

*Crack* — I fell backwards, writhing.

Rahab forced memories one after the other in a movie of Violet's Worst Moments: assaulting Rebel, whilst under the influence of the witches' potion, Marking Rebel against his will, abandoning Harahel to abuse, attempting to kill my own father... Every action, for which I ever felt guilt, replayed in multicolour, *over and over and over and...*

I keened, scratching at my face and slicing my lips in my distress, splashing side to side, until a sudden surge of copper lime and the Bailey was awash with Anael's blood.

The tendrils snapped back into Rahab, as he wailed, bent over and scrabbling his hands through the blood that was being washed away by his own storm in horror. "Zophia, what have you done?" He gasped.

Mischief pushed himself up, opening his wings, until he

towered in glory. "I believe I promised to make the *hope real*...?" He wiped his hand through his wet hair, smoothing it back. "Isn't it obvious? I've teleported the stored blood from the Bleeding Chamber out here to drain away." He tapped his broken lip. "Oh dear, does that mean no more slave army?"

Rahab roared, surging towards Mischief, but this time Mischief was the one lashing Rahab; Mischief threw out a lasso that caught Rahab around the chest. When Rahab struggled, I leapt up, adding my magic to Mischief's. Together, we dragged Rahab to the whipping post and hung him, roped in silver, facing the post.

The storm died down; I might even get my rainbow moment. Rahab, however, had started weeping.

The shadows slipped back inside me.

Mischief met my gaze, and we grinned at each other. When I turned back to the Bailey, however, I realised that the remaining Brotherhood, who hadn't yet been taken out with the vampires, were watching us in shock. Anael had been backed into a corner by a gang of mages, who didn't look down with the liberation program.

I wet my bleeding lips: time to play my part. "I may be your champion and queen, but every one of you can rise." The mages glanced around at me, then their broken leader strung up on the whipping post. "You've nothing to prove, fear, or feel guilt for. One thing I've learnt, it's not how you're born — Glory, Wing, magical, Child of the Seraphim or Fallen — that makes you who you are but what you bastard *do*. Fly in the world and open your eyes because there's magic everywhere, even in human music, the Fallen's anarchy, or a Glory's love. *This* is the Brotherhood rising: *Rise!*"

*Lazarus rises! Rises! Rises! And we will rise!*

The mages burst into passionate chanting as they rose in rippling golden waves, followed by their Phoenixes, to fly to Neptune's Courtyard.

I sagged against Mischief, whilst my fam who weren't herding the unusual mix of vampires and angels off the island, gathered around me.

Rebel clasped Mischief with the intensity of a bloke who'd been forced to watch his fam's near death (and I knew how that felt).

Blaze and Spark slipped either side of Rahab, as if on guard duty, and Firebird clung to Spark: I should've known my shy vampire Halfling would be playing big brother to the angel Phoenix.

Anael rested his hand on the base of Drake's neck in a casual display of older brother dominance, but it still shook.

Ash curled himself around me, resting his head on my shoulder.

"Are they likely to become Mage Munchies as the vampires' Blood Lovers?" I asked.

Ash waggled his hand in the universal sign for *fifty-fifty*. "Are the mages likely to force Compulsion Collars on the vampires?"

Anael's mouth curved wickedly, as if already imagining it. "Only if they enjoy playing. Do you, soldier?"

Both sides of my nature rose in possessive rage. *My brother was putting the moves on Ash...?* "Stand down, bitch. No one's collaring the Brigadier again."

I scowled at Anael, whilst winding my fingers through Ash's feathers.

Ash grinned. "You're hot when you're in Silver Queen mode, monkey muffins."

Anael snorted with laughter.

*Yeah, there was my older sister respect blown.*

I pinched Ash's hip. "The Silver Queen can get even more creative than garlic crushers and butter knives..."

Ash rubbed his head against mine. "Never doubted it, babe."

"I apologise for interrupting the prattle of your vampire whore." Drake winced, when Anael increased the pressure on his neck, but he still continued, "Allow me to remind you that we yet have the most powerful mage in the Legion tied to the whipping post. What do you propose to do to him?"

Drake quickly averted his gaze. He hadn't said *father*, but I'd heard it: I had his father bound in front of him.

Rebel had been forced to watch, whilst his own father had been executed by Drake on the Matriarch's order.

Could I put both Anael and Drake through that, even if they'd chosen me...and freedom...over their father?

After all, I'd sacrificed mine to save the world from an apocalypse; Lucifer had been taken back by the Matriarch as her forced Wing.

*Why should their father be spared?* And would my fam ever be safe again if he was?

I wriggled free of Ash, stepping in front of Rahab.

Rahab lifted his head, trying to swallow his sobs, even though his eyes were red-rimmed. He looked so much younger *and achingly alike to Drake.*

**This isn't Snape, Violet-crush, it's Voldemort. I'll read you until you die and rise again that this is your chance—**

*To become an executioner?*

**Why, girl, of course not. This is your chance to become a true leader.**

When I raised my hand, sparks danced on my fingertips. Rahab's startled gaze met mine, before he glanced around the now empty Bailey and slumped against the post again.

Mischief strode behind Rahab, shaking out nine strands of silver in a fizzing whip.

*Rip* — Mischief tore Rahab's shirt in half, revealing his unmarred back.

Then he raised the whip and slashed it down.

*Swish — thud.*

I jumped on Rahab's hissed groan.

*Was this justice? It sure as hell felt like vengeance.*

Then I noticed how ashen both Drake and Anael had

255

become.

"I'm sorry, does it hurt?" When Mischief *cracked* the whip against the ground, Rahab flinched. "Only, you ordered ninety-nine more strokes like that for Rebel, who you professed not to wish to hurt. But then, you also *hung* him. So, busy day ahead of us: shall we get going on the flogging first?"

When Mischief lifted the whip again, however, it was Rebel who curled his hand gently around Mischief's, stilling it. I stared at Rebel in shock: Rahab had whipped his back to ribbons. The punishment had haunted me. How could Rebel not want it repaid in blood?

"It's like this, see, the bad bastard is banjaxed already. He's lost his family, reputation, and home. He's made a balls of everything, and sweet Jesus, do I understand that. But I don't want to be like him." He glanced at the whip, before adding softly, "*We* shouldn't be like him."

Rahab barked a deep laugh, before choking on a cough. "I told you, Zachriel, that you were *too good*. Do you finally believe me?"

"You'll not talk to him, Mr Bound at My Mercy, or I'll add a special Violet sprinkle into the arse kicking." I sidled closer.

Rahab writhed, trying to look over his lashed shoulder. "D-duma...my prince...A-anael... I never meant my names for you to mean... *You are still my sons.*" His howl echoed around the courtyard. I shivered, wrapping my arms around myself. My gut roiled at his devastation. For once, he wasn't playing to an audience or long game: his agony was real. *Why did there have to be something real underneath?* Tears slipped down his cheeks, as he rested his forehead on the post and murmured, "How could you take away my sons?"

"I am *not* your son." Anael's arm tightened around Drake. "I'm nothing but a trained weapon, like all your boys. And you don't deserve your true son."

Drake's lips were pinched, but he flushed. "You wished I hadn't been born, father. This is surely your wish come true."

Suddenly, the skies darkened with clouds, before the ground shook. I staggered, stumbling to my fam, who clasped each other's hands in an instinctive circle.

*Nope, not looking like a rainbow on the horizon...*

"This is my island, and if you're not my sons..." Rahab hissed, even through his tears, "then I can take life, as easily as I grant it."

*A growling rumbling.*

"No one ordered a freight train did they...?" Ash asked, even as he cast a concerned glance at me.

"Holy Mary preserve us..." Rebel pointed at the sky above the castle.

It wasn't a train or rainbows that hung above us but a wall of water.

*Rahab had summoned a tsunami to destroy us all.*

"I love you," I hollered above the roar because suddenly in the exhilaration of knowing we were about to die, I knew my last words.

Mischief seized the back of my head, crashing his mouth against mine. In the desperation, magic, and love, I tasted the blood of his torn lip. Then, whilst the first droplets of seawater fell on us, he bit my lip and sucked.

When the wave thundered down, I was swept away in a swirl of silver.

# 30

When my powers had arisen phoenix-like from the ashes of my human life, I'd torched my mum's court in Angel World, then stolen my dad's light from the Under World.

Now I'd cheated my brother of his magical birthright, whilst I'd shattered the world of our false mage father.

Yet did that make me the destroyer or saviour? The Beginning or End? Birth or death?

Both light and shadow, I was the Phoenix and Silver Queen.

Yet did that make me an exploder of myths? Or simply a better storyteller?


*Feathers, copper, and ash.*

I spluttered on the taste of Mischief and magic.

*Death.*

Then I booted out in my panicked confusion because the world had been transformed to soft feathered violet.

*Was this...hell or heaven?*

I snatched at fistfuls of silky hair, wings, and tails. A tangled pile of soft arms and hard chests.

"Sweet Jesus, woman, would you stop that? I'm not a cow to be milked," Rebel's voice broke into my alarm.

"And my tail's not a wee comfort blanket," Blaze grumbled.

I stilled. In one hand I clutched Rebel's hair, in the other, Blaze's tail. I lay in a tangled pile of fam: angels, vampires, Phoenixes, and Halflings.

After everything — when I'd expected a *nothingness* at this moment of death — I'd been rewarded with all I'd ever desired.

*Fam.*

Maybe wishes did come true. I'd acted the leader and saved my people, even if I'd have given anything for my fam not to have died with me. I'd promised Rebel *light* and I bubbled with silvered delight that it hadn't been a lie.

I squirmed around, kissing lips, wings, tips of elbows, nipples, and backs of knees: every surface of skin that my exulting mouth could reach. My blokes laughed and jostled, but both sides of my nature glowed with such intense joy that I vibrated with it.

*Hell, I'd never expected to feel so alive in death: again, with the irony.*

The only angel missing was Rahab. It'd be even more ironic, if he hadn't been judged *worthy* of the light.

"Not to interrupt your fun," Anael slouched up onto his elbow, "but you do know where we are, surely?"

I blinked. "Together."

He rolled his eyes. "And...?"

"Heaven...?" Suddenly, as the high began to fade along with Mischief's potent blood, I became less certain about what had happened in the moment before the wave had hit. The blur in front of my eyes began to clear.

Anael waved a lazy hand. "Stand up."

When I stumbled to my feet, I noticed that Mischief hadn't been in the cosy group snuggle, but was hunched to the side with his arms crossed. He wouldn't meet my gaze.

My feet sank into the mountain of violet feathers. I stared out over a valley of glowing bones, choking on the stink of ash. The skies raged, *burning*: I shielded my eyes, backing away, until I bumped into Drake's shoulder. He steadied me.

The land of feathers and bones from my visions: *they were*

*real...?*

Or had we been transported into my mind and dreams?

"Where the hell are we?" I demanded.

"Calm yourself. We're alive, although how long we shall survive in this realm of gods...?" Drake shook his head; his curls fell over his eyes. *Gods...?* He attempted a smile, but it barely curled the corners of his lips. "Do I still have so little skill as a kisser that you must choose to swap saliva and blood with Zophia and drag us to the Realm of the Seraphim?"

The realm of the deadly and ancient *angel gods...?*

I twisted to Mischief, who bowed his head under my scrutiny. "But you told me only the Emperor's son could...?"

Mischief finally raised his gaze to meet mine; his eyes twinkled. "Ta da!"

I flushed hot and cold: *Mischief was the Archduke of the Seraphim. And he'd known all along.*

Anael's gaze was assessing. "What a naughty secret to hide from us."

Rebel burst up, snatching Mischief around the neck and dragging him closer to me; Mischief didn't struggle. "You great idiot; we trusted you."

Drake's icy glare made Mischief shrink back. "You truly are a traitor."

I traced Mischief's cheek with the back of my knuckles, whilst Rebel fisted his long hair, holding him still. Yet I knew Mischief was allowing himself to be manhandled: he'd taken on Rahab with me. He was the *Archduke*.

His powers were no longer hidden.

When I lowered my hand around Mischief's throat, however, he remained unresisting. "Your mother was right: you're a *Sly Imp*." Mischief's eyes gleamed with tears but he defiantly didn't let them fall. It ached to flay him like this, but he'd lied and masked himself for too long, and now we were stranded in the world of my nightmares. My steel nails shot out, grazing his neck. Mischief hissed but he didn't pull back. "I swore to behead you, if you tricked me again. Tell me how everything you pulled back in Castle Drake wasn't one big illusion?"

Ash slinked up, prowling between us: The Brigadier comes to the party. "Enemy terrain. Unknown hostiles. No backup." Ash stabbed a finger at Mischief's chest. "No executing the Imperial Highness, whilst we need a guide or hostage." Then he shrugged. "At least we finally know who the true Emperor is..."

Why did it excite me that I wasn't alone in the royalty gig, at the same time as my angelic and vampiric sides seethed to hear *Imperial Highness* on Ash's lips? And why didn't it surprise me that Mischief was the rightful son of the *Emperor of the gods*, despite having been treated as an Undeserving?

"I was saving you all," Mischief's voice was low and brittle. "Saving my family."

I huffed. "You scheme and plot; it's what you do. All I wanted was for Rahab to notice and train me: *just like you with your daddy*. Now, thanks to our help, you've jumped realms. Don't pretend that wasn't your true plan or that you haven't dreamed about it since you killed the bloke who raised you."

This time, the tears did escape Mischief's eyes.

When I caught Rebel's gaze, I hadn't expected the sad reproach. Hell, even if I was right, I regretted voicing the words: Mischief had told me something agonisingly private, and I'd used it to shank him. J had taught me that, yet only now did it feel *wrong*.

Mischief slumped; his wings drooped. "Despite what you clearly believe, from the moment my brothers and myself were held on that damned island, my dreams were focused on one thing alone: saving the Broken, Phoenixes, and Undeserving. To free *my people*." He raised his gaze to mine: sharp as ice. "I sincerely doubt that I shall be invited into the loving arms of my true father. I was, as you know, abandoned as a bastard son." I flinched at the raw pain that bled through his steely tone. "Put aside your unwarranted mawkishness," his gaze softened for a moment as it flickered to Ash, "and execute me because I have no value as either guide or hostage."

When I trembled, my nails nicked Mischief's neck.

At a sudden yank on my skirt, I glanced down.

Firebird knelt amongst the feathers, glancing between Mischief and me in agitation. "Please, if he has done wrong, he can be punished but not...? He's loved by the Phoenixes because he's our Defender."

Mischief swallowed hard. "Turn away," he whispered. "Grant me this one thing: do not watch."

Hell, Mischief was begging his own *brother* not to witness his death, even if his brother only knew him as the Defender of his kind.

My nails retracted so quickly that I staggered backwards. Then I launched myself at Mischief, snatching him away from Rebel and clasping him.

Mischief blinked. "Perhaps you have a different definition of execution...?"

"Perhaps I'll never kill one of my own, even if they are Machiavellian Archdukes. And perhaps I'm just buzzing that we're all alive."

Spark's ears twitched. "Aye, but we're also above a valley of bones in the Realm of the Seraphim. The Seraphim—"

"Right, like we know anything about those bastards," Blaze scoffed. "That's why you'd be a head case to go exploring here." Blaze beat his wings, rising into the smoky air. "Just like the head case Seraphim. The numpties declared themselves gods and swaggered off to this world centuries before we were born."

I raised my head from Mischief's shoulder: we truly were in the realm of the gods. And I'd struggled to accept bastard *magic*...

"They're shifters," Mischief muttered (and I didn't need *like me* tagged on to get his flush of shame). "It'd be just like the arrogant deities to have been walking amongst us, spreading tales of their deadly nature and glory. They certainly spread their *seed*." He grimaced, and I nuzzled along his jawline in reassurance. "But we can't know."

**Maybe your Scottish fox brothers should watch their colossal mouths, Violet-divinity, or they'll find**

**themselves with more than ears and tails. Plus, the Unicorn Kid needs his cute mouth washed out...**

*J, where the hell have you been? We rewove the Legion's story. Plus, our Sugar Plum Angel hid—*

**Excuse me, I was busy gagging on your hypocrisy.**

**How many secrets are *you* hiding? Have you told anyone about the voice who speaks to you?**

***Who am I, Violet?***

Cold washed through me, as I recoiled from Mischief. He furrowed his brows in confusion.

"My Queen?" Drake strode towards me, but I waved him back.

My heartbeat was suddenly too loud; my mouth too dry.

*No, no, no...*

J had always been *my* secret: he'd raised me, saved me, and never abandoned me. As a kid, unlike my parents and the angels, he'd always answered when I'd called.

*Almost.*

He'd only gone silent, when I'd demanded to know *who he was*...

I loved J, even if I'd never known whether he was real. Yet what if he *was* real...?

*"Well, my son and the Silver Queen seeking an audience with my fabulous self. I'm honoured."*

I froze: J's voice burst into my head. *Except, not J's voice.* It was similar but colder, harder, and regaler.

When I glanced around, however, everyone else had also stiffened.

I rubbed my foot through the feathers. "Any chance I was the only bitch to hear that?"

A sea of shaking heads.

**I tried to warn you. You've demanded trust, but you held onto the only secret that mattered.**

***Me.***

*Who are you, J?*

**Haven't you guessed yet? Don't you know me well**

263

**enough after all these years?**

*Jahael?*

"I don't believe we formally requested to see you," Mischief said, stiffly.

A delighted laugh. *"Sure you did: blood called to blood. BAM! Don't try to trick your daddy, I know how much you wish to show off your skills."* I didn't miss the warning edge, nor did Mischief who cast a troubled glance at me. *"I know who's naughty and nice because I have the inside track, darlings. And one of you naughty creatures has hidden me inside their heads from the moment of their birth."* I panted, pressing my nails into my palms to control my rapid breathing. *Don't say it, don't say it, don't...* Rebel studied me, cocking his head; his eyes narrowed in both concern and sudden understanding. *"You wondered how I walk amongst you...? I've been there all the time: inside your Silver Queen."*

I stared down at my boots, unable to look up at the *gasps* and shocked whispers.

*"We Seraphim are angel gods, but say hello to my creation: A Fallen god."*

Rich frankincense, then I was cocooned in the safety of violet wings. "I always knew there was something extraordinary in your mind." Drake rested his forehead against mine. "Did I not tell you how special, important, and powerful you are?"

"I lied," I whispered, "I'm sorry, sor—"

Drake's lips pressed against mine, and there was heaven in the flare of frankincense infused stars.

When he drew back, he placed one final chaste kiss on my lips, before insisting, "You have no talent for lies, and I should know, since I've lived my life amongst them. If you'd known you housed a god, you'd have been considerably more insufferable than you already were."

Rebel sniggered.

Anael raised an eyebrow. "My sister, the insufferable god."

"What happened to worshipping deities, bitches?" I growled.

Mischief twirled me away from Drake. "At least we know

264

what's up with the *kneel* thing now." I tried to cross my arms, but he caught my hands between his instead. "Childish."

When I licked the end of his nose in retaliation, he trapped me with his wings. "Let's put on a show for daddy dearest. After all, he's *inside* you. He's seen...everything...you've done from the moment you were born." I flushed: I'd thought Lucifer's spy lights intrusive but to think Jahael had seen *everything*...? Strike that...*was* watching everything...? Mischief grinned wickedly. "We're *both* children of the Seraphim: we shan't be invisible again."

I wriggled my feet more firmly into the feathers, staring down at the valley of bones.

*This was my land*: ancient, deadly, and secret.

Yet here I was finally free of all secrets to be myself, just like Mischief, even if I was trapped in a mysterious realm, cut off from my own world with my fam.

**I swear on all the sequins on Broadway, I'm still the bitch who raised you.**

**Don't forget, I love you.**

*You betrayed me.*

*All these years I wanted you to be real...but now I just want you out of my head.*

**You still need me. I promise, I won't abandon you.**

I stared up into the fireball sky; it flared in crimson streaks.

So, the Emperor of the Seraphim wanted an audience with the vampire god?

I grinned: *bring on the fireworks.*

Because in this world of gods, the Seraphim had just welcomed in a monster.

*They were in for a hell of a shock.*

The End


Ready for the next instalment in the Rebel Angels series?

Check out **VAMPIRE GOD!**

https://rosemaryajohns.com

Did you enjoy **Vampire Mage: Rebel Angels Book Four**?

Let me know by leaving a review!

# Love Reading Addictive Fantasy?

Sign up to Rosemary A Johns' *VIP* Newsletter List to be notified of new promotions, secret bonus content, and never miss out on hot new releases.

Plus you'll also receive Rosemary's FREE and exclusive novella "All the Tin Soldiers".

It's our gift to you.

Visit Rosemary's website to subscribe and become a Rebel: rosemaryajohns.com

# Hooked on the *Rebel Verse*?

### Series in the Rebel Verse

Rebel Vampires
Rebel Angels

### Read More from Rosemary A Johns

Website: https://rosemaryajohns.com
Bookbub: https://www.bookbub.com/authors/rosemary-a-johns
Facebook: https://www.facebook.com/RosemaryAnnJohns
Twitter: @RosemaryAJohns

# ABOUT THE AUTHOR

ROSEMARY A JOHNS is a USA Today bestselling and award-winning fantasy author, music fanatic, and paranormal anti-hero addict. She writes sexy angels, savage vampires, and epic battles.

Winner of the Silver Award in the National Wishing Shelf Book Awards. Finalist in the IAN Book of the Year Awards. Runner-up in Best Fantasy Book of the Year, Reality Bites Book Awards. Honorable Mention in the Readers' Favorite Book Awards.
Shortlisted in the International Rubery Book Awards.

Rosemary is also a traditionally published short story writer. She studied at Oxford University and ran her own theatre company. She's always been a rebel...

Want to read more and stay up to date on Rosemary's newest releases? Sign up for her *VIP* Rebel Newsletter and get a FREE novella!

# Member of a Book Club?

Why not share *Vampire Mage* with your group?